STORMFRONT

R S SUTTON

STORMFRONT

THE BOOK GUILD LTD

First published in Great Britain in 2021 by
The Book Guild Ltd
9 Priory Business Park
Wistow Road, Kibworth
Leicestershire, LE8 0RX
Freephone: 0800 999 2982
www.bookguild.co.uk
Email: info@bookguild.co.uk
Twitter: @bookguild

Typeset in 12pt Adobe Jenson Pro

Printed on FSC accredited paper
Printed and bound in Great Britain by 4edge Limited

ISBN 978 1913913 137

British Library Cataloguing in Publication Data.
A catalogue record for this book is available from the British Library.

ONE

Apart from Elvis straying through an open window, reminding anyone who was still unsure that Heartbreak Hotel was at the end of Lonely Street, all was quiet along the esplanade. It was just turned six in the morning. The last mistimed streetlight gave up its rebellious struggle and switched off. A young couple crossed the road and jumped onto the sandy beach. Fresh in the passion of new love, they embraced between lingering kisses.

Looking over the boy's shoulder, the girl pulled away. 'Someone's dumped some rags in the water.'

The boy half-turned and looked the fifty yards or so along the shoreline. 'So what?' He shrugged, pulling the girl closer. She held the flat of her hand against his chest and walked off.

Getting closer, the mixture of faded colours resolved into a clearer picture. A leg was skewed up the sand as an arm bobbed around in the gentle waves. Swallowing hard, she slowed until, just a few yards away, she stood still, letting the water swirl around her shoes.

'Dear God.'

Face down, the body of a man had deep parallel gashes across his back, the last of which all but severed his head. Again she swallowed, but was unable to stop her shaking legs from edging closer. He wore a single deck shoe and the remains of a pair of jeans. What was left of a T-shirt clung to a broken arm.

Her boyfriend stayed away, asking his obvious questions from a distance. The girl flashed anger as she looked back.

'What the bloody hell do you think it is?'

Feeling compassion for the body in front of her, and contempt for the boy's stupid enquiries, she knelt in the shallows.

'Stop acting like a bloody fairy, and get help.'

TWO

UNABLE TO WORK OUT HOW TO CHANGE THE RINGTONE, Valerie cursed as the aggravating chimes bounced around the walls. She was lying neck-deep in hot suds when the phone broke, or rather barged, into her consciousness. Moments of luxury were scarce, so she could do without the interruptions. She eased round and rubbed a small circle in the steamed-up porthole. Skimming an overhanging willow, a two-man scull glided past, the slender hull barely leaving a ripple as it disappeared. Apart from a pair of swans, the river was deserted. She turned back, laying on the folded towel that rested against the bath rim. It didn't matter how much electricity she used, it was all, or mostly all, free.

She lived in a houseboat on a short stretch of the Thames, with just two or three other boats as neighbours. Along with a nearby business park, the supply for the few houseboats had been rerouted. For some reason, best known to the developers, the contractor had been changed halfway through erecting new units. Valerie had been left with a connection to keep her going, for which there was no charge.

'Because of all the upheaval, madam.' The apologetic developer had come around in person to explain the situation.

When the work had been finished, she wound up with one electricity supply through the meter to the lights and the other straight off the grid to the power circuits, including the greedy immersion heater. She did get the odd query from the guy who read the meter, but he was easily brushed off.

'Only use the lights, and I have a log burner for heat, so I'm afraid I'm a bit of a disappointment to EDF.'

'No worries, Miss,' the meter reader had said, feeding the figures into his consumption monitor. 'I get paid the same no matter what, not like the chief executive. Needs all 'is fingers to count 'is wages.'

'And his bonus?'

'Yeah.' Closing his monitor, the man had scowled. 'And 'is bleedin' bonus.'

Now, as usual, because she was in the bath, the phone was not about to stop.

'Hell's teeth and buckets of blood!' Like a winter athlete descending the slalom course, a tablet of Lux negotiated a shapely breast before disappearing into the soapy abyss as Valerie left the most comfortable place she'd been in all morning. With water dripping from her naked body, she snatched the receiver from its cradle. 'Yes?'

'We got a big one,' said an excited voice.

'Who's that? And we got a big one what?'

'It's Jane. We got a job.'

'Dear God in heaven, what part of *you're fired* are you having problems with?' said Valerie, staring at the pool of water gathering around her feet. 'I've got no money, can't afford to pay you. You've got your P45, now take a hike, get your arse off to the job centre.'

'But we've got a job and it's a biggy.' Catching the edge of excitement in Jane's voice, she let her continue. 'Should keep us going for up to a month… if we play it right. And the good news is you don't have to pay me.'

Valerie pushed out her bottom lip and blew at the cluster of soap bubbles on her nose. 'Suppose you're going to work for free?'

'No,' said Jane. 'Government's got another of their brilliant schemes going, massage the figures, make them look like they're doing more than sitting on their butts while picking their friggin' noses. You know, make us feel like our money is being used for something positive. All you've got to do is fill in some forms, or rather, all I've got to do is fill in some forms for you. I read somewhere that some pillock called it The Big Idea. Just got to be a man. Probably pay him six figures to come up with gems like that.'

'For crying out loud, have they nothing better to do with my taxes?'

'Tax? Never known you pay tax, least not while I've worked for you. The Valerie Stone creative bookkeeping system gets there first.'

'Okay, okay,' said Valerie, 'I'll be in as soon as I get dressed.'

Towelling herself down, she smoothly brushed recently highlighted hair behind her ears. The stroking of a sharp antiperspirant concentrated her stare into the mirror, but as in the four preceding years, the solitary reflection mocked at the loneliness. There was no one looking over her shoulder.

The drifting deodorant bought back the intense thoughts and feelings once again. But as usual she pushed them away and pulled on a white T-shirt. The yacht-club logo was faded to near obscurity, but a pair of brand-new Levi's balanced the image. The man's American leather flying jacket had been taken in, but not by so much that it spoilt the way it hung, and when it was finished it had only been necessary to reposition one of the badges. Lipstick and makeup were ignored as words from another world echoed around the cabin.

'You can't improve on perfection, Val.' She could still see the smile that, at one time, enfolded her life.

On her way out she stooped at the door. 'I don't need reminding,' she said, pulling the cream envelope from between a B&Q sales leaflet and Red Cross appeal. From the prepaid stamp on the front to the green crest on the reverse, it was all too familiar. 'It's on standing order. Why do I have to look at it every month?' She tossed it unopened onto the side table and dropped the flyers into the waste basket. What the envelope contained was a statement of where most of her income went every month.

Clients stuck with defending divorce petitions, and the others wanting rid of their other half, seemed to be as cash-strapped as she was. 'Pay you half now and half later,' had become all too familiar. And the pay-you-later part of the deal often turned into picking up forms from the small claims court. With so little money to spare, the car hadn't left the garage in six months.

She glanced at the watch that never left her wrist, as she quickly walked along the towpath. Sunlight that had avoided the hawthorn on one side and long water reeds on the other, sparkled on the river. Up above on the bridge, it was only a short wait before a hybrid Routemaster lumbered towards her and slowed at Valerie's outstretched hand. Grabbing the plastic-covered handle, she swung onto the platform and poured some silver into the driver's bowl.

'Gone up, I'm afraid, Miss,' he said, scooping up the coins. 'Need another five pence.'

'Since when? I was only on the bus last week.'

'This morning, I'm afraid.' He drizzled the coins into their respective dispensers. 'Still trying to memorise the new tariffs.'

Valerie rummaged through pockets as an overweight mother, pulling a toddler and pushchair, pressed from behind. Finding one two-pence and two one-pence pieces, she smiled at the driver. 'Sorry, not got another bean. Must have left my change in another jacket.'

The driver winked. 'It's okay, you can owe me your body.'

Moving down the bus, she could hear the mother with a now-crying child, and pushchair that refused to collapse, drop her fare into the metal bowl. 'Don't suppose you want my bleedin' body?'

No vast expanses of glass, no fancy door or slick signage. This was an office in a rundown part of town with a low, or as low as possible, rent. 'Stone Detective Agency' had been applied to the door in neat DIY lettering.

'Hello, Jane.' Valerie pushed firmly at the sticking door. She was directly off the street, no corridor, no anteroom, just straight into the one office with adjoining washroom and toilet. Accommodating two desks gave a cramped feeling that was not alleviated by the intense orange blinds. The computer, a sometimes-connected phone and a free Viking calendar were on Jane's desk. Second-hand filing cabinets, finished in MOD green, were to one side. Valerie's desk on the far side was clear except for a desk tidy. High on the wall behind, a narrow window let in a little extra light.

At twenty-one, the pretty girl sitting by the window was six years Valerie's junior. The blue eyes and petite nose were neatly complemented by baby-pink lipstick and natural blonde hair. The smell of pencil shavings hung in the air.

'Morning, Miss Stone.'

If ever there was such a thing as a rescue girl, then Jane was it. She had worked at her desk for the last two years. Two years of up-and-down wages since she had been liberated from the life of the damned, in pornography and prostitution. She was just sixteen when she had been carefully groomed by a piece of slime called Vinnie. Vinnie the pimp, Vinnie the porno film-maker, Vinnie the "anything to do with sex, drugs and money" merchant. Small time, but he had a few brain cells and managed to stay on the correct side of the big boys and on top of the ones under his greasy thumb. Early one cold morning, Valerie had arrived at her office to find Jane huddled up against the door.

'Not today,' she had said, pushing past with a key in one hand and half a pint of semi-skimmed in the other. Jane had looked up, revealing a swollen lip, bruised eye and hair caked with blood. 'Christ almighty, what the bloody hell happened to you?!'

All Jane could do at the time was groan in attempting to rise to her feet. She'd been well and truly worked over.

Unable to find where Jane lived, if anywhere, Valerie spent the next two months taking her to hospital, the counselling centre, sexual health clinic, keeping her off the Smirnoff and generally looking after her, while telling Vinnie that if he came anywhere near her again she would enlighten the police as to his views on a suitable age for sex workers. It was down some side alley that Jane had been jumped, so whether it was Vinnie teaching her a lesson for keeping too much of her earnings to herself or a perverted customer, neither of them knew.

'Honest to God, it wasn't me,' Vinnie had said, holding his hands up as Valerie pushed him into a corner. 'Just ain't my style.'

So, for now, like a faithful puppy, Valerie seemed to have

her for the foreseeable future. Wasn't there some religion that said if you saved someone's life, you were responsible for them from then onwards?

'It should be the other way around,' Valerie muttered, pushing the door shut with her backside.

'What?' Jane inclined her head. She was a girl that, only giving a half-smile, communicated a sparkling nature that was never far away.

'Nothing, nothing. Go on then,' said Valerie, 'let's have it, starting with your job.'

'Like I said, Miss Stone, the Department-of-Whatever has decided to start another let's-help-the-unemployed-get-a-leg-up-campaign.' She picked up a slim buff file and dropped it onto Valerie's desk.

'This the form I have to fill in?'

'No, no, I'll do that; you can sign it later,' said Jane. 'This is the new job.'

'Okay,' said Valerie, pulling the few pages from the folder. 'What's it about? And what's the money?'

'The money's good.' Jane bubbled with her usual enthusiasm. 'Some guy washed up on the south coast. The insurance company want us to look into it.'

'Why us?'

'Someone from Southern and East will be here soon – that's the insurance company.' Jane sat on the desk, rotating the papers. 'They'll fill us in.'

'How much?' Valerie pulled the pages back.

Jane slid from the desk and closed the blind before pushing the bolt across the door. 'Better get changed, she'll be here soon. Tell you all about it.'

Valerie took off her jacket, put it on the hook in the washroom, along with her T-shirt and jeans, then took a blouse and skirt from the coat hanger and laid them across the chair. Taking a suspender belt and stockings from a bag hooked behind her desk, she put them on.

'Straight?' she asked, nodding over her shoulder at the line of butterflies ascending each stockinged leg.

'Yeah, yeah, sure.' Jane screwed her face up in disapproval. 'Ever considered coming into the twenty-first century?'

Valerie buttoned up the blouse before sliding the zip up the black skirt. 'What? Tights? You serious? I'm a woman, not Sir Walter bloody Raleigh.' Hopping around on each foot in turn, she pulled at the burgundy high heels.

Jane rushed to the window, flicked up the blinds and drew the bolt on the door in one slick movement as someone made an attempt to get in.

'Good morning. Come in, please.' The perfected business manner greeted their visitor. 'Think the door was stuck.'

'Good morning.' Peering into the office, the woman, smartly dressed in a navy suit and white blouse, removed a glove as she looked around. 'Miss Stone?' Before Valerie could answer, the woman held out a hand and, sitting down, neatly crossed her legs. Only after continuing the inspection of her surroundings did she release the handshake and look at Valerie. 'Benson. Rosemary Benson.' She handed a card across. 'Southern and East. We heard about you from…' She stopped and, removing the other glove, placed a Gucci handbag on the desk. 'Well, it doesn't matter where we heard about you. Let's just say we know you can be discreet.

'We have a Mr Alan Preston washed up on the beach at Weymouth. Boating accident, cut up by a propeller, or so it seems.' Mrs Benson revolved a photo between her fingers. 'Now we wouldn't normally question this beyond ID, etcetera. But the only photo we seem to have of Mr Preston is this.' She pushed a creased image across the desk. Valerie looked at the blurry picture of a few men sitting around a table outside a pub. 'On the left.' Mrs Benson reached across and tapped the photograph.

'Is this it?' said Valerie. 'It could be almost anyone. Who identified the body?'

Mrs Benson carried on with her fast, clipped delivery. 'His personal assistant did the identification. Very cool, apparently, didn't turn a hair. Just said yes, asked if she had to sign anything and left.'

'DNA?'

'Yes, it all checks out. The confirmation is in the file.' Mrs Benson passed another photograph across. 'His only living relative we think, brother.' The eyes of a respectable-looking guy in his thirties stared confidently from the photo. 'Normally we investigate any high-value accounts ourselves, but we're up to our eyeballs in a company restructure and everyone, including the assessment department, has several weeks of work scheduled.'

Valerie looked at the file, wondering just what she was being hired for. 'And you're suspicious?'

'No, no. Well, not sure. His brother is the only relative and we got the claim while he was still away overseas.' She leant back, replacing crossed legs with one ankle placed behind the other. 'The boat he presumably fell from is a yacht. It's in a small marina on the River Exe. And it's registered to his brother.'

'Off using it when he shouldn't have, was he?' Still looking at the brother, Valerie drew the last few words out slowly: 'Then got into trouble.'

'Yes, maybe, we're just not sure. Just seems a little... cloudy, although there may be nothing in it. The police aren't involved as such, but the inquest has been opened and adjourned. Although the body has been released.'

'So, where do you want me to start? And what do you

want me to look for?' Valerie thought it was all a little vague, but maybe she could stretch it to a couple of weeks.

'The boat, his brother and anywhere it leads, I think. We have to be sure on all pay-outs, especially large ones.' Mrs Benson scooped up her bag. 'Oh yes. It's in the details, but the remuneration is expenses plus point seven five per cent of the sum insured.'

Valerie frowned. Point seven five per cent, she thought; even at a hundred thousand the pay-out would only be a lousy seven hundred and fifty quid. She could earn a lot more than that in two weeks of divorce cases.

'And,' Mrs Benson added, 'three per cent if it's fraudulent. Don't think it will be, but we never know, do we? It's all in the folder.'

With her hands behind her back, Jane had been leaning on her desk for the last few minutes. 'There is the boat retrieval to the Medway at normal delivery rates, I understand.'

'Yes, of course, if you could arrange that too,' said Mrs Benson, getting up.

Jane ushered her out before Valerie could say anything more than thank you and we'll keep you up to date.

'What have you got us into? And at what fee?' Valerie pushed her lips together before continuing. 'We're not in business just to turn money over. Thought you said pay-out would be good? Point seven five per cent! Are you mad?'

Jane persisted with her smile. 'And three per cent if fraudulent.'

'What?! All I can do now to make anything out of it is to massage the expenses.'

Jane suppressed a giggle. 'You've not asked what the sum insured is.'

'Go on, point seven five per cent of what?'

'Or three per cent.'

'Yeah, yeah, of what?'

'Three million.' Laughing, Jane smacked her hands together and threw her head back. 'Twenty-two and a half thousand, or do you know what three per cent is? Ninety grand.' She repeated the sum slowly: 'Ninety bloody grand.' Then, before Valerie could say anything, she reminded her of the boat delivery on top.

'Ninety? Are you sure? Christ almighty.'

No, calm down, thought Valerie. *It's straightforward, and twenty-two and a half would solve an awful lot of problems. Two, maybe three weeks of creative expenses then a cheque for twenty-two and a half. That's fine, and if we make up a lovely thick, impressive report, another job. Although, as it's from a large company, the payment would be declarable to the chancellor. It has to go through the books, more's the pity.*

A fair amount of her business was from clients who paid in cash and didn't throw up a query when she "forgot" to give them a receipt. In those cases it was straight into her pocket.

'Need a car.' Valerie clenched a fist as she screwed up her face in satisfaction. 'Off to the marina first, I think, see if there is anything that's been missed.'

'Make more money taking yours – we can charge by the mile. A hire car is a hire car, just pass on the invoice.' Jane picked up the phone. 'Shall I put it on cover? Have you enough money?'

'The card's not maxed out… yet.' Valerie threw her wallet across the desk. 'Put it on the Barclaycard, I only have enough in the bank for day-to-day expenses. Don't forget to say it's a classic car and I only—'

'I know,' said Jane, 'built in nineteen sixty-one and just three to four thousand miles a year.'

'That's right, keep the premium down. If the mileage starts to climb, I'll disconnect the speedo.'

'Don't know why you have it connected anyway,' said Jane, 'you never look at it!'

Someone else was pushing at the door, and after a couple of tries it opened.

'Hello, Valerie, hello, Jane.' A man of about forty came in, smiling as he approached Valerie. 'How are you, beautiful? Thought you were going to phone?' He pushed at his thinning hair before removing his glasses and bending to kiss her on the cheek. 'Dinner date? No?'

'Oh blimey, Nigel, sorry, had to see a client, couldn't phone. Dropped it in the Thames.'

'What, phone or client?' said Nigel, trying to connect with a smile.

'Phone, silly.' She gave him a peck on the cheek.

Although hopelessly in love, it was unrequited. Not that she disliked him; he was quite nice, and spoiling her was a regular occurrence: flowers, chocolates, and of course only the best restaurants and theatre seats. He owned several shops, filling stations and flats. A redevelopment company, and more besides, added to his happy empire. He was nice to be with, funny, witty and knowledgeable, but he didn't ring the bells; didn't even come close.

'What about tonight? There's a great little Italian opened up just off the Strand. Let's have a meal there before it gets too well known and crowded out.'

'Love to, Nigel, but I'm looking into something for a client, sorry.'

Having had plenty of practice, Nigel hid his disappointment well. With what he was worth, and his kindly disposition, he could have had a choice of many. But he had been bitten and the wound was deep. There was only one woman for Nigel and, until she was put out of circulation, he would forgo all others and stay faithful. Apart from the lack of sex in their relationship, he was pretty sure he was the only man in Valerie's life. So he was now relaxed with his place.

'Okay. When you get back?'

'Of course, love to.' Being given a more intimate kiss, he looked embarrassingly at Jane. 'Don't worry, Jane's seen it all.' The remark was friendly banter, but it still took the smile from his face. 'Don't have a spare phone, do you?'

'Sure, I'll get it from the car.'

'Could do with some fuel as well.'

'No problem,' said Nigel on the way out. 'You taking your own car?'

'Yes, give it an airing; it's been gathering cobwebs for too long.'

Nigel returned and handed her a Samsung. 'Use it as much as you want; it's a spare so it won't be going off every ten minutes with someone asking you to build them a new house. I'll call the service station and tell them. You can fill the car up when you get there.'

'Thanks, you are a sweetie. Now I have to talk with Jane.'

'Oh, yes, of course, I'll get off. See you later.' He shuffled from one foot to the other as he felt the embarrassment of stealing another kiss. 'Are you okay for money?'

'I'm okay, Nigel,' said Valerie, opening the door. 'Sweet of you to ask.'

Jane took the phone from Valerie and copied the number onto her own.

'What was it you wanted?'

'Nothing, just wanted to get him on his way.'

'Nick his phone and petrol then kick him out – there's a name for women like you.'

'Look,' said Valerie, 'he's gone off on cloud nine, happy as Larry with a few kisses.'

'Oh, dispensing therapy,' said Jane. 'Didn't realise you were an angel stepped down from on high.'

THREE

Leaving the houseboat with a grip containing spare clothes and toiletries, Valerie jumped on the next Routemaster.

Half-closing her eyes, she let her head rest against the back of the seat. In the four years since opening the agency, four commissions had come from companies. While they were, in general, satisfied with the reports, a request for further information always followed. It never seemed sufficient to say that a particular enquiry had been unproductive. A page summing up a particular line that had been investigated inevitably brought a follow-up request for further information. The lesson was quickly learnt: a ten-hour day at the computer, turning the original A4 sheet into a dozen, was as lucrative as it was easy. These companies just had to have some middle management justifying their salary.

She looked out onto the day that was now producing a little sunshine. *Good*, she thought, *roof down, blow away the crap*. Though better weather could not burn away dominating thoughts of money. Twenty-two and a half thousand. Two for Jane, a bonus, no problem. Twenty in the bank, five hundred for something frivolous. A Christian Dior dress? She'd be two grand adrift, but massaging expenses would get her there.

Edging down the bus at the first change, a caress smoothed across the top of her jeans. Hand raised, she swung around just as a young lad, not yet north of sixteen, pulled away. 'You're going to get into trouble, son.' She grabbed his fingers and bent them back before propelling him into the corner. 'Keep your hands to yourself until the lady gives you an invitation.'

Forty-five minutes and another change later, she swung from the platform and crossed the road. The building in front of her had once been a large Ford dealership but now was one of Nigel's petrol stations. Behind the fuel pumps on the forecourt was a large white garage, typical of those built just after the war. The plate-glass windows, that stretched along the entire length, had vintage oil and petrol adverts hiding the interior. Following a side passageway around to an office, Valerie knocked on the door before entering.

'Miss Stone.' The station manager put his pen into a Goodyear mug and looked up. A pleasant smile revealed a broken tooth, reputedly from a car accident. The broken veins on his nose and cheeks were just starting to distract from his looks.

To the one side, away from a line of filing cabinets, was a photograph of a brilliant yellow Lancia barrelling along a forest rally stage. Valerie had heard that, at one time, the man behind the desk had been quite a tasty driver.

'Nigel said you'd be by to pick the car up.'

From the highest manager in his company to the newest apprentice, they called him Nigel. It was one of the company's foundation stones. 'We're all in it together,' he told them. 'Everyone is important.'

'I'll come through with you.' The manager leant back in his chair and passed his finger across several hooks before picking out two keys attached to a worn leather fob. 'We've drained and changed the oil, new filter, been round with the grease gun, replaced the plugs and checked out everything else.'

'Blimey,' said Valerie, looking at her watch, 'you must have worked at light speed.'

'Not really. Nigel told us to service it a few weeks ago. Said you hadn't taken it out in a while and thought you couldn't hold out much longer before you'd need a "fix".'

'He was probably right.'

Valerie followed him out, passed a couple of hydraulic ramps, to where, in its own private bay, the outline of a car stood under a light nylon cover. Dropping her bag onto a nearby stool, she helped him pull the protective cloth over the back of the car.

Like a stage magician, the manager held out his hand as he moved to the side.

'There she is.' He pulled a large yellow duster from his back pocket and needlessly wiped at the flawless black paintwork. Miniature stars sparkled from the chrome wheels and trim under the cold strip lights. 'You know what Enzo Ferrari said when he first saw the E-Type?' he said, putting Valerie's things into the boot. Although she heard it all before, Valerie let him carry on. 'He said it was the most beautiful car in the world.' He smiled while flicking at an imaginary piece of fluff. 'And by God, was he ever so right?'

Taking Valerie's silence as an approval for more historic reminiscing, he continued. 'When it made its debut at the New York motor show, Frank Sinatra jumped onto the Jaguar stand, pointed at the Series One and said, "I want that car." Did you know that?' Valerie drew a short, silent breath and gave a little, polite shake of the head. 'And this is the one, of course. The later series and the V12 were great cars, but this one, the original flat floor three point eight, alloy dash, this is the daddy.' She knew this well enough but continued to feign interest. 'I know it's commonplace now, but when it was launched it was a big deal, doing over a hundred in third. I wouldn't change a thing.' Grinning, he opened the door. 'With the exception of that bloody Moss box.'[1]

'Better get it filled up,' said Valerie, quickly cutting him off before the odd anecdote became a flood of quotes about the legendary car.

She eased into the driver's seat and turned the key. The fuel needle flicked to a quarter as the ignition and oil lights came to life. When the petrol pump had stopped rattling out a succession of clicks as it filled the fuel line, she pressed the black button. The engine turned slowly two or three times then burst into life, giving out the familiar Jaguar ring as the open flywheel disengaged from the starter.

A smile spread over the manager's face as she blipped the throttle a couple of times. 'Music.' He briefly closed his eyes, listening to the exhaust note. 'Pure bloody Mozart.'

'Better make that Elgar.' Valerie glanced at the oil pressure as she released the handbrake. Then, carefully threading the car past a couple of bollards, she drove out into the sunshine.

At the first pump, a motorcyclist removed his crash helmet, put it on the machine's seat and turned to his mate. 'Now, ain't that the best thing you're going to see all day.'

'Thought you'd be along for a fill-up.' Soothing a stiff leg, the attendant left the kiosk. 'Need a hand?'

---

1   The 'Moss Box' refers to the gearbox fitted in the early E-Types. It had been used by Jaguar in their cars through the fifties and was quite crude by modern standards (no synchromesh on first). It was replaced around 1965 when the 3.8 engine gave way to the 4.2.

'Thanks, Jack.' Valerie smiled. 'Still doing a bit?'

'Yeah, still helping out now and again, Mr Nigel don't mind me dropping in. Like to think I'm still useful.' Holding the trigger against the grip, the old man filled the Jaguar with one hand while leaning on the waste bin with the other.

'Must get some funny looks when a petrol assistant pops out?'

'Don't do much "popping" nowadays, but they don't mind. Get some pillocks, but people's mostly nice. It's like going back to the nineteen sixties.' He took a piece of muslin to the small spill on the paintwork as the pump automatically cut out. 'Put it on Mr Nigel's account, shall I?' He put the nozzle back in the cradle before snapping down the filler cap.

Valerie nodded as she slid back into the creased and polished oxblood leather. 'Please, Jack, yes.'

'Good lass. Love Mr Nigel like a son, I know he can afford it. Always gives me something in an envelope at the end of the week, 'e does, and not just a couple of quid.' He pushed the car door shut. 'When you going to marry 'im?'

'Marry! What, Nigel? You serious? When you're around getting a pension and some folding stuff every week? I'd marry you first!' She kissed her fingers before pressing them to the old man's cheek.

'Ha,' he laughed, shaking his head, 'if I become available, you'd be trampled to death in the bleedin' rush.'

When a safe distance from the pumps, she stopped and searched around in the glove compartment. Removing a pair of aviators, she pulled a cable end around each ear, before taking a pack of Disque Bleu and Zippo lighter from her jacket. Selecting a cigarette, she put it between her lips, flicked at the lighter and drew in deeply.

With half-closed eyes, she held the smoke momentarily in her lungs before letting it drift into the still air. She raised a hand to the old man reflected in the mirror, then, sliding the Jag into first gear, pulled out into the traffic.

Filling his Astra, the young man's grip on the fuel trigger slipped as Valerie drove off. 'Jesus Christ almighty!'

'As you so rightly say, son,' said Jack slowly, as he made his way back to the office, 'Jesus Christ almighty.'

FOUR

THREE HOURS LATER, THE SATELLITE NAVIGATION, which had been fighting for attention with the Pointer Sisters for the last fifty miles, guided her into the car park next to the marina on the River Exe. Pushing fingers through wind-ruffled hair, she closed her eyes. Breathing in the familiar smell of the sea, she sat silent for a minute. Misty words from another time drifted back. 'Sailors call it the smell of the land. In fact, it's neither land nor sea. What you can smell is the shoreline where land and water meet.'

She could still recall slapping his shoulder and pushing him along the jetty. 'Okay, Sir Frances Drake, it's the smell of the ruddy shore.'

Pushing old memories away, she grabbed the case file and, squeezing between closely parked cars, made her way alongside a red brick wall entangled with ivy. Towards the corner an attempt had been made to remove the invasive climber, but the wall beneath was crumbling. So an unlikely alliance had been struck between the two, both vine and wall supporting each other.

To the other side of the potholed tarmac, the river provided a watery boundary between the car park and marina. The harbour master's office at one end, a temporary porta-cabin, was beginning to look like it was there for the duration. The part-completed building to the side had been abandoned, allowing the ivy to send out an exploratory tentacle.

Removing her sunglasses, Valerie pushed at the part-open door. 'Hello?' Peering over frameless glasses, the uniformed man kept his forearms resting on the desk. He said nothing. 'I've come to look over *Sun Dancer*, the yacht that was towed into the marina a few weeks ago.'

'Another one?' He got up, shaking feeling back into his wrist. 'It's causing a lot of interest, this boat. Got authorisation?' He threw his pencil on the table as Valerie pulled an A4 sheet from the folder and handed it over.

'Know anything about it?' Blinking once or twice as her eyes became accustomed to the dark room, Valerie watched him run a finger down the paper. 'Or was it just towed in?'

'Just towed in. Not much else I can tell you. Couple of fishermen found it driftin'.' He moved over to the door and motioned with the sheet of paper towards two men. 'Young Ben over there next to the railings, he was one of them. He'll tell you all, or as much as he can about it. Just buy him a pint.' He returned the notes and started riffling through the desk drawer.

'Thanks.' Valerie stood in the doorway, replacing the paper. 'I'll have a word with him.'

'Keys.' He threw a ring of three across the room. 'You'll need those.'

The young men were at the corner of the car park, where it narrowed alongside the river. The tarmac gave way to a pathway of uneven flagstones held down with iron fixings. Further along, fishing boats moved gently at their moorings.

One of the men was gesturing across the harbour, while the other seemed more interested in Valerie as she approached.

Valerie tapped the file on her knuckles. 'I'm looking for Ben.' The taller of the two had black hair permed in unfashionably tight curls, the over-gelled locks catching the flashes of sun.

'Why? What's up? Who wants... to know?' The last couple of words fell away as he looked her up and down. 'Well, well,' he said, recovering. He was one of the few in the male population afflicted with a high registering, squeaky voice. There was an attempt to shift it down to a more manly octave. 'What have we here?' He flicked at his long hair, letting it fall again over the collar of his red bomber jacket. 'Not often we get the pleasure of such a lovely piece of work.'

From the immature chat-up line, and eyes that roved between her breasts and crotch, she presumed the nearby BMW, with the over-wide wheels and bean-can exhaust, belonged to him.

'Turn it up, Sid.' The young man she now knew as Sid looked at the ground, kicking at an imaginary stone. 'Never stop going flat out, do you?' *Thank God for that*, thought Valerie as who was who became clear, *couldn't be doing with much of Sid.*

The one she now presumed to be Ben looked a little younger than her, but his face was already being worn by persistent sun and wind. It was not possible to say if his blond hair was natural or the result of weather and saltwater.

'Got to get after it,' said Sid. 'We'll all have to stop when we're dead.'

Can't come soon enough for me, thought Valerie. 'I'd like to have a word with Ben, if that's okay with you, Romeo?'

'Sure, okay. Carry on.' He leant back against the railings and pulled out a rather nice, silver cigarette case. It was finely engraved, with an enamelled flag in one corner. Valerie guessed it to be from the nineteen thirties. 'Would you?' He pressed a button and the lid flew open, revealing a few cigarettes rolling around the gold-plated interior.

'No thanks, I'll stick to my own.' Besides being a status symbol, she guessed the case was to hide the fact that he bought the cheapest cigarettes on the market, or didn't like looking at the compulsory artwork each pack carried. 'I'd like to talk with Ben alone. If that's okay?'

'Oh, right, sure.' He stopped leaning on the fencing and flicked at his cigarette. 'Don't forget to get in touch if you want showing around. Just ask at the pub, everyone knows me.' A sharp gust of wind blew at his hair as he went over to the BMW. 'See you later, Ben.' Along with Sid, the smell of cheap aftershave disappeared.

'Jesus,' said Valerie, 'he's a bit of an acquired taste, isn't he?'

'Oh, don't mind Sid.' Ben nodded towards the car as they were battered by a chorus from the harsh exhaust. 'Weird, but harmless.'

'I understand you brought in *Sun Dancer*?' Valerie looked across the river towards swaying masts and small powerboats pulling at coloured warps. 'By the way, where is she?'

'Yeah, over there, the cream one with the blue boot topping.' He nodded over the river to where a yacht, that must have been all of forty feet long, was tied up.[2]

'Can you take me over? I understand a pint or two wouldn't go amiss for your troubles.'

The young man looked at his watch. 'Sure, make it lunch and you've got a deal.'

'Yours?' asked Valerie as Ben untied a small dinghy from the harbour wall.

---

2   The 'boot topping' is the line of contrasting paint at the waterline along the length of a boat between the topsides (hull above the water) and the antifouling (protective paint below the water).

'Anyone's, really.' Steadying the small craft with his foot, he offered an outstretched hand. 'As long as it's returned to where you found it, no one minds. We take turns to chuck a litre of varnish over it now and again.'

The tide was on the ebb as Ben, rowing at an angle, kept them on course for the marina. He bent into the smooth, regular strokes that only comes with habitual boat work.

'What's to do with it then? We've already had the police and harbour authorities going over her like ruddy surveyors.'

'Southern and East want a report. You know, insurance. Then it's somehow got to be taken back to the Medway.'

'That's all?' he asked as they approached one of the larger floating jetties.

'Loose ends, always loose ends. Someone's got to tie them all up.' Perfectly balanced, she walked confidently across the forward thwart and onto the jetty.

'Not the first time you've done that,' said Ben, throwing a clove hitch around the nearest bollard.

Valerie looked up at the mast before pulling the keys from her pocket. 'Impressive boat.' She jumped into the cockpit.

'Knock a bloody big hole in two hundred thousand.'

Valerie opened the aft hatch and disappeared down the steps. 'Lights?'

'Switches by the chart table.' Hanging on to the sliding roof and swinging down, he followed her into the cabin. 'The rocker switches to the side of the radio will get a little light going.'

Valerie did as she was bid and the cabin came to life as the strips stopped flickering and settled into a steady illumination.

'Master cabin behind you, others are forward. Galley is starboard.' Ben swept an arm around. 'And this is the main lounge area.'

'Did they race it?' asked Valerie. 'Hell of a waste if it wasn't raced.'

'Don't know, but I suppose it must have been at some time,' said Ben. 'There's racing pennants in the lockers, and the deck layout looks like it was. Tactical compasses, multi-geared winches and all unnecessary cabin clobber is easily removed.'

'You can earn your lunch,' said Valerie. 'Have a look around the pointed end. I'll search around here and the master cabin.'

'What are we looking for?'

'No idea.' Valerie pushed her hair back. 'Anything, anything that looks... I don't know... anything.'

The aft cabin had a king-size bed neatly in-between the perfectly fitted drawer and wardrobe units. A small dressing table and stool stood next to the entrance to an en-suite shower. Like all vessels, it had been designed with "a place for everything and everything in its place" firmly planted in the architect's mind.

'Anyone been on this boat?' she asked, meeting back up with Ben in the main cabin.

'Police, harbour authorities, customs,' replied Ben. 'And now you. Why?'

'There's nothing here, just like it's been cleaned from top to bottom. Few clothes, sailing stuff. But that's it. It's as clean and tidy as, I don't know. Even the books and charts are ranked in size like a public library. It's just too clean and... and, nothing. I don't get it. Come on, I'll buy you lunch.' Ducking her head, she made her way back on deck.

Ben received envious looks as he ushered Valerie across the stone floor towards the bar in the Harbour Arms. The girls that he usually had in tow could never be described as plain or ordinary, but the woman he was now motioning to a bar stool was: 'Bloody gorgeous,' the barman said quietly through the side of his mouth to a nearby customer.

'Bloody right,' said the man with a beer halfway to his lips. 'Couldn't I just—'

'Ben,' the barman put a cloth to a dripping beer tap, 'what will it be?'

'Guinness.' Ben briefly rubbed his hands together. 'Pint.' As he turned, he realised he did not know Valerie's name. 'And, for you…?'

'Valerie, Valerie Stone.' She looked around the busy, low-ceilinged room festooned with hop vines and glass fishing floats. 'Diet Coke or Pepsi, as long as it comes from a bottle, lots of lemon.'

'Only on tap.' The barman shrugged his shoulders. 'Sorry.'

Valerie leant on the bar and looked at the cooler shelf. 'J2O orange, industrial amount of ice. Got a menu?'

'It's quiet at the moment, so just the specials.' The barman finished polishing a glass and nodded towards a chalk board displaying a menu written in perfect italics. Around the board a large Donald Duck, with one foot missing, looked out of place hanging from the few yards of oiled netting.

'One of the lads pulled it up in a lobster pot,' said Ben in reply to Valerie's incredulous expression.

'In?' said Valerie.

'Yeah, in. That's what he said. Not sure if someone was using it as bait. But if they were it worked. There was a ten-pounder in there. Must have eaten Donald's foot.'

Returning to the menu, she ran an eye down the list and looked back at Ben. 'All good?'

'Usually, but steer clear of the curry. The chef's from the sub-continent, thinks we need gastro education. Never uses one chilli when six will do.'

'Only the brave,' said the barman handing over Valerie's drink, 'but to be fair it does say "hottish" underneath.'

'Think I'll have the spicy chicken salad,' said Valerie. 'As long as it's not—'

'No, no,' cut in the barman, 'just normal spicy.'

Closing his eyes, Ben savoured the creamy top of his beer before wiping the back of a hand across his lips. 'Fish and chips.'

'For a change.' The barman shouted the order through the hatch, before returning to glass polishing. Just as she was about to start a little small talk, Valerie's mobile went off. Sliding from the stool, she closed her eyes and blocked out the background burble with a free hand.

'Jane?'

'Yes, Miss Stone. Any joy?'

'No, nothing. The boat looks like it's just come off the production line. Clean as a new pin.'

'I've been having a bit of a think,' said Jane.

Jane's ideas were seldom useless, but Valerie still put a sarcastic slant to her answer. 'Oh yeah, about what?'

'Bringing the boat back from the Exe is going to be quite expensive. Why don't we… er, you do it? More money for us. You used to race a lot, didn't you? You know one end of the boat from another.'

'Yes, but I'm not all that hot on navigation,' said Valerie. 'It's got to be a couple of days from the Exe to the Medway. And it's a bloody big boat. Not sure.'

'Course you can, get help from someone. All you have to do is sail along the south coast then turn left when you get to the end. Simple.'

'Oh yeah, simple,' said Valerie. 'And what about the car?'

'Store it at a garage for two or three days, then more expenses picking it up again,' said Jane. 'If we've got a licence to print money for a few weeks, let's get the presses running.' She let Valerie think for a minute before adding, 'I'll make an appointment to see this guy Preston next week, it'll fit in perfectly.'

'Leave it with me,' said Valerie, looking across to the barman carrying a tray, 'lunch has just arrived.'

Taking a fork to the middle of his mushy peas, Ben made a well and filled it with vinegar and black pepper. 'All right?' he asked, pointing to Valerie's plate before tasting the mixture in front of him. More dashes of vinegar followed before he pronounced the concoction satisfactory by starting to clear the plate.

'Fine.' Being rather more interested in Ben's culinary modifications, she leant her head to one side and gave him a friendly frown. 'Yours okay?'

'Yeah. Fresh cod.' He jabbed a bent fork towards the fish. 'It'll have been landed this morning. One or two of the boats go out line fishing the wrecks. Sell the fish door to door and around the pubs.'

Valerie mulled the job over in her mind while looking around. A large copper urn of dried flowers was conspicuous in the fireplace. Highly polished brasses decorated leather straps and horse hames were fixed either side of a warped darts board. She guessed the pub was little used by tourists, which gave it a homely feel.

'What you doing for the next few days?' Unless she uncovered something pretty quickly, or thought of some way to string it out, the whole case was going to come to an abrupt halt. Two or three days delivering a boat would help money-wise.

The young man suddenly perked up. 'Nothing, nothing,' he said enthusiastically. 'What did you have in mind?'

'Steady up, Casanova, don't turn into your hot-blooded mate, for God's sake. Fisherman, right? Go to sea day and night?'

'Sure,' said Ben. 'Why?'

'Done any sailing?' Valerie pushed the last third of her lunch to one side before laying the knife and fork across the remains.

'Yeah, some racing, some cruising, makes up the money when the fishing's 'ard.'

'So, you can navigate? Read charts? Get from A to B?'

'Yeah, of course,' said Ben. 'But you don't need much nowadays. With satellite navigation you just switch it on and away you go, just like in your car. Easy.'

Valerie thought of the ever-narrowing lanes the car navigation system had sometimes led her along. 'Really,' she said wearily, thinking that if it was up to her the boat would probably end up at a Premier Inn somewhere up the M20.

'Want to get *The Sun Dancer* back home, do you?'

Valerie nodded. 'That's the idea. What about it?'

'My turn to ask if you can sail a boat? Or am I going to end up single-handed on a forty-foot yacht?'

'Yes, sure I can sail, racing mostly. How would you like to earn a few days' wages taking the yacht back to the Medway?'

'With you?' Attempting to look nonchalant, he swung around, leaning his back to the bar. 'A few days on the boat with you?'

Valerie put a twenty- and ten-pound note on the counter and pushed them towards the barman. 'Don't get any ideas, sunshine. Since I was put up for canonisation, the Pope insisted I put a restriction notice on them.'

'What?' Ben eased from the stool.

'My knickers, they carry a no-entry sign.' An old man seated in the corner coughed as his gin and tonic momentarily went the wrong way.

'Yes? No?' said Valerie, making for the door.

'Yes, of course,' he said, then added softly, 'Pity about the knickers.'

'Don't want to know what the money is?' said Valerie.

'Er, I—'

'Don't worry.' She took cigarettes and lighter from her pocket. 'I'll not rob you.'

Walking back across the car park, Ben looked at his watch. 'Tide won't be on the flood for a while. Anything you need to do?'

'Get this to a safe place.' Valerie nodded towards the Jaguar as she put the Zippo to a cigarette.

'Bloody hell. It's sex on wheels. Yours?'

Blowing smoke away from Ben, she nodded. 'Any ideas?'

'Sure, my place. Er, me mum's place.'

FIVE

To the side of the council house, the gravel crunched underneath the tyres as the E-Type was squeezed next to the wisteria.

Ben's mother looked on from the kitchen steps as Valerie started pulling the cover over the Jag.

'Well, give her a hand, yer great lummox.' Between the occasional tut and head-shaking, she turned back into the kitchen. 'Sweet Jesus and little fishes. Men.'

'How long will it take?' Valerie asked Ben. 'Here to the Medway, I mean.'

'Couple of days, if the wind's okay.' Behind the small vegetable plot of runner beans and sprouting potatoes, the ash trees swayed in the rising breeze. 'Shouldn't take any longer. Come on, let's get inside.'

'Tea?' Ben's mother rubbed pastry remains from her hands with the corner of a gaudy-coloured apron.

'Yeah, we've got time.' He looked accusingly at his watch. 'Any sign of Uncle Dan?'

'He'll be here, give him a chance,' his mother replied. 'You only called him a few minutes ago.' She continued to pour out tea before placing dark, sticky flapjacks on the table.

'Uncle Dan will help us fuel up and get a few stores in,' Ben explained between guzzling tea and filling his mouth with honeyed flapjack. 'And there's the harbour master to clear and coastguard to inform.' He casually threw deck shoes, jeans and a jumper into a backpack. 'We'll need him if we're going on this tide.'

Ben's mother disappeared, returning moments later with socks, underpants, spare jeans, shirt and an oil-stained sailing jacket. 'Men!' She hid her mother's love inside the rebuke while throwing the lot across the table.

After ten minutes of mother-son banter, a dilapidated green Land Rover drew up at the front door. The grinding of rusty door hinges announced the arrival of a wizened older version of Ben. Uncle Dan was soon putting Valerie's grip and Ben's backpack in behind the seats, along with a flare pack.

'Don't know what condition the ones on the yacht are in. Those are new.'

'Blimey, Dan, it's the Medway.' Ben managed a look of respect mixed in with the scowl. 'We're not off to the roaring bloody forties.'

Taking a flare from the pack, Dan waved it under his nephew's nose. 'You never know.'

'Okay, Dan.' Ben took the flare and threw it back in with the others. 'Okay.'

Valerie sat squashed between the two men on the front seats as Dan drove towards the harbour.

'You get down to the harbour master. This young lady can make my day and come along to the coastguard with me.'

Valerie smiled. There was no threat, no snide meaning behind his words. 'Okay, Dan, I'll come along with you.'

The worn suspension on the Land Rover gave it a rhythm not unlike a boat, as they navigated the narrow gap between cars half-parked on pavements. The smell of burnt engine oil and fish was largely suppressed by the thick clouds from Dan's pipe and the, mostly, fresh air coming from under the floor.

Ben jumped from the Land Rover as they passed the harbour master's office, leaving Valerie and Dan to go to the coastguard.

'You both found *Sun Dancer* adrift, I think?' said Valerie as they walked across to the office.

'Yeah, me and Ben work our fishing boat between us.' Dan pulled a pipe from his smock and stuck it into his mouth. 'Just driftin' around, about ten miles out.'

'Tell me, Dan, was it as clean and tidy as it is now, or were there any signs of anyone being on board?'

'Same as now, I suppose. I never set foot on it. Ben took the tow across; I never left *Fresh Dawn*.'

'*Fresh Dawn*, your boat?'

'Yeah, our boat *Fresh Dawn*, named after Ben's mum. Me sister.'

'Oh, I see. Where's Ben's father?'

The old man's reply was flat, devoid of expression. 'Dead.' He took the pipe from his mouth, tapped it on his palm, then replaced it between clenched teeth. 'Dead.'

'Oh, sorry,' said Valerie as they climbed the few steps to the dark blue door.

Inside, the usual office equipment was augmented by walls crowded with colourful posters instructing the public on what to do, and not do, at sea. And reminding anyone calling 999 with a sea-related emergency to ask for the coastguard.

As Dan pushed the door behind them, the officer got to his feet, deep lines emphasised across his face. 'No smoking.' He thrust a long finger at the lopsided sign.

'It's empty, yer bleedin' pillock.' Dan returned the growl in equal measure. He took the pipe from his mouth and shook it upside down. 'See?'

As his face gave up the struggle, the coastguard offered a hand from a sleeve heavy with braids. 'How's things, Dan?' A smile revealed a gold tooth amongst uneven neighbours.

'Oh, clinging to the wreckage, you know. How's things with you?'

'Too busy with bloody fools, as usual.' Momentarily the frown returned. 'Don't know why the arseholes...' Looking at Valerie, he touched his cap. 'Pardon my French, Miss.' She shook her head and let him carry on. 'Don't know why the cretins can't go and jump off a bloody bridge somewhere, instead of getting us and the lifeboat involved. You know, yesterday, the full crew spent the morning looking for some ruddy speedboat, and all the time they was pissed up in the Harbour Arms!' Again, he apologetically pulled at his cap while looking at Valerie.

Dan let the minor outburst subside before half-turning to Valerie and gently putting his flat palm to her back. 'Like you to meet me girlfriend.' Although friendly, the smile was still mischievous. 'Valerie, this is Leonard, our esteemed coastguard, Lenny to his intimates.'

'Girlfriend, is it? You wish. You bleedin' old villain.'

Feeling the niceties were beginning to take on a life of their own, Valerie cleared her throat.

'Oh, yes. Got the papers?' Dan took the folder and passed it to Lenny. 'Valerie and Ben are going to take *Sun Dancer* back home to the Medway. Want to get out in the next half hour or so, give them some daylight to get along the coast a bit. They can anchor in Seaton Bay till morning. It'll be sheltered enough tonight.'

Lenny scrutinised the schedule and copied the relevant information into the office log. 'Ben navigating?'

'Yes.' Valerie was quick to assure him there would be no wild goose chase looking for an inept sailor. 'But I know what I'm doing too. I've got my day skipper and used to race a lot, Six Metres mainly.'[3]

'Six Metre yacht racing,' said Dan. 'Now there's a classy boat if ever there was one.'

'Bloody handful in heavy weather,' added Lenny.

'You can say that again. Had some big days in a Six Metre…' Valerie thought better of admitting to nearly sending one to the bottom during a race, even if it was gusting seven at the time.

Lenny handed the papers back. 'Warning of squalls maybe tomorrow, so keep an ear to the forecast. Don't forget to radio in as you leave.'

Ben was waiting on the quayside as they came out. 'All clear to go?' Dan shouted out as they crossed the car park.

'Yeah, fine.' Swinging his rucksack across his back, Ben handed Valerie her bag. 'Coastguard happy?'

'Yes, we can leave.' A playful grin crept across Valerie's face. 'Could be squally.'

'That's okay,' said Ben, 'a few squalls ain't going to bother *The Sun Dancer*. You still want to go?'

'No problem.' She took out a cigarette and accepted Dan's match. 'Let's get over to the boat.'

Being low on money, only a minimum of diesel was put into the tank. So, with the current to help, Ben kept the revs low as the yacht moved out into the river under the power of

---

3   A Six Metre yacht is a boat built more or less purely to race. It is decked fore to aft with just a cockpit for the crew. They are not six metres in length, as one might expect, but designed to an involved formula allowing the architect to have leeway in the plans. Most are between ten and eleven metres. They are extremely graceful, especially those built between the thirties and sixties.

its own engine for the first time in weeks. Dan waved a few times, letting it get a couple of hundred yards downstream before turning away towards the Land Rover.

To the side of the quay, tall drying sheds leant precariously from years of being pounded by storms coming up the channel. A man in a dark suit stopped relaxing against one and popped a Polo mint into his mouth. He removed a grey plastic mac from his arm, threw it over his shoulder and walked off quietly towards a mud-splattered Toyota. He sat behind the wheel, closed his eyes for a few minutes, then made several phone calls. Tossing his mobile on the passenger seat, he took one last look out to sea, then headed up the winding lane towards the main road.

SIX

BEN THROTTLED THE ENGINE BACK A LITTLE, POINTING the boat in a more easterly direction.

'Better get the sails up when we're clear of the river mouth, save what little fuel we've got for heading up the Medway.' Then he added quietly, 'And any emergency.'

'Okay. By the way,' said Valerie, looking at the fuel needle that was barely above the reserve mark, 'I'd never get paid for any surplus, so I wasn't going to deliver it full of diesel.'

Ben raised his eyebrows and passed a hand around the back of his neck. 'Well, there's no fear of that.'

They motored on for another ten minutes, then, pointing the yacht into the wind, it was left to gently tick over.

'Jib's down the fore hatch. Can you bend it on while I get the main sorted?' Ben received no querying looks as he threw out the occasional technical term.[4]

'Sure, no problem.'

---

4   To "bend on a sail" is to attach in position. In this case, being the jib, it is fixed to the forestay.

He pulled a harness from the locker and threw it across. 'Better put that on. Prop's still turning, don't want you going over and coming out the back as best mince. Can't say I fancy explaining that one to the insurance company.'

Valerie slipped it on, connected the carabiner to the safety wire and walked up past the mast, unclipping and re-clipping at every stanchion along the deck, each manoeuvre accompanied by a rearward sarcastic smile and spasmodic flash of tongue.

The jib fell onto the deck as Valerie upturned the sail bag. She found the head and shackled it to the halyard. 'Hoist a little,' she shouted back along the deck, 'while I get the rest of it on.'

The jib secured, Valerie made her way back to the cockpit. She looked at the array of tailed-off halyards at the foot of the mast. 'Which one?'

'Blue.' He took a shackle pin from between his teeth and nodded to the coils of rope. 'Get the main up first… you feed, I'll winch.'

Valerie stood by the mast, making sure the main went up its track as Ben wound smoothly on the winch handle.

'How long to that bay we're stopping at?' asked Valerie.

'Seaton?' said Ben, looking around. 'Wind's good, we'll be there before dark.'

Uneventful and quick. They were soon at the overnight anchorage. Valerie dropped the jib as Ben paid out the anchor.

'It doesn't hang back, this boat, does it?'

'Yeah, it's quick,' said Ben, moving his attention to the main. 'A bit hairy in a blow, but yeah, it fairly bowls along.'

'You been out on similar boats?' Valerie shook a Disque Bleu up from the pack. 'You seem to fall into its ways very quickly.' She flicked at the Zippo as Ben refused an offered cigarette.

'Yeah. Crewed in races and helped deliver boats, mostly into winter storage.' He coiled the last rope and sat down. 'What the bloody hell are those?' He waved a hand across his face as the smoke blew past. Valerie held the pack up. He pressed his lips together and gave a slight shake of the head. 'Never heard of them.'

'French.'

'Which cabin?' Ben got up and pulled off his deck shoes, before using the chrome rails to slide below.

'Don't mind.' She threw the part-smoked cigarette overboard and followed him down. 'What's that?' she added as he pushed down a couple of switches.

'Riding lights. It's quiet in this bay, but we don't want to be run down by some half-asleep trawler skipper.' He motioned his shoes towards the master cabin and yawned. 'I'll go forward.'

The slap, slap of the waves echoing around the yacht had a comforting effect that soon had Valerie asleep.

***

'Takes all sorts,' said Valerie, ringing a spoon on the Charles and Diana mug. 'Tea.' She put it down on the bunk side table and gave Ben a shake. 'Tea,' she repeated as he opened his eyes. 'You want something to eat?'

'Yeah.' Ben moved his head back as if trying to focus and frowned at the mug. 'Any chance of an egg?'

'Between bread, okay?'

'Sure, no butter, but sauce if there is any, tomato or brown, don't mind, whatever there is.' He swung his legs from the bed and scratched vigorously at his unkempt hair. 'Yuk.' Looking into a nearby mirror, he clicked his tongue around his mouth. 'Glad Mum threw a tube of Colgate in.'

Ben still had the remains of the butty between his teeth as *Sun Dancer* swung round to reach out of Seaton Bay.

'You want to take her?' he said, rising from the tiller. 'I'll check the weather.'

'Sure. Keep heading east?'

'Yes,' Ben waved his left hand, 'just keep the land on this side.'

'Very droll.' Valerie took the helm and slid across the seat.

Ben was below for quite a while, and as the wind rose and swung a little more from the north towards the east, Valerie had to harden the sheets, bringing *Sun Dancer* from a close reach onto a beat. The starboard rails dipped as the port side rose high into the clear wind. With the superior gearing, she pulled the jib in, quickly followed by the main. Now, with the boat really starting to heel, Valerie moved to the windward side of the cockpit, watching the sea bubble and pour along the now-submerged leeward rail.

Spray started to fly along the deck, but she still managed to light a cigarette. The speed dropped slightly as the boat went past its optimum angle, but Valerie didn't stop. Pulling at sheets until both sails were bar-tight, the boat began to smash through waves and troughs.

'Blood and friggin' sand!' shouted Ben, crawling and falling from the cabin hatch. 'What the bleedin' 'ell's going on?!'

Jamming a foot against the cockpit side and holding on to a winch top, Ben steadied himself against the violent pounding. With his free hand he grabbed the traveller control and, with one upwards jerk, released it, sending the mains carriage flying down to leeward and crashing against the stop. *Sun Dancer* immediately obeyed and, recovering her composure, came up to a more comfortable angle.[5]

---

5   The sheets (ropes) that control the mainsail are fixed to the deck beneath the boom. Nowadays it is rare that a sailing boat will have just a single anchorage point. The blocks (sheaves) are on a carriage allowing the anchor point to travel the width of the boat on a rail. In severe weather the blocks on the carriage are eased to leeward (opposite side to where the wind is coming), thereby allowing some of the wind to spill from the sail and depower it.

'If you're trying to win the Fastnet, you're going in the wrong bloody direction!'

'Just seeing what she'll do,' said Valerie. 'Getting a bit of excitement.' She flicked the remains of her cigarette overboard.

'Seeing what she'll do!' Stepping and tripping over rope ends that had emptied onto the deck, Ben took the tiller. 'What as, a bloody submarine? Carry on like that and something will give.'

'What? On a boat of this calibre? Give me a break.' She started down the cabin steps. 'Want a drink?'

'Beer.' Sliding to the windward side, Ben pushed a hand through his tangled hair. 'If there's none on board, try my rucksack.'

When she returned, Ben had eased the controls and the yacht was creaming along at full speed. She threw him a can of Stella and pulled the ring from a Diet Coke.

'What was all that in aid of?' Ben wedged his knee under the tiller and opened the beer. 'Sailing the ruddy thing on its ear?'

'Oh, I don't know, live a little closer to the edge, I suppose.' She took a swig from the can. 'Don't you ever get fed up with the dullness of it all, want to go out and do something? Leave your mark?'

She hadn't finished a cigarette all morning, so drew one out now they were set on a steady course. 'That's nice.' A long stream of blue smoke disappeared over the stern.

'You not worried they'll kill you?' He motioned towards the cigarette between her fingers. 'Jesus Christ, they're not even bloody tipped.'

She took a piece of tobacco from her tongue, shrugged her shoulders and pointed to a structure a few miles out into the channel. 'What's that?'

Ben wiped spray from his face and slid round. 'Second World War fort. Kept us safe from Hitler. Some, outside territorial waters, were used as pirate radio stations in the sixties.'

'Let's go and have a look, spin the delivery out a bit.'

'Naw,' said Ben, 'it's only some empty towers strung together with rotting walkways. Likely to get yourself hurt getting on and off.'

Valerie un-cleated the jib sheet and flicked it from the winch. 'Good grief, Ben. Get out into the channel and stop being such a wuss.'

With the jib flogging out of control, Ben had little choice if he didn't want the sail damaged. He eased the helm and set out towards the rusting structure.

Valerie smiled as she set the sail on a reach. 'See, it's easy, have a nose around and earn a little extra for you and me.'

Ben settled back into the remains of his beer. 'Got a boyfriend? You've no wedding ring, and anyway, I can't see a husband putting up with what you do, sitting around the kitchen waiting to hear if you're coming home in the next few days.' Valerie drew on the last of the Disque Bleu before sending the spinning stub overboard. 'Or girlfriend?' added Ben, looking at the man's wristwatch.

As all Ben got by way of reply was Valerie staring out into the channel, he tried another approach. 'Been in this business long? Investigating, I mean?' He crushed the empty beer can and dropped it over the side.

'Four years or so.'

'And before that?'

'Oh, this and that,' said Valerie. 'Change in circumstances set me off in a different direction.'

'You work for the insurance company?'

Valerie leant back, stretching her arms along the safety wire. 'No, no, I work for myself. Investigating anything as long as there's money at the end.' She trimmed the jib sheet, giving the sail a little more fullness. 'There's life cover involved, and Southern and East wanted this accident looking into. All their assessors were tied up, so I got the job. Wouldn't tell me how or why – maybe they put a pin in Yellow Pages.'

Three orange buoys, tethered to each other, passed down the port side. 'They're not warning markers this far out in the channel, are they?'

'No, they'll be lobster or crab pots. The amount of wrecks around the south coast is mindboggling. Anything down there,' he said, motioning over the side, 'is going to attract fish and shellfish. Bloody big conger in some of them too, like ruddy serpents. We sometimes arrange fishing trips for guys wanting a bit of sport. We had one of our customers catch one just short of a hundred pounds last year. You should have seen Dan, he doesn't like congers – disappeared into the wheelhouse and locked the door.'

'You're kidding.' Valerie leant back on the hatchway and laughed. 'Looks as hard as nails.'

'Oh Christ, he is. No one better when the going gets hairy, only don't chuck any big eels into the boat.'

The buoys vanished in the troughs as the wind started to whip the odd top from the waves. A few minutes later, a large power cruiser passed fifty yards or so on the shore side in the opposite direction. Valerie responded to the friendly wave from a couple up on the flying bridge.

'Looks vaguely familiar,' she said as it carried on westward.

'You know them?' said Ben.

'No, no. The pennant on the stern. I think it's one of the clubs on the Solent.' She shrugged her shoulders and watched a dozen or so small fish scatter across the surface in panic. 'Wonder what's after them?'

Ignoring her, Ben kept probing. 'Where did you learn to sail?'

'Out on the Solent. Like I said before, used to race on a Six Metre.'

Ben nodded approvingly. 'Never set foot on one myself, but lovely boats to race, I should think.'

'Incredible,' said Valerie. 'We only left the mooring to race or tune it up. They're built for nothing else.'

'Your boat?' said Ben, keeping up his enquiries. 'Or—'

'Someone else's,' cut in Valerie. 'The skipper, me and a couple of guys. Four up. Perfect. Some go with five, but if you're up to it, four's fine.'

'Not tripping over each other,' said Ben.

Looking up at the flying wind indicators, Valerie nodded. 'Lean and fast.'

'Successful?'

Valerie thought back to the autumn's end in the yacht club. 'Armfuls of silver every end of season. Winning isn't everything, but losing is nothing. Who the hell wants to be anywhere but upfront fighting for the lead?' Valerie gave out a little smile. 'Hoisting the winning flag at the end of the race is what it's all about, and if you weren't in the first three it was a disaster... Although the skipper put it a little stronger than that at times.'

'Not just doing it for the sport then?' said Ben.

'No way. Love sailing but could never understand crews coming into the clubhouse smiling after finishing in the last half dozen.'

'You still race?' asked Ben.

Valerie got up and turned to go below. 'No.' Disappearing into the cabin, she pulled the hatch shut.

Twenty minutes later, Ben called her back on deck. 'We're here. Better come up and give me a hand if you want to save your precious diesel.'

Valerie went forward as Ben put the yacht head to wind and stopped short of the rusty ladder. She tied off before going back and helping with bringing the sails down. With her neck craned upwards, the swaying boat gave the illusion of the towers moving against the sky.

Each of the five structures sat on four legs and were joined to each other by walkways. The accommodation on top of the supports gave the strange impression of oversized stools. There were the remains of radio masts on the towers, some with lengths of wire flapping in the wind. On the furthest one was what looked like a flagpole held up by frayed stays. Rust dripped from the concrete where iron reinforcing rods poked out into the sea air. What colour the towers had been was no longer possible to determine. The little paint that remained was a pale grey.

'Coming up?'

'You go. I'll get some lunch together. And be careful,' he called as Valerie scrambled up the ramshackle ladder. 'Don't want to be phoning Southern and East to tell them you fell down a bloody hole.'

'Well, Ben was right about there being nothing here,' Valerie said to herself, rubbing the rust from her hands. She moved from empty tower to empty tower, each one connected to the next by a paint-flaked, corroded walkway, until the last, that looked so unsafe she turned around.

Back in the first tower, and before descending to *Sun Dancer*, she drew a shoe across the floor. Curiously, as if it had been swept, there was no dirt, no dust.

'Well, was I right or was I right?' said Ben as he pushed a lunch of tinned tuna and salad across the table.

'Yeah, right. Nothing but a few rotting cables hanging from an old junction box.'

'What were you expecting, the ghost of Tony Blackburn playing "Get Off of My Cloud"?'

'Think you'll find he was further east, on Radio Caroline… And anyway, he's not dead… allegedly.' Valerie pushed a hand into her jacket pocket. 'Music system on board, do you think?' Like a valuable jewel, she produced a USB.

Ben motioned over his shoulder. 'By the chart table.'

Valerie pushed the memory stick into one of the inputs on the front of the brushed silver panel, scrolled through the index and pressed play.

'Didn't think you looked the type,' said Ben as Bruce Springsteen blasted out across the cabin.

'The boss?' said Valerie. 'One of the best.'

'What else?' said Ben, putting the last of his tuna between two slices of bread.

'Everything… Stones, Oasis, Little Richard, Pink Floyd, Beethoven, Etta James. You name it.' She pushed her hair back behind her ears. 'Only things I can't be doing with are Benjamin Britten and rap.'

'Bit ancient. You're not much older than me, and who's Etta James?'

'Oh, good grief.' Valerie gently shook her head. 'I was injected with the good stuff by…' She stopped, scraped her plate into the bin and turned to the bottom of the cabin steps. 'Been in my blood for too long. And there ain't no cure for rock 'n' roll. Come on, Ben, let's get going fast and hard like we were racing.'

'So, it was a conversion?' said Ben as they peeled off from the rotting structure. 'Rock music, I mean. Like on the road to Damascus.'

'More like on the road to Brighton, winter weekends when we weren't racing.' She stopped and began tending sails that were perfectly set.

And that was as much as Ben got out of her. Deeper questions were given generic answers or met with silence.

Later the next day, *Sun Dancer* was using up the last of the diesel as Ben guided her along the Medway to her berth.

'Good couple of days,' said Valerie, pocketing the keys and jumping onto the jetty. 'Thank you, sweetie.' Ben had an extra bounce in his step as he followed her from the yacht. 'Not you,' she said, noticing the smile, 'the boat. But thank you, too.' She stroked one of his cheeks, while kissing the other. Then as he stood there looking at her, she drew him forward and kissed him intimately with slightly parted lips. Minty breath from freshly brushed teeth, mixed with Giorgio Armani, briefly swirled around as she ruffled the back of his neck.

Ben cleared his throat. 'Anytime.'

Valerie looked at the serious expression as his face flushed. 'Surely you've been kissed by a girl before?'

'Exactly,' said Ben. 'By girls, and not like that.'

'Going to have to go out and get yourself a woman then, aren't you? Find out what life's about.'

Ben threw his bag over one shoulder and followed her across the floating pontoons to the taxi rank.

***

'Look after the car.' Valerie stood back from the train as she saw him off on his way back west.

'Sure.' This time Ben had to make do with a farewell handshake.

'Got to go and see this guy's brother. Then I'll be along to pick it up and give you some loot.'

It was not until he was sure that Valerie was on the next train back to the city that the man returned to his car, put his plastic mac on the rear seat and pulled out his mobile.

'On her way back.'

Ending the call, he thoughtfully tapped the phone on his knuckles before dropping it onto the passenger seat. He then took a fresh packet of mints from his pocket and tore away the outer wrapper.

SEVEN

Before keeping her appointment with the late Alan Preston's brother, Valerie returned to the houseboat, took a shower and changed. Chewing on the last of a slice of toast, she looked in the mirror, wondering about lipstick. She held her image for a second or two, then, with a fingertip, wiped a last crumb from the corner of her mouth. Taking out a gold tube, she stroked on the mid-red Estee Lauder, then moved closer to the reflection and pressed her lips together.

Grabbing a coat, she checked her watch and, as much as high heels allowed, ran along the towpath to the bus stop.

The meeting that Jane had arranged, or more accurately Preston had suggested, was at the Four Seasons. Walking in through the impressive marble entrance, she briefly thought of the last time she was there: another life, another time. Deliriously happy times. Although young, she had recognised the times as the best, the happiest and that more was to come. It would just go on for ever. So deeply enveloped in what was happening in her life, and being able to know just how fortunate she was—

'Madam?'

Valerie's melancholy thoughts were brought to a halt as she approached the reception. 'I'm here to meet a Mr Preston. Do you know…?'

'Yes, madam. It's Miss Stone?' said the immaculately dressed young man behind the desk. 'Mr Preston left word you'd be coming.' He pointed across the foyer, to where a man she recognised from the photo was holding a hand towards a black leather chair.

The man stood up, offering his hand as Valerie approached. 'David Preston.' The smile was deep, extenuating the lines either side of his eyes. 'Nice to meet you.'

'Yes.' Valerie flashed a business-like expression. 'Sorry about the circumstances.'

'Yes, quite,' he cut in, quickly moving the conversation onto a friendlier level. 'I have a table booked. Shall we talk over lunch?'

A waiter in a gold waistcoat guided Valerie to a plush red velour and black-framed chair, before seeing to Preston. In one swift move menus were placed on the deep mahogany table. Red walls decorated with red paintings in black frames complemented the rich oriental ornaments on side tables. The whole room breathed top restaurant, in a top hotel, in a top city.

Valerie steered clear of dishes on the menu that stirred up memories. It was a betrayal of sacred times. Although her mind flooded with items from the exquisite menu, she chose a simple lunch of avocado followed by salmon, new potatoes and salad.

'Not very adventurous, from such a menu. Are you sure that's all you want? Would you like something to drink?' Preston gave her a reassuring smile. 'Miss Stone, are you all right?' he said in response to Valerie's silence.

'Yes, fine, fine. Can I have a Coke or Pepsi? Don't mind which as long as it's bottled. Two slices of lime and plenty of ice.'

'We can put the meeting off to another day if you like?' He leant forward slightly.

'No, I'm sorry,' she said, pulling herself into the present. 'Just thinking of something I have to do later.' The smile was warm and directed towards her dining partner. It touched her vivid green eyes but went no further. Valerie's smile no longer smouldered from the beautiful emerald depths. 'I'm fine, honestly.'

Studying his features, she sat back in the chair. Smart, well-groomed hair and freshly manicured nails hinted at the pride he took in his appearance. The pale blue tie against the slightly darker blue shirt went well, as did the dark charcoal suit finished with fine blue stripes. Not a designer suit; this man did not follow the pack, neither was he concerned about the latest trends. The classic single-breasted suit had been made to measure, and she was quite sure it had a wardrobe full of companions.

'Now what can I do to help? I'd have thought it was all pretty straightforward: Alan fell from *The Sun Dancer* and was unfortunately killed by the propeller.'

'On his own? It's a pretty big boat to take out single-handed. I sailed it back from the Exe with another guy, and he was experienced. Wouldn't have wanted to do it on my own.'

'Yes, well, as you said, sailed it. My brother wasn't sailing; he was under power, as I understand.' Preston took a sip of water, then patted his lips with the crisp linen napkin. 'I was out of the country, so I don't know what he was doing. Taking it from one marina to another, I should have thought.'

'What about the insurance? There's no will, so it goes to you, next of kin.'

'Yes, I suppose. Not sure why he took out such a large amount. He was engaged at one point, maybe he took it out then. He has no family, and Mother and Father are both dead. Bit of a mystery, but nothing illegal.'

'No, no, nothing illegal. It's just the circumstances and the large sum. Southern and East want to look through it, that's all.' Valerie fiddled with the stick in her drink, pushing at the ice and lime. 'What about *Sun Dancer* being in your name? You've been abroad for a while. What's behind that?'

'I was coming back a while ago; we were going to race and maybe some coastal cruising, so I bought the boat. It was in my name, I did the deal, but it was our boat rather than mine. We did some racing, but not as much as I'd have liked.'

'When's the funeral?' Thinking only of how to extract as much out of the case as possible, Valerie carried on with irrelevant questions. 'The body's been released, somewhat early, I'd have thought, but—'

'Last week,' Preston cut in. 'No point delaying, and in any case, I wanted to get it done. Although we didn't see much of each other, we were pretty close. I owe him a great deal – he's the…' He stopped to correct himself. 'He was, the brains. Anyway, wanted to do him one last service.'

'Yes, sure.' Valerie pushed her plate to one side. 'Where have you laid him to rest?'

'Cremated, and ashes scattered off the coast.'

Well, that puts a full stop on things, Valerie concluded. *Where do I go from here? If anywhere. Seems like Jane's little money-making scheme has come off the rails. Go and get the car, call into Weymouth on the way back, and that will be about it.*

Finishing the lunch and polite chitchat, Preston waved his Platinum Visa at a passing waiter. 'Can I give you a lift somewhere?' he asked, breaking into her money-stretching plans.

'Yes, thanks.' She gave the street nearest to her office. It had a little class about it; she never gave clients the downtrodden area the office was in if she could possibly help it. She had occasionally toyed with the idea of using the houseboat but didn't want people coming around at all hours, moaning down her ear about the terrible life they were leading and expecting her to kiss it better.

Valerie had assumed Preston was not short of the folding stuff but was taken by surprise as a midnight blue, highly polished S-Class Merc stopped outside the hotel. The chauffer that opened the door for them was around six foot two and, to Valerie's eyes, about the same across the shoulders. And on top of that he was a tough-looking sod. Sinking back into the cream leather, she pondered why he would want someone that looked less like a driver and more like a bodyguard.

She had become quite expert at fending off any probing questions into her past. On the ten-minute journey, Preston had to be satisfied with a general conversation, punctuated by smiles that, although lighting up her face, had no intimate communication. That had stopped four years ago.

Preston turned to her as the chauffer opened the door. 'Have you a card?'

'Card?' Valerie slid out, brushing imaginary creases from her coat. 'Why would—?'

Before she could finish, Preston leant out. 'Your secretary didn't give me your phone number.'

'Why would you want my number?' The defence was slight but deliberate. 'I—'

Again Preston interrupted before she could continue, this time with a smile. 'In case I can think of anything else that may be of importance. Also, if I haven't your number, how can I ask you out to dinner?'

Valerie patted her pockets, looking for non-existent cards. 'Sorry, don't seem to have one on me.'

'Phone number?'

Valerie took the mobile from her pocket and looked up its number. 'There you are,' she said. 'Can never remember it myself.'

Preston took the phone and tapped the number into his own. 'Thank you, Miss Stone, or may I call you Val?'

Standing on the kerbside, Valerie's face drained of colour as the smile vanished. 'It's Valerie,' she said, pushing hands deep into pockets. 'Please don't call me Val. Thanks for lunch, must get off.' Without looking back, she walked off down the busy pavement.

'Bloody hell, boss,' said Preston's chauffer. 'I think you pressed the wrong button there.'

'Think I did, Kenny.' His eyes did not leave the elegant figure until it vanished in the crowd. 'Think I did.'

Turning down a quiet alley, Valerie took the last Disque Bleu from the pack and struck savagely at the Zippo. Drawing deeply on the smoke, she walked back to the office.

'Train back to Exeter, Jane,' growled Valerie as she opened the door. 'And bloody first class, too.'

'Cripes, who's crossed you?'

The small glass pane in the door rattled as she crashed the door shut. 'Do you know if I have a packet of fags left?'

'If you do, they're in your desk drawer. If not, you're back on the Dunhill's.'

'For crying out loud,' said Valerie, opening the drawer, 'nothing.'

She pushed the usual desk rubbish about until, among the paper clips and rubber bands, she pulled out two wedding rings tied together with a piece of dark green ribbon. She held the gold bands in the palm of her hand for a few seconds, before placing them back.

Jane knew. Once, when Valerie had drunk too much, the whole story had come out. Until that evening Jane had thought her own history was pretty dire, but compared with what Valerie unravelled between swigs of iced Southern Comfort, it was not the end of the world she had always imagined.

***

Only taking time to call off at one of the last tobacco specialists in the city, Valerie made her way to the train station with two hundred of the more expensive cigarettes available in the UK tucked under her arm. Tipped this time; she'd only had the plain before because the shop had run out.

'Bit strong, Miss Stone,' the old man behind the counter had said. 'Have a couple packs of Benson's or Dunhill's. I'll have the tipped back in tomorrow.'

Valerie had scooped up the two blue and white packs.

'No, thanks,' she had said, dryly.

EIGHT

BEN'S MOTHER DID NOT SEEM TO HAVE STOPPED WIPING her hands on the flowery apron from when they had last met.

'Should be back soon. Not sure where he is. You could try the boat; it's about two hundred yards downstream of the coastguard's office.'

Valerie rolled back the cover on the Jag before realising she had given the keys to Ben's mother for safekeeping. 'Have you got the keys?'

'Ben's got them on his ring.' She noticed the quizzical look on Valerie's face. 'Don't worry,' she said, turning to go back inside, 'it's been nowhere.'

Valerie rolled the cover back over the car and started off to the river.

***

Aboard the boat, a familiar figure was hunched over a couple of lobster pots.

'Permission to come aboard, Dan?'

The old man stretched his back as he turned around. 'Hello, gorgeous. What are you doing around here?'

'Just come to pick up the car and pay Ben, so I thought I'd come and see you before I went back. He's not on board, is he?'

'Naw, gone to get a couple of shackles. Cup of tea?'

'Got coffee?'

'Sure, careful on the gangplank, it's a bit wet.'

Dan pointed to the skipper's seat as he boiled up the water. 'Milk, sugar?'

Twisting the seat around, Valerie leant on the wheel. 'Just milk, please, Dan.' She looked around at the faded and torn photos, mostly of Dan and Ben, pinned to the woodwork. There was a photo of Ben's mother that had been torn from a full print. Just an arm was visible of whoever had been at her side. 'Tell me about Ben.'

'Why?' Dan passed the battered enamel mug over. 'What's he done?'

'Nothing, just wanted to know about him. He wasn't very forthcoming on the boat, just kept asking me questions. What happened to his father?'

'Boating accident. He got tangled up and pulled overboard.' Raising his eyebrows, he held up his pipe.

'Sure, carry on.' She pulled out a fresh pack of cigarettes and stripped them of the cellophane.

Reaching across, the old man offered a match before attending to his pipe. 'Bloody awful. We were just a hundred yards or so from the shore. A gentle swell and clear blue sky. When that kind of thing happens, it brings to mind big seas and driving sleet stinging your eyes. It seemed to make it worse, people on the sand having a good time.' He shook the match and dropped it on the floor. 'Ben was on board and it was all I could do to stop him going over after his dad. I managed to cut one of the lines but he'd been dragged down too far. By the time we got him up he was dead. It was two years before Ben would talk to me.'

'Not letting him go after him?'

'Yeah, but we're okay now. As he let the time go by, he realised I did the right thing. I'd have been coming back to harbour with two corpses instead of one. Telling me sister she was a widow was bad enough, couldn't have hacked telling her she had no son either.'

Although it seemed the case was petering out, Valerie still had little doubts that refused to go away. 'What can you tell me about coming across *Sun Dancer*? You told me before she just drifting?'

'Yeah, just driftin' about.' Dan's pipe gurgled as he continued puffing. 'Like the *Mary* bloody *Celeste*, except the sails was down.'

Valerie looked out along the deck as she sipped at the coffee. The boat was well looked after. The gears on the winch must have been lubricated that morning; large lumps of grease sat undisturbed on the cogs. Only small dribbles of rust came from the odd piece of equipment. The dark blue deck had been recently painted, as had the white superstructure. A couple of small nets hung over a stack of lobster pots. Ropes and wires were neatly coiled, set around the central hatch.

'Peculiar, that, isn't it?' she said. '*Sun Dancer*, just sitting there. Waiting for you to come along.'

'Yeah, and the funny thing is, we'd never have found it if Ben hadn't insisted we went fishing away off where we normally go.' Dan swilled round the last of his coffee before finishing it.

'Did he say why?'

'He said a couple of boats had had a good haul and kept it to themselves, but he thought he knew where they'd been.'

Valerie took a last drag of her cigarette before sending it spinning into the river. 'You never went on board, did you?'

'No, not until we were back here on the Exe. Why you askin' all these questions anyhow?'

'Got to put something in the report, Dan. If I can beef it up a bit, you know, make it look better than it is, I might get some more work out of them. At the moment it's looking pretty thin.'

'No galvanised in two-inch,' Ben called as he walked across the gangplank. 'Had to get stainless at twice the bloody price.' Two shackles dropped with a clunk onto the chart table as he jumped into the cabin. 'Oh, hello. Come for a visit?'

'Yes,' said Valerie, sliding from the seat, 'and to pick up the car.' She pushed her hand into the inside pocket of her jacket and produced a brown envelope. 'Bit of brass, keep the wolf from the door.'

'Blimey,' said Ben, looking at the wad of twenties inside. 'Thanks.'

'That's okay, you earned it. Here,' she laid a piece of paper on the table next to the shackles, 'put your moniker on this.'

'Oh, bloody hell, Valerie.'

'Anything will do,' she said, reading his mind. 'It ain't going to get back to the chancellor.'

'Mickey Mouse?' he asked, while writing Charlie Jones on the bottom of the receipt.

'Come on, Ben,' she went over to the door and turned, 'you can walk me back up to your place. Okay, Dan?'

'Sure, we're just about finished here.' He made an exploratory prod at his pipe before producing more clouds of smoke. 'See you tomorrow, Ben.'

**

Ben helped Valerie pull the cover from the Jag. 'Happy to have *The Sun Dancer* back, was he?'

Valerie was quiet for a minute while they rolled up the light nylon. 'Sure you don't know this Alan and David Preston?' She slowly, deliberately drew the words out.

Ben was surprised, like a kid caught with his hand in the sweetie jar. 'Know them? Why should I know them? Course I don't, never heard of them before you turned up.' He recovered his composure a little but still continued talking too quickly. 'No, no, course I don't.' With a slightly nervous hand, he extracted the car keys from his own ring and passed them over.

Valerie threw the cover into the boot before putting a cigarette between her lips. 'Okay,' she said slowly and quietly. 'Okay.' Then, drawing a gentle hand down his cheek, she flicked the Zippo into life. 'You sure you know what you're doing?'

Glancing at him once in the rear-view mirror, she shifted through the gears. 'Hope this isn't your last chance, Ben.'

***

By the time she was halfway back to the city, Valerie had dictated the report directly to Jane. 'Get it off to Southern and East. Email.'

An hour later, Valerie's hands-free broke into Van Morrison.

'Miss Stone? It's Rosemary Benson, got your email.'

'Blimey, Jane, that was quick.'

'Pardon? It's Rosemary Benson, Southern and East.'

The engine note and rushing wind calmed as Valerie eased off the accelerator. 'Sorry, I'm in the car, just slowing down. I can hear you now.' Valerie's speed dropped even further as the dual carriageway funnelled into a single lane. 'You have the report?'

'Yes. Can't let it go now, can we? Things don't add up. As long as you're sure in what you've put?'

'Could be nothing, but the way they found the boat, and one thing and another.'

'One thing and another, such as?'

'I'd rather keep that to myself at the moment. Don't want to start, and then make a fool of myself.'

'Okay, Miss Stone, we're happy to let you carry on. We can delay settlement for a few weeks without causing any problems. It's a large sum, no one is going to think a delay unreasonable.'

'Talking about payment, we can't keep going on just expenses, I—'

'No, no, that's fine. I'll transfer some money into your account today.'

'The bonus,' said Valerie, 'that still stands? We're not giving that up for a few weeks of salary.'

'Of course,' said Mrs Benson. 'Point seven five, or three, whatever it is.'

'Okay, we'll get after it.' Valerie hung up and slowed even more as the drivers ahead rubber-necked Stonehenge.

An hour later, Valerie was entering the city outskirts and called Jane again.

'Going back to the houseboat,' she said. 'Need to see Preston again, but don't want to get pushy. I'd like him to call first, but if he hasn't done so in a couple of days, I'll have to accidently bump into him or, worse, call him.'

'Oh, I don't think it will be that long,' said Jane. 'My bet is tonight or tomorrow morning.'

Valerie pushed the windscreen-wiper rocker in response to a few drops of rain. 'You gone all clairvoyant on me?'

'No, can't claim that, or any insight into the male psyche. We've got an office full of red roses, arrived about an hour ago. And no, they're not from your good old standby. There's a card, says, "To Valerie, thanks for a lovely lunch." And Valerie is underlined twice.'

NINE

Valerie was towelling off her hair and wondering how she was going to work the next few days with Preston, when the phone broke in.

'Valerie.' She could sense he was smiling, stressing the name carefully, making sure she understood it was an apology. 'How have you been?'

'Oh, hello, Mr Preston, I believe I owe a thank you for some lovely roses?' She threw the towel onto a stool then flopped into the nearby chair.

'Mr Preston… Can't ask you out to dinner with you calling me Mr Preston all night.'

Valerie curled her legs beneath her bottom and put the phone on loudspeaker. 'All right… David.' With exaggerated care, she started manicuring her nails.

'That's better,' he said. 'How about dinner… Tonight? We can go to a nice little place I know on the river.' Valerie took a sip of mineral water before selecting another emery board. 'You still there?' asked Preston after a short pause.

'Sorry, David, just finding the diary. Trying to work something out.' With an accompanying frown, she blew the dust from her nails. 'Give me a minute, let me have a look.' After inspecting her other hand for a few seconds, she continued, 'Can't tonight, got a couple of clients I have to catch up with. They're both in a bit of a tizzy, you know, need someone to reassure them, hold their hand.' She thought for a split second, wondering whether to give him tomorrow or wait until the next day. String him out, she decided. 'Day after tomorrow is okay, any good for you?'

'Yes, of course, day after tomorrow, I'll pick you up. Where do you live?'

'You could pick me up from the American Bar if you like, I'll be in town most of the day, should be through by six. Six-thirty any good?'

***

A couple of days later, the taxi driver was looking at the refined reflection in his rear-view mirror. 'Where to, Miss?'

'American Bar.'

For a moment the driver held the vision in his mind as he pushed the indicator down. 'And bloody right, too.'

'Sorry?' said Valerie, popping a Tic Tac into her mouth.

'Well, you wouldn't be going down KFC looking like that, would you? What time you got to be there?'

'Six-thirty.' She leant back in the seat, rolling the small mint around her mouth. 'But take the scenic route, let's make it around seven.'

'Just like my missus, she used to keep me waiting. Still does. She was a looker, just like you.'

'Was?'

The taxi driver pulled the wheel around as they left the end of the road. 'No. Not was. Is. Swear she hasn't put on more than two or three pounds in the last twenty years. Still makes me feel like a million dollars when she's on me arm.'

'Sounds like I'll be doing all right if I look like her in a few years.'

With his arm leaning out of the window, he smiled. 'You will, Miss. You will.'

Waiting in the rank on the Strand, Valerie looked at her watch as it moved to seven, then took some notes from her wallet and folded them in half. 'Thanks,' she said, putting the money into the hand passed through the glass division.

'Have a good time, Miss.' The driver waved the money as she left the cab. 'And keep him dangling. Keep 'em all dangling.'

Instead of putting her coat on in the conventional manner, Valerie slipped it over her shoulders. Preston was seated in the foyer watching the comings and goings through the main entrance. The slight look of irritation was replaced by a smile as Valerie walked in.

'Sorry.' Valerie handed her coat to a waiter and sat down. 'Client kept going on and on, never thought I'd get away.'

'It's not a problem. Drink?'

'Southern Comfort.' She looked up at the young man with a tray beneath his arm. 'Highball glass, two slices of orange, up to the top with ice.'

'We'll be in the American Bar,' added Preston before looking back at Valerie. 'Had a busy day?'

'Very.'

With Preston by her side, Valerie crossed the chequered floor and onto the thickly carpeted bar entrance. Pulling back a blue tub chair, Preston momentarily stood in attendance as Valerie sat down, crossing her ankles, the suggestion of a suspender outlined on each thigh.

Pieces of ice cracked as the waiter removed the thick-bottomed glass from a silver salver and placed it on the table.

She whispered a very private "thank you" to the young man, and asked him if he would request the pianist to play "On Green Dolphin Street".

She raised the glass slightly towards Preston and took a sip. Then, momentarily holding a small amount of the golden liquid on her tongue, she let it gently burn down her throat.

'Would you send a drink over to the pianist, please?' Preston waved the waiter back and told him to take over whatever the musician usually had, with the lady's compliments.

Valerie smiled. 'He drinks the same as me.'

'Been here before?'

'Now and again.' Valerie looked around the familiar room. 'Never tire of this bar. Glass, chrome, slick service.'

'That's unusual,' he said, pointing to her watch. 'Man's Rolex Submariner. Old one, you can tell by the dial – the figures go a creamy colour. Probably worth two or three times the price of a new one. Father's?'

'No, no.' Cutting him off sharply, Valerie slid a hand over the watch; Preston had trampled into somewhere he was not welcome. 'It's just a watch.'

With the slightest of nods, he acknowledged the accidental trespass. 'Tell me, how did you get into this business of yours?'

'Oh, kind of fell into it, I guess. Helped someone out with a problem. Then this other guy heard about it and said he'd pay me to sort out some pilfering from one of his outlets.'

'That was lucky,' said Preston, 'getting a client straight away.'

'Would be if I hadn't been stuck with him from then on.'

'Keeps coming back, does he? Can't say I blame him.'

'Oh, he's all right, feel sorry for him. My fault, really, never told him to get lost.'

'And what about your family – do they approve of your business?'

Valerie took another sip of the spicy bourbon, letting it roll around her mouth once more. 'No way,' she said after swallowing the wonderful nectar.

'Not in the same trade, as it were?'

'No.' Deciding to let a veil drop to the floor, Valerie smiled. 'I come from a village in the Midlands, a few miles outside Worcester. My father's a solicitor and mum's a doctor. I'm a terrible disappointment to all, I'm afraid. Especially as my brother is now a surgeon.' Valerie raised her glass towards the piano player as her request wafted across the room.

'Oh dear, I can see how that might be a problem,' said Preston, getting her attention back. 'They don't have anything to do with you anymore?'

'No, they're fine. Can't pretend to have been thrown out in disgrace, and I didn't run away from home when I was thirteen.' Once again, the laughter did not reach her eyes. 'They're loving, but perplexed.' Valerie swirled her drink around, watching the thick liquid cling to the sides of the glass. 'I sometimes get this vision of them praying every morning that I go back and finish uni.'

'Men?'

'Ooo,' she said slowly. 'Straight in with the biggies.' Valerie let her words hang in the air for a moment. 'Sometimes.'

Looking like someone about to hit the buffers, Preston finished his drink. 'Shall we get off to this restaurant then?' He got up, raising his hand to a nearby waiter. 'Lady's coat and the bill, please.'

Valerie was unsure how Preston's driver did it, but just as they stepped onto the pavement outside the hotel, the dark blue Merc appeared.

'Boss.' The driver held the door while ushering them in.

Preston let Valerie slide across the leather, then got in beside her. 'The Riverside, please, Kenny.'

The restaurant, about forty minutes out of town, was perfect. It was a converted mill set by the side of a gin-clear river. Visible by the underwater lighting, white-flowered water-crowfoot wafted around in the current to the side of the wooden walkway. Stopping by the railing, Preston pointed into the slack water towards the tail of some weed. A native brown trout sat patiently, its tail moving slowly as it kept station. After a minute it rose to the surface and, leaving the slightest of ripples, sucked a delicately floating blue-winged olive below.

Reluctant to move, Valerie rested her arms on the wooden rail. 'It's beautiful.'

'And deadly,' said Preston. 'You do not want to be a fly floating downstream towards the Prince of Darkness.'

After watching another rise, Valerie followed him into the restaurant. 'Don't think I want to eat one ever again.'

Spread over three floors, she guessed it could do sixty covers, maximum. As they were seated, she looked around at the machinery that once powered the building and was now decorating whitewashed walls. Every one of the generous tables was taken.

'Busy,' said Valerie. 'How ever did you get us in at such short notice?'

'Oh, that's an easy one,' said Preston. 'We, or should I say I, own the place.'

'Well, that would help.' She smiled as a waitress asked what they would like to drink.

'Southern Comfort, or something else?' Preston asked.

'Erm—'

Before Valerie could say anything else, he said, 'Or we could order the wine now. Any preference?'

'Chablis.' The reply was automatic, said without thinking then immediately regretted.

'Good choice,' he said, turning to the waitress. 'A bottle of Chablis.'

Valerie resolved to take a break from feeling guilty, at least for the evening. The innocent look was accompanied by a finger to her lip. 'Can I be a peasant?'

'I think you'd find that very hard, but go ahead. What did you have in mind? Please don't say you want it with ice and slices of orange.'

'No, no. Could we have it cold, not just cellar cool?'

'Oh dear, nearly as bad. That is being a peasant.' If there was any anguish in his reply, he hid it well. 'Okay. Make it cold, Janice.'

The waitress, with her nose in the air, left the table as if she'd been invited to take part in something that should only be experienced on a pornographic website.

'I think I've upset Janice,' said Valerie, hiding behind the menu as they perused the list of dishes. 'Hope it's not a capital offence.'

'Could well be.' Preston pulled down the top of Valerie's menu. 'Janice is a highly qualified and knowledgeable sommelier. She came here straight from Claridge's.'

'Ah,' said Valerie quietly. 'Better get the food right, or I'll be floating downstream towards that trout.'

Preston laughed. 'Well, we'll try not to let that happen,' he said as the waiter approached to take their order.

'So, what about you?' said Valerie when they had ordered.

'What about me what?' he said.

'Well, you know all about me.' Placing her elbow on the chair arm, she rested her chin on an upturned palm. 'What about you?'

'I know just about as much as you want to tell me, Valerie. There's a lot more about you than I think you'll ever tell anyone. But me, I have no secrets. I'm just what you see,' he said, holding out his hands. 'I, or should I say we, me and my brother, were left money by our father. Not a fortune, but enough to start a loan business… and no, before you ask, not lending to vulnerable people at five thousand per cent.' He leant back in his chair as the first course of sliced melon with lime dressing was placed in front of him. 'We were fortunate like you: a guy with a great business idea but no money came to see us.' He motioned to Valerie's bowl of fresh tomato and basil soup. 'Okay?'

'Yes, perfect,' she said. 'I've made it myself many times, but always fall a little short. Have to get your chef to come around, show me where I'm going wrong.'

The very cold Chablis arrived and Preston took a sip from the offered glass. 'Now I've got a problem,' he said, as Janice made no effort to hide a pained expression. 'Insult one of the finest wine experts in the south or upset my guest.'

Valerie waved a hand. 'Don't worry,' she said dismissively. 'I've been upset before and I dare say it'll happen again. But not over a glass of wine.'

Janice, on the other hand, didn't look like she was about to give in gracefully, ever, even if Preston was her employer.

'Well, there's no denying that we are losing a little on the taste. But…' he drew the word out slowly, 'I can see where Miss Stone is coming from; it has a definite and pleasing way about it.'

'Very neatly put,' said Valerie. 'I'll settle for that.'

'If you'd like to have a taste, Janice, take a half bottle out of the cellar and try it cold. Split it with the manager, I'm sure you'd both like to give it a go.'

Leaving the table, Janice resumed her disapproval by putting her nose back in the air. 'Yes, sir,' she threw over her shoulder, 'I'm sure we both burn with curiosity.'

A cheeky smile flickered across Valerie's lips before she returned to the conversation. 'So, you lent money for a business start-up and never looked back?' she said.

'Yes, but came damn near to losing it all at one go. The guy fell in a big way, along with all our investment.'

'You obviously didn't go down, though,' she said.

'No.' Preston waited until the table had been cleared and the main courses put in front of them. 'My brother had great faith in the business and suggested we bought the guy out with what little we had left.' He took another sip of his wine. 'Beginning to grow on me,' he said, holding up the glass in mock inspection. 'But don't tell Janice.'

'And?'

'Oh, yes.' Looking thoughtful, he returned to his story. 'We took it over and he cleared his debt. We… or rather, my brother, put it into profit in twelve months. I'm afraid the gentleman with the idea took it very badly, threatened us with all sorts, but history is strewn with business opportunities won and lost. He took us to court, but it was a waste of his time. All he's done is given himself a debt he will never be able to repay.'

'What was the business?' she asked.

'Computers,' he replied, 'like most everything else in this world. Can't pretend to know much about what was so revolutionary with his idea. I'm just glad he put a good team together, because without my brother I'd be lost.'

'And that was the start of a mighty empire,' said Valerie.

'I think "mighty empire" is a little bit of an exaggeration, but yes, once we had that going, everything else we touched seemed to turn into gold. Lucky.'

They continued with the small talk for about forty-five minutes before Preston looked up and nodded to someone behind Valerie. 'We'll have to move into the lounge for coffee. Promised the head waiter we wouldn't be too long. The restaurant has a three-month waiting list at the moment and the manager's doing what I pay him for: keeping customers happy.'

Once again Preston followed Valerie's swaying hips into the lounge.

'Brandy? Something else?' asked Preston as they sank into large, caressing chairs.

'Southern Comfort, two slices of orange and plenty of ice.'

'Is there nothing you don't have chilled to death or served with mountains of ice?'

'Like I said before, just a peasant, I guess.'

'Change of subject,' said Preston. 'You don't work weekends, do you?' As all he got in reply was a furrowed brow, he carried on. 'Having one or two friends over for the weekend, going to take *The Sun Dancer* out, shake her down, blow away the ghosts.'

Valerie looked at him for a few seconds. 'Sorry,' she said, knowing he'd said something that once again rang a bell. 'What did you say?'

'Would you like to come out for a sail this weekend?' he said slowly.

Valerie sat back in her chair, cursing the law forbidding her to smoke indoors. 'Excuse me a moment,' she said, pushing up on the chair arms, 'I'll just go and wash my hands.'

'Sure,' said Preston, half-rising.

Valerie looked at herself in the mirror as she ran her hands beneath the water and thought, *What the bloody hell is this all about? What's with the friggin' mystery; if they know each other, why did Ben deny it and look so nervous?* She put her hands into the hot dryer and spoke out loud. 'Well, what now?'

'Beg pardon?' Valerie hadn't been conscious of the door opening, nor the elderly lady now leaning on an ornate walking stick.

'Sorry.' Valerie rubbed her drying hands. 'Thinking out loud.'

'Oh dear,' the lady smiled as she inclined her head, 'that doesn't usually happen till you reach my age.'

Pulling her hands from the swirling air, Valerie looked thoughtfully at the old lady. 'Ever wondered why someone is lying when there is no apparent reason to do so?'

'Oh yes,' said the lady as Valerie left, 'I have grandchildren.'

Do I come right out with it? Valerie sat back down, her mind preoccupied. *It's all a bit bloody thin. The guy's just lost his brother and all I've got is maybe his brother knew Ben. If he's dead then he's dead. An accident and that's it.*

'Well?' said Preston. 'You up for a couple of days' relaxing?'

'As long as it's in a group,' said Valerie.

'I do believe you don't trust me.'

TEN

'THAT'S IT,' SAID JANE, HANDING THE SINGLE SHEET OF A4 to Valerie. '*Sun Dancer*'s been in nearly every port and harbour from Plymouth round to Yarmouth. Most of all the Medway of course, but Poole is used a lot. She was on the entry lists of a few yacht clubs, but nothing at the moment as far as I can find out.'

'Okay, so where does he live?'

'He's on the voting registry in Poole.' Thoughtfully, Jane tapped a pencil on her teeth. 'Sandbanks, if you please.'

'Christ,' said Valerie, 'that's serious money.'

'And that's the one we know about.'

Valerie scanned the few lines on the sheet of paper. 'Think I'll go along to the Poole Harbour Master.'

'Stretch out the expenses,' said Jane, 'good idea. Any chance I'm in for a bonus?'

In an effort to look stern, Valerie narrowed her eyes. 'About the only thing that's going to get us ninety grand is suicide, but I'm not holding my breath. We're clutching at straws. I think David, er, Preston is going to get his three million.'

'Twenty-odd, plus a good massage of the expenses, ain't going to hurt now, is—' Jane's musing was interrupted by the phone.

After answering with the normal greeting, her face fell. 'No way, I've told you before.' She spat the words back at the caller. 'Get lost! I'm finished with all that; I don't work on my back anymore.' Valerie leant back against her desk, knowing that nowadays Jane was quite capable of looking after herself. 'It's taken me two years to get back onto this planet, and if you think I'm returning to your bleedin' sewer you've not just got a slate loose, your whole bloody roof is suspect. Now piss off, Vinnie! I wouldn't work for you for one hundred per cent of my earnings.' She slammed down the receiver. 'Fucking arsehole,' she said while giving Valerie a forced smile. 'Sorry.'

'No, no, very ladylike if he was asking you what I think he was asking you. Is that the first time he... you know... since you...?'

'No, it bloody well isn't.' Anger brought a deep flush to Jane's face. 'Been on at me for months, even come around to me flat.'

'You've got those innocent schoolgirl looks back, that's what it is... can't wait to get you into a grey skirt and white blouse for the dirty mac brigade.'

'Yeah,' said Jane. 'One of his girls really looks about fifteen; five hundred quid a night. Bastard,' she blasted venomously.

**

Valerie learnt very little about Preston or *Sun Dancer* at the harbour master's in Poole. Except that one of the super-yachts along the quay, looking more like a block of flats on the move, belonged to his brother.

'Quite something, aren't they?' the officer said, looking out the window. And before Valerie could ask, added, 'Ten million, some of the larger ones like your friend's.'

Curiosity getting the better of her, Valerie drove off to Sandbanks.

Leaving the Jaguar in the car park, she walked along the sea road until, standing outside Preston's house, she blew out her cheeks in appreciation. The building, looking out over the water, stood on twin piers so as to accommodate parking under the main house. From the roadside she could see great slabs of smoked glass set into brilliant white stonework.

The main part of the house, resting on the piers, stood two storeys high, and Valerie gauged the whole place to be set on a double plot. To the right and nearer to the road was what she presumed were staff quarters. Guessing that the Merc and a lime green Lamborghini parked between the piers meant Preston was at home, she walked back along the road.

Sitting in the car, Valerie closed her eyes and let the sunshine warm her face before picking up the mobile. 'Take an early weekend,' she said. 'I've been invited on a cruise-cum-party.'

'Oh yeah,' said Jane, 'anyone we know?'

'Well, I know him,' said Valerie.

'Oh, it's a him, is it? Can only be Nigel or Preston.'

'David Preston, okay? Weekend on his boat!'

'Going at a bit of a break-neck speed, aren't we?' said Jane. 'You've only known him a week. Anyway, thought you were signing holy orders, giving up men for good? Well, except for Nigel, but I don't think that poor sod counts.'

'Well, nothing seems to be making much sense... I can't see Preston being involved with anything dodgy, but I'm pretty sure he knows Ben and yet he's keeping shtum for some reason. And he was away at the time. So maybe he's protecting his brother… smuggling? I don't know. Hold on.' She stopped and took a cigarette from the pack and tried juggling it along with her phone and lighter. 'Damn, hold on, Jane.'

'Allow me, Miss.' The man moved his plastic mac to the other arm and, hanging it over his shoulder, reached in with a lit match. She hadn't time to exhale the smoke before he was gone. Valerie twisted around but only had the vague impression of someone disappearing behind a four-by-four.

'Sorry, back again. Some of his friends will be coming as well, so don't get the idea we'll be rolling around the ocean in a frantic forty-eight hours of wild passion. Anyway, it's been so long I'm not sure if I can remember what to do.'

'Don't worry, it'll come,' said Jane. 'Like riding a bike, if you'll forgive the expression.'

'Thanks, Jane.'

'Just don't fall off.'

'Not sure holy orders wouldn't be simpler,' said Valerie quietly as she hung up.

Satisfied he knew where she was going, the man took a cold mineral water from under the car seat and, taking a sip, pulled out his phone.

***

The yacht had been moved from the marina where Valerie and Ben had left her. She was now moored alongside the quay, the last in line of five other boats, all looking like they were about to go out to sea.

This side of the complex appeared a lot more affluent than where Valerie had walked off the floating jetties. Bentleys and Audi R8s stood side by side, along with the occasional

Ferrari, the green Lamborghini among them. Two cafés and a chandlers' store bordered the car park and, further along towards the river mouth, dinghies were pulled up outside a yacht club. The club burgee, fluttering above the clubhouse, was at half-mast.

'One of the hierarchy must have gone for a final beat down the channel,' Valerie breathed quietly.

Dressed in white shorts, a blue La Martina polo shirt and Ralph Lauren deck shoes, Preston looked every inch the successful entrepreneur as he waved from the foredeck of *Sun Dancer*. 'Valerie.' He walked down the short gangway and onto the pontoon. 'So glad you could come.' He risked a peck on the cheek as he took her grip. 'Yours?' he said as she locked the car.

'Yes.'

'Early sixties?'

She nodded.

'It goes with the watch.'

'Will it be safe here?'

'Safe as houses; we're in a locked compound. But you can put it in the store house over there if you prefer.' He pointed to some blue double doors to the side of the chandlers.

'No, here's fine, as long as we're in a secure area.'

Preston waved her in front, following Valerie's shapely bottom and hips. 'Jesus,' he said quietly.

'Sorry to be a bit precious about the car, it's just that—'

'No, no,' he said, skipping a couple of steps to catch up. 'I'd be precious about something like that.'

***

Two days later, Preston walked her back across the car park.

'Lunch tomorrow?'

Valerie reached into the pocket of her jacket and took out the worn fob and keys. She'd gone onto the boat, forty-eight hours earlier, still firmly rooted in the past. Now she was happier than in a long time. Was it time to move on, take a step away from the past? All on just a weekend? She'd had four years with him and now four years without him. Could she let him go? Break the ties? Jump ship and land, if not in paradise, then another place?

The weekend had been a break away without much thought about anything she'd left ashore. She had thought about him – he rarely left her mind – but now memories were not pulling as before. And another plus: the two other couples on board were not what she had expected. They were rather pleasant and not the brainless, champagne-swilling, cocaine-snorting cretins that she'd uncharitably planted in her mind. And apart from Preston having to pull up one of the men about calling her Val, they were perfect company. And this time even that was not really a problem. Someone calling her Val did not bring the usual, almost uncontrollable mixture of pain and anger. Anguish had been blown away on the breeze.

After clearing the river mouth, one of the girls had suggested that as it was getting hot, they should go below and get changed while the men, 'Did the only thing they were good for, and sail the boat.' And it had been easy to join in the giggling and general deriding of men as they changed into swimwear.

'Knew I should have packed mine,' one of them had said, admiring Valerie's one-piece, classic black swimsuit. 'Why do I always go over the top? Bloody bikinis.'

Valerie found herself back in the familiar master cabin, the only one en-suite.

'Thought I'd let you have a little space to yourself,' Preston had told her. Although unsure of where she was heading, but being more at ease with herself, Valerie decided to give him a glimpse of the prize that might be his.

She knew he would pass her door on the way to the main cabin when he came below to make a radio check. And knew it would be a pretty safe bet that if she left her door ajar, he would glance in as he passed. At the sound of his footsteps she left the shower, water dripping from her naked body.

The success of her plan was confirmed when, during lunch in the cockpit, Preston had said, 'I'll be getting the lock on your door looked at next week, but in the meantime give it a good pull; it doesn't always close properly.'

In reply, Valerie had removed an apple from the bowl and polished it on her breast before taking a bite and tossing the remains to Preston.

'Understood,' she'd said with the suggestion of a smile.

***

Only the tyres were visible beneath the cover hiding the familiar shape, but it brought immediate guilt swimming about her brain before funnelling through her body.

'Valerie?' Preston repeated. 'Lunch tomorrow?'

She pulled a pack of Disque Bleu from her pocket and tapped one out. Only when she was emptying her lungs of smoke did she speak. 'Sorry, I wasn't listening. What did you say?'

'It's okay,' he said. 'Let me help you.' They both peeled back the cover.

'Sorry,' Valerie said, putting her bag and car cover in the boot, 'I was miles away, thinking about a client I have to see later.'

'You didn't touch one,' he said, nodding to the cigarette, 'while you were on board, I never saw you smoking.'

'Oh that. Don't go thinking I've an iron will. Got NiQuitin patches when the need arises, you know, so I don't go climbing the walls if I can't have one.' She smiled. 'But I don't like it if there isn't a pack in my pocket.'

'Never saw a patch.'

'My, my. And here's me thinking you were the observant one. You don't have to wear them on your shoulder, you know.'

'Oh, I see. Lunch tomorrow?' he asked again, closing the car door as she slid behind the wheel.

'Not sure, I'll call.'

As he bent to kiss her on the cheek, she put a hand to his face and turned his eyes to hers. Letting her lips relax, she gave him the gentlest of warm kisses, then, opening her mouth slightly, she turned away, leaving a sweet, moist memento.

Drawing away slowly, the light smile on his face turned to one of deadly seriousness.

***

Instead of using the hands-free, Valerie pulled into a cliff-top car park and called Southern and East, then the office. Jane's trembling voice dragged her from the last two days, sharpening her concentration.

'What's the matter?' she asked.

'Bloody Vinnie sent two of his scumbags around to try and persuade me back onto the game.'

'Hurt you?'

'No, just pushed a pile of twenties onto the desk and asked why I was here, instead of making easy money.'

'Right,' said Valerie. 'Lock up the office and get yourself round to the houseboat. Make sure you're not followed, change buses, swap to a taxi. Just make sure you get there alone. There's a spare key on a hook under the gangplank.'

'Okay,' then after a couple of seconds, she added, 'we're not being a bit Secret Service, are we?'

'Just do it, Jane.' Valerie threw the mobile onto the passenger seat and re-joined the road.

***

By now the sun was shining down out of a clear blue sky, so the man decided to use his mobile while having a coffee on the terrace of the roadside café. He made several calls before reporting back.

'My guess,' he said, 'is that she's just pushing up the expenses as much as possible.' Nodding occasionally, he listened for a few seconds while playing around with a sugar cube. 'I might be wrong; this lassie could be a lot sharper than we think. I spoke to that contact we have at Southern and East a few minutes ago. They said she wants them to send someone down to the boat and check for any trace of narcotics.'

He threw the cube back into the dish and listened a little longer. 'No problem. I'll keep on it.' He got up, dropped a few coins on the table, picked up his plastic mac and left.

ELEVEN

With only a towel wrapped around her, Jane stood in the middle of the main cabin, rubbing vigorously at her hair. 'I took the liberty of freshening up,' she said. 'Wanted to wash those two morons away.'

Valerie hung her jacket on the back of the door and walked into the galley. 'Coffee?' She took a couple of mugs from the shelf and flicked a switch.

'Please, I'll get dressed and come through.'

'Well?' said Valerie as Jane plonked herself on one of the bar stools.

'He just keeps going on,' said Jane. 'It's like water dripping on stone. Bleedin' relentless. Gets me down at times. The bastards won't accept I've turned a corner and ain't going back. Joined the living, as it were. And then one of his goons slaps this on me.' She dropped a pile of twenties on the table.

'What about an ASBO?' said Valerie. 'Take it to the law, get him sworn off.'

Looking for inspiration, Jane stared into her coffee. 'ASBO? He'd think it was some long-lost tribe from up the friggin' Amazon.'

Valerie put a hand under Jane's chin, bringing their eyes together. 'You're not going back.'

'No, no,' said Jane, 'that ain't even on the agenda.'

'Even if it means you work for me forever,' Valerie added under her breath.

'I'd better get off,' said Jane, sliding from the stool.

'Go tomorrow, stay tonight.' Valerie picked up the wad of money. 'I've just got to go out for an hour.' She leant on the doorframe, flicking through the money. 'You can make us something for tea, look in the fridge.' She pocketed the twenties and left.

***

Once the height of fashion, the bright green tiles either side of the peeling front door were now chipped, along with rectangles of crumbling cement showing where the odd one had been broken away. The Beggars Hat public house was just about the last of the rundown pubs in the East End and was destined for renovation or demolition. From years of pushing hands, the only clean part of the door was the brass plate. The rest looked like it hadn't seen a paint brush in years.

Valerie dropped her half-smoked cigarette into the outdoor ash box and walked in. A chorus of whistles spread around; whether from appreciation or surprise it was impossible to say. Sarcasm was more likely, Valerie thought.

A few years ago, she would have been making her way through thick smoke, but it all looked rather strange in a now fug-free atmosphere. There were still signs of days gone. The ceiling was a rich orange and no attempt had been made to fill the holes in the tables where the ashtrays had once been nailed down.

'Now what can I get you?' The barman wiped the counter with a grubby tea towel before replacing it over his shoulder.

'Bottle of Diet Pepsi,' said Valerie, looking at the battered cooler cabinet. The barman knocked the top off and was going to pour it into a glass, but Valerie, seeing the grey water in the sink, held up a hand. 'From the bottle.' She snatched it away before he could empty it into something unsavoury and put a five-pound note on the counter.

While waiting for the change, she glanced around. Vinnie was in a corner holding court. An expensive haircut, designer suit and highly polished shoes could not change the slimy aura that surrounded him. He'd noticed her but hunched up and pretended to be in earnest conversation with the man opposite.

His eyes stayed focused on his companion, as Valerie dragged a chair to his table and sat down. 'Hello, Vinnie, and how's life treating you?'

Not knowing if Valerie was a loner or could back any little chat they might have with real muscle, he looked slightly nervous. 'Well, er… it's Miss Stone.' He smiled. 'I'm fine, just fine, and how have you been? Not seen you for a long time, must be—'

'Up to naughty ways again, aren't you? Thought I'd warned you off. Jane's no longer in your line of work, but you just don't seem to be getting the message. Now what does it take, Vinnie, a little visit from the Gendarmes?'

Vinnie held his hands out in defence. 'Just trying to help an old friend,' he said. 'I'm sure Jane could do with a bigger pay packet. I mean, you can't be paying her four figures a week, now, can you?'

Valerie took an instinctive wipe around the bottle top. 'She's out, Vinnie. No longer interested.'

'Okay, okay, it's not a problem, no more calls.' Taking a mock oath, he held up his right hand. 'Promise.'

A couple of men started moving towards the table, but Vinnie gave a slight shake of the head. 'What about a decent drink?' he said. 'Shake hands, just a misunderstanding.'

Inspecting the half-full bottle, Valerie declined then looked around. 'And how's your business then?'

'Oh, can't complain, keeping the kids in shoes.' He inspected his fingernails and eased back into the worn leather. 'What are you up to?'

'At the moment? Just a little work for an insurance company. Jane's a great help, clever girl.'

'Yes, bright lass, always was.' Vinnie took a swig from his vodka and orange. 'Now there,' he added, nodding towards the door, 'is a hard piece of work and no mistake.'

Valerie half-turned as a tall, thin man walked across to the bar. His receding hair was cut short but was compensated by a handsome handlebar moustache. Strangely enough, the butterfly perched on a rose tattooed on his neck did not distract from his striking angular looks.

'How's that?' she said, returning to her drink.

'You pay and he'll come with real muscle.' Vinnie waved across. 'Hello, Charlie, how's it going?' With her back to the room, Charlie didn't notice Valerie.

'Who's he work for?' asked Valerie as his raised glass was reflected in the old brewery mirror.

'For 'imself, ain't beholden to no one,' said Vinnie. 'He's a bit like the Lone Ranger, except he does it for money. Them that don't want to get their hands dirty call for Charlie. You get an alibi, go on holiday for a couple of weeks and leave it to 'im. Some say that there's one or two who ended up face down in the Thames, were down to Charlie. I'm not so sure. I reckon it's just something he likes people to think is true. But

I do know that whatever they dun in the first place, they don't go doing it again.'

'Well, have to get off.' Valerie reached into her inside pocket. 'Yours, I think,' she said, dropping the wad of money onto the table. 'I've taken out sixty, fifty for upsetting Jane and ten for petrol.'

'Sure, sure,' he said, reaching out his hand as Valerie got up.

Being conscious that this was the bad lands, she thought it better to take his hand before leaving.

TWELVE

VALERIE LOOKED OVER JANE'S SHOULDER AT THE SHORT
email. 'Well, they were quick if nothing else,' she said. 'But it
doesn't help. Signs of smoking dope and a few dregs of coke
down the back of a chair.'

'Well that's it,' said Jane. 'Sex and drugs and rock 'n' roll.'

'Not the crime of the century, though, is it?' As if waiting
for divine inspiration, Valerie sat down and stared at the
ceiling.

'Why, what were you expecting?'

'Oh, I don't know, maybe the traces of smuggling, that's
about all I could think of, really, but this is just recreational
stuff, illegal but it ain't going to set the world on fire. I think I
can see a brick wall looming out of the fog.'

Deciding that whatever was going on, if anything, it had to
be all down to Alan Preston, she picked up her phone. 'David,
it's Valerie. I think we need to talk.'

'Oh dear,' said Preston. 'That's the usual preamble to it's all
been very nice, but goodbye. And we've hardly said hello.'

'No, no.' Her words were measured and deliberate. 'I want to ask you a few things about your brother, Alan.'

'Okay, how about dinner tonight?'

'No,' she said. 'Straight questions. I'd rather meet—'

'Somewhere a bit neutral, as it were,' he said, cutting her short.

***

The big chauffer stopped a little way from the park bench where Valerie sat throwing the occasional piece of corn to the ducks. 'You can wait in the car, Kenny, I shouldn't be too long.'

Walking the rest of the way on his own, he sat down beside her. 'Different T-shirt,' he said, pointing to the Pink Floyd illustration.

'Yes,' said Valerie quietly, 'different T-shirt.' She threw a few more pieces of corn towards the lake while they sat in silence for a minute or two.

'Well?' said Preston. 'I think one of us should say something... if it's only goodbye.'

'Yes,' she said, throwing a few more pieces of the cereal.

'Well?'

Valerie brushed the last of the crumbs from her hands and looked at Preston. 'Alan.' She stopped and pulled a pack of Disque Bleu from her pocket. 'Okay?'

'Sure. Don't think they've banned it in this park. Yet.'

'Do you think your brother could have been up to anything without you knowing?' She flicked at the Zippo and drew in a lungful of smoke.

'Such as?'

'Wish I knew, it's just that...' She paused and examined the end of the glowing cigarette. 'There's a young guy down on the Exe. Fisherman. He helped me bring the yacht back.' She drew in more smoke. 'He got very nervy when I threw your names into the conversation. And…' Flicking ash to the ground, she hesitated.

'Well, go on, let's have it.'

'He also found *Sun Dancer*, seemed to go straight out to where it was floating around. So…'

'All a bit coincidental,' said Preston.

'Yes, but how did he know where to find it, and why was it spotless when it arrived at the marina?' She ground the cigarette under her trainer as some children sat on the grass close by. They licked at deep yellow ice-creams, one of them chasing a dribble down his arm with a quick tongue.

'So, my brother was, what?' he said, turning to face her.

'Exactly, your brother was, what? I'm afraid all I've got is a nervy lad with a homing instinct when it comes to yacht salvage.' She thought it better to keep the last piece of information, tying Ben to Preston and the boat, to herself. 'Ben, that's the young fisherman, must have been told by someone about the boat and to go out and bring it back. And,' she stressed, 'go over it like a demented friggin' chambermaid.'

'Valerie!' The mock castigation and smile did little to raise the atmosphere. 'Never heard you swear before.'

Valerie laughed. 'Moderated it because of the kids over there.' She nodded towards the children still engrossed in their fast melting ice-creams. 'But I know one or two when the brain's idling in neutral.'

'So, we have Alan doing something that is connected to your young friend and a mysterious, unknown person.' He stopped for a few seconds before adding, 'Maybe.'

'Yes, but who and, more to the point, why? Not to put too fine a point on it, you're as rich as Croesus, so I'm not sure it's money.'

'Power?' threw in Preston, trying to be helpful. 'Blackmail? That's about as far as my thinking goes. What are you going to do?' He squeezed her hand. 'After having lunch with me, of course.'

***

'Go and see this Ben,' said Preston as he watched Valerie stirring her coffee. 'Ask him straight out. Put the screws on.'

'Yeah, suppose,' she said absentmindedly. 'Have to go by train – something wrong with the alternator on the car, it's not charging properly.'

'Come on,' said Preston, rising from the table, 'let's get you some wheels. I've got a car you can use. I have it for running around town.'

***

'Running around town?' Valerie looked at the dark blue Golf R sitting in the parking bay. 'Only a man could have a rocket ship for nipping down to Sainsbury's.'

Preston put his head through the open window and began showing Valerie the relevant switches and controls. 'All very simple,' he said. 'Flappy paddles each side of the wheel, but to tell you the truth you don't really need them; the computer keeps it all under control. Just use your foot to go and stop.'

'Thanks.' Valerie fondled the back of his neck as she returned a kiss. It felt warm, desirable and, for a moment, she did not let him go. Parting her lips, she willingly accepted the close contact with a man. Still holding the back of his head, she drew back, a resolute look on her face. Signalling that the moment had passed, Valerie stroked the side of his face and gripped the wheel.

'Oh, one interesting thing,' he said, clearing his throat. 'Press that.' He pointed to a button to the side of the gear lever. Valerie did as she was told and a selection of driving modes came up on the screen: Comfort, Normal and Race. 'If you touch that one,' he said, pointing to Race, 'tighten your seatbelt.'

'That for when the bad guys are after me?' she said, driving off.

***

'Ben,' she said as he leant against the wheelhouse door, 'stop messing me about. Try and think of this as a "this could change your life" situation.' Whoever was frightening him, it was obvious Valerie was coming in a pretty poor second. 'What's it all about?'

'Change my life?' he said. 'Don't get so bloody melodramatic. I did some work for him. Picked people up, dropped them off, that's all.'

'What else?' she said, thinking he had given in rather quickly.

'I don't know anything else. The only person I dealt with was Alan Preston. He gave the orders and I did the gofering.' Ben shrugged his shoulders. 'A little tax-free, that's all.'

Valerie still had the feeling he was supplying the minimum information possible. 'What about his brother, David?'

Ben kept strictly to the "volunteer nothing" method of counter-interrogation. 'Never knew he had a brother, not until you mentioned him. Honest.'

Valerie said nothing as she looked out across the river. Car headlights reflected off the water as the light faded. On a nearby yacht, a lone seagull lurched as it attempted a landing on a rolling mast.

'Okay, okay.' For a moment, Ben's breath drifted around in the dropping temperature. 'Picked up some packages and dropped them off at the boat. Probably wacky baccy. What's the problem?'

'And coke?' she said.

'Okay, okay,' said Ben. 'But so what? Smoke it, shove it up your nose. What's the bloody problem?'

'And what about your connection with the paranormal?'

'Paranormal?' Ben looked quizzical as he drew away. 'What the frig you on about?'

'How did you know where *Sun Dancer* was? And don't give me that guff about just going out fishing – that ain't going to wash.'

'Got a phone call. Someone said to come out while they stayed on board, stop any nosey bugger from butting in. Then when we come chugging over the horizon, they'd sod off. And before you ask, Dan had nowt to do with it, okay.'

'And that's it?'

'Yeah,' said Ben, 'that's it. Whoever it was just wanted the boat cleaning up. End of story. What you going to do?'

'As far as you're concerned? Nothing. As you said, smoke it, shove it up your nose, what's it matter?'

THIRTEEN

Looking at the report for Southern and East, Valerie decided not to spend any more time on stretching it. She scribbled her signature on the bottom before passing it back to Jane.

'We want some more work out of this company if we can,' she said. 'Better not milk it. Or at least, not obviously.'

'Back to spying on marriages that are no more, or never were in most cases, is it?' Jane pushed the wad of A4 pages into an envelope and ran her tongue along the edge. 'I heard someone invented flavoured gum somewhere.' She banged her fist along the fold, then opened the desk drawer. 'Cadbury's Fruit and Nut would be nice.'

'Get tidied up, then take a few days off,' said Valerie, putting her jacket on.

'Off to see you-know-who?' said Jane, searching for stamps.

'Need to think,' Valerie replied. 'I might have come to a crossroads.' She pulled the door behind her and set off down the road in search of the Golf.

***

Valerie's unnoticed tail took his phone and tapped the first autodial number as he followed on the other side of the road.

'Time to invite her in?'

He listened hard but the traffic kept breaking into the conversation. 'Hold on.' He pushed past a couple of pedestrians and into an alley. 'That's better. What do you want me to do?' To aid his concentration, he closed his eyes and leant back on the wall. 'Okay, okay, not a problem, forty-eight hours. Then where do you suggest?' He nodded a couple of times. 'Okay, sure.' He listened for a few more seconds. 'No, I won't lose her. Besides, I've a pretty good idea where she's off to.' He made a couple more calls, then pocketed the mobile.

Valerie's ever-present shadow was correct. Preston had called on her return from seeing Ben and invited her round to his flat overlooking the river. 'Besides,' he'd said, 'I'll need my town car back.'

Valerie picked up the Golf and drove down to the river and around the back of the apartments. 'Just got to be it,' she said to herself, looking around the parking area before driving straight into the space signed "Penthouse".

The main glass door was released by an attendant whose accent made her think of Eton and Winchester. 'Miss?'

He was tall, around six feet. Slicked-back hair and a full beard surrounded brown eyes and a large nose. His mouth was all but hidden behind the luxurious growth. Whoever had designed the uniform had missed the target. Braid and oversized buttons made him look more like the guy in the Booking.com advert than someone in charge of an exclusive block of apartments.

'I'm here to see Mr Preston, David Preston.' Obviously taking his duties very seriously, he managed to look down his nose and raise his eyebrows at the same time. 'Sorry,' said Valerie, wondering why someone so obviously well-educated was working as a glorified doorman. 'Stone, Valerie Stone.'

He picked up the phone and put in a couple of digits. 'Good evening, sir. There's a Miss Stone to see you.' He listened attentively for a few seconds before responding in a slow and measured tone. 'Certainly sir. Right away, sir.' He replaced the receiver as the defensive frown turned into a polite welcome. 'If you'd like to come this way, Miss. Mr Preston has asked me to show you up personally.'

As the lift arrived at the floor below the penthouse, the concierge pressed an illuminated button. 'Robins here, sir. I have Miss Stone with me. May we come up?' A couple of lights flashed on the control panel, then the lift resumed its journey to the top floor. 'Miss Stone,' he said as the door slid back.

Valerie left the elevator, but before she could thank him, Robins disappeared behind the sliding door. Descending the single step into the room, she flicked her shoes to the side before stepping onto the thick, cream carpet.

'Think I might need a Garmin to see me through this,' she said, running a foot from side to side.

The all-leather furniture was made up of two large settees and three chairs. Running down one side was a chrome and glass sideboard supporting a hi-fi system and enough drinks to start a serious party. To the right were two doors, and straight-ahead sliding glass panels led to a balcony. The contemporary pictures on the wall were by nobody Valerie had ever heard of. In the centre of one wall was a large photograph of *Sun Dancer* going flat out in a force five to six. An oblong coffee table, supporting a chess set, sat in front of one settee.

'Lovely to see you, Valerie. How did it all go?'

'Fine, good advice. Gave it to Ben straight and got what I wanted. More or less. I think.'

Lightly holding her arms, Preston gave her a kiss. 'What are you going to do now?'

'That's it,' she said, 'report's been sent. End of story. I think all your brother was up to was smoking dope, maybe some cocaine, maybe not, could have been his friends. All Ben did was to clean up after them. Some well-wisher tipped him off, you know, remove anything incriminating from the boat.' She decided to soften the blow by not telling him there was someone on the boat. She couldn't see that it was relevant. Fell off on his own or fell off when someone else was with him.

Preston rubbed a couple of fingers across his forehead. 'Drink?'

'Bottle of Coke or Pepsi, diet, please. Lots of lemon.'

'Will a can do?'

'Yes, sure, just can't be doing with that damn draft stuff.'

Preston handed the drink over and sat down, looking at the ceiling as he let his head fall back.

'Oh, Jesus,' said Valerie, going to sit beside him. 'He was your brother and all I've done is slag him off. I'm so sorry, just thinking of what it meant to the case, and all the time...' She broke off and took his hand. 'It's okay, David, no one will find out from me, and I don't think Ben will incriminate himself. Bit of dope is no big deal. No deal at all, as a matter of fact.'

'It's okay, I'm okay.' He took a sip from his gin and tonic and gave her a polite smile. 'Just, you know...' He got up and went across to the terrace window. 'Come and have a look at the view.'

Valerie joined him in the cool evening air and leant on the stainless rail. 'What's this, the view money can't buy?' Stroking his hand, she gave him a warm smile. 'Or rather, can.'

Preston stared out over the river. 'I'd give it all to have him back.'

Valerie placed her drink on the nearby table and put her arms around his neck. 'I know.' The kiss was tender and warm. 'It's bloody hard.'

He pulled back slightly. 'That sounds like someone's been there before.'

'Been there, done that,' she said, picking up her drink and going back inside.

'Got the T-shirt?'

'Oh yeah. Been every inch of the nine yards. Fully paid-up member.'

He followed her in and, saying nothing, crushed her to his chest. 'Music,' he said. 'Enough of this misery.' He picked up an iPad, put in a couple of commands and handed it to Valerie. 'Have a look, there's thousands in there.'

Valerie scrolled through the Tidal menu. 'Good choice,' said Preston as the opening chords to Supertramp's "Give a Little Bit" erupted from the giant KEF speakers. 'No need to turn it down,' he said as Valerie reached for the control again, 'a bomb could go off in this place and you wouldn't hear a thing beyond the walls.'

Preston went over to the fridge. 'Surprise,' he said. 'Had it in here for hours, it'll be freezing.' He pulled the cork from a bottle of Chablis.

'Good job Janice isn't here,' said Valerie, taking a glass.

'Don't want anyone else here.' He lightly put the rim of his glass to hers.

The music continued and Valerie wasn't sure if an hour had passed, or two, or more. She hadn't looked at her watch nor wanted to; she didn't care but was quite content to grab a lift on the passing cloud. For the last few tracks, the music had got softer and slower as she flowed along. With only drinking one or two glasses of wine, it wasn't from too much alcohol that she now felt comfortably warm.

She again put a hand over her glass as Preston offered a refill. 'No thanks,' she said, reaching for a chess piece from the board in front of them.

'Do you play?' he asked as she playfully tapped the rook against her teeth.

'Play? I know *how* to play,' she continued, with a flirtatious grin. 'I'm afraid there's a big difference.'

'Well, I'm not all that great... shall we? We could have a small wager.'

'What were you thinking of?'

Preston made a playful effort of thinking. 'If I win, you come to bed with me.'

'Oh. Heavy stakes.' Valerie now stroked the chess piece against her cheek. 'Throwing all your money onto the table in one go, are you?'

'Can't think of anything I'd value more,' said Preston. 'Not even your car.'

'And what if I win?'

'Name it. But I own nothing that would even come close.'

'Well, you ain't getting the Jag.' Rising to her feet, she slowly removed one piece of clothing after the other, before, with a final flourish, she dropped her knickers onto the chess table. 'Oh,' she said, holding a hand to her mouth in mocking innocence, 'I just knocked the king over... I must have lost.'

With a sweep of her leg she sent the chess set into the thick carpet. Then, standing on the coffee table, she held her hands behind her back.

'Happy birthday, Mr Preston.' She coyly put one ankle behind the other. He rose to his feet and, with an outstretched hand, ran the back of his fingers down her cheek.

'But it's not my birthday.'

'It is from where I'm standing.'

***

Valerie slowly opened her eyes and reached out into an empty, but still warm, space. The sensations and colours of the previous night still journeyed through her mind. But it was a clear mind. Not one swamped with stale alcohol. There had been no lovemaking in a haze concocted by a distillery. It had been sharp, almost cutting, in its exquisite execution.

The bedroom was just as she imagined, understated. Crisp white bedding. A cream carpet. Two Chinese cabinets, one to each side of the bed, and no television. Everything else was behind a door to a walk-in dressing room and wardrobe.

'Morning, sleepyhead.' With a piece of toast between his teeth, Preston kicked the door shut with his heel. 'Breakfast?' He placed a tray on the bed and removed the piece of toast. 'Made it myself.'

'You made some toast...' she said, revealing creamy white breasts while pushing herself up. 'Escoffier is alive, and living on the bank of the Thames.'

'I made the bread that made the toast.'

'Oh, I see.' She took a piece of toast from the silver rack and laced it with butter. 'Not just a bloody sex machine then?'

'Me? Jesus. I seem to remember a certain lady going at it like it was her last day on earth.'

'Hold on,' she said, 'I'll just see if I can find my complaints book.'

'Ha. Shouldn't think there's many entries in that.'

Valerie pulled *The Telegraph* from the tray. 'What's happening in the world?' said Preston, lightly touching a pink nipple.

'Just having a look in the stop press, see if a certain riverside apartment had been reported at the centre of a seismic shift last night.'

'What are we going to do?' he asked, lying back across the bed.

'Well, I can give myself a couple of days off. So, you say.'

'No,' he said, rolling onto his stomach and looking up. 'Us?'

'Us?' she repeated. 'Steady on. I've only just beamed down from the mother ship, don't know which side is up and which side is down yet.' She got up and made her way to the shower, her perfect bottom moving like a poem across virgin parchment. 'Can I pinch some shower gel and shampoo?'

Preston shuffled lists on the iPad as he shouted from the lounge. 'Like classical music too?'

'Sure, blast away.'

It was the wrong music, and it sent Valerie into a descending spiral.

Almost anything else would have been fine, but now she felt a downward pressure of guilt crushing her brain, her body, even her soul. She could listen to all the old music without it being accompanied by pain, but after a night in Preston's bed this piece was too much.

She slumped to the shower floor, tears mingling with the drenching water as the music thundered around. The piece had been played as they left the church surrounded by friends and relatives. And after that he had made a ritual of playing it full-on while bringing her breakfast after Sunday-morning lovemaking.

Lovemaking in green fields and haystacks. Between silk sheets. Other times and places. He always made it special. But Sunday morning, accompanied by Widor's Toccata, was sacred.

'Valerie! Valerie!' Preston's voice broke into this most private grief. 'Christ, what's the matter?'

Quickly recovering her wits, Valerie dragged herself away from the mental precipice. 'Stupid bitch I am,' she said. 'Slipped, banged my arm.'

He threw a towel around her shoulders and helped her back into the bedroom. 'Sit down a minute. It's a bit early for a brandy, unless you think you need one?'

'No, no, just banged my arm, that's all,' she said, rubbing at the phantom injury.

FOURTEEN

No matter where she started thinking about Preston, it all came around in a big circle: a mixture of guilt and wanting to break out. Is this what she had to settle for, she wondered, nudging the office door with her hip. The door bounced back as a large boot was jammed against the frame.

'Miss Stone? Miss Valerie Stone?' The man in the dark suit eased past and dropped his plastic mac on Valerie's desk. 'We would like a word with you.' He motioned through the window to a double-parked car across the street.

'Oh yes.' Valerie followed his gaze through the crooked blind, 'And who's we?'

'Us.' He pulled out a warrant card and held it up. 'To be exact, me, DI Simonds.'

Before he could put it away, Valerie took the card and scrutinised the photo. 'And what's it all about?' she said, handing it back.

'A word, somewhere in private, discuss a couple of things.

Nothing wrong, you're not in any trouble if that's what you're worrying about.' Pocketing the card, he looked around the office.

'And you can't tell me what it's about?'

'Not can't, Miss, just better back at… somewhere else. Somewhere a bit more secure.'

'Secure?' said Valerie. 'This is hardly the bloody Kremlin.' His smile was polite but firm as he grabbed his mac and held the door open.

'After you, Miss.'

The journey to the nearest police station was quick and uninformative, as the inspector restricted his conversation to the weather and how it would affect the running in the two-thirty at Kempton.

The police station, constructed during the optimism of the nineteen-fifties, stood back at the top of five wide steps. Once again Simonds courteously held the door for Valerie.

A uniformed sergeant looked up from his desk, pointing his pencil along the corridor to the side. 'Along there, second door, he's waiting for you.' Uninterested, he went back to checking a file of papers as they passed.

The inspector led the way along a discoloured passageway. 'Miss Stone, sir.' His expression unchanged, he held the door to an office with the minimum of furniture.

'So good of you to spare the time to come and see us, Valerie.' The man, with a rich baritone voice, rose from the only comfortable-looking chair and held out his hand. 'I'm Thompson, and this gentleman, as you know, is Simonds.' He shook her hand, before waving her to a chair that wouldn't have looked out of place in a Victorian classroom.

She looked at the two men. Thompson, in his sixties, was probably approaching six feet tall and, with a clipped moustache, just had to be ex-army. Simonds, the man that had brought her to the station, was younger, a strong, fit-looking man of about forty.

'Simonds,' said Thompson as they sat down, 'has been keeping an eye on you, making sure you didn't come to any harm.'

'I didn't notice him,' said Valerie. 'But what's more to the point, why? Why should I have come to any harm?'

Thompson smiled. 'He'd have been back in the office and behind a desk if you had seen him. And why…' said Thompson, 'is a little more involved. For one thing you're on the inside and we're not… at least, not anymore. So we… let's see, how can I put it, wanted to sound you out on something, see if we might be able to help each other.'

Valerie moved her eyes from one man to the other. 'Help each other is usually a euphemism for I help you, and if it coincides with me getting what I want then lucky me.'

'No, no, no,' said Thompson. 'We are people of honour.' He talked slowly while raising an eyebrow towards Simonds. 'That's more than can be said for the people you've been running around with for the last couple of weeks.'

'Oh yes?' said Valerie. 'And what do you know about the people I've been running around with?'

'We'll get to that,' cut in Simonds. 'How do you feel about helping your country?'

'What?! Some poor sod falls from a boat and suddenly I'm working for the police? I work for myself: private investigator, emphasis on the private.'

Thompson shook his head as Simonds was about to speak again. 'We're not the police. Simonds here carries a card for, let's say, convenience. Saves a lot of explaining.'

'Oh God,' said Valerie, 'spooks.'

'No, we're not anything like that.'

Thompson pulled a cigar tube from his inside pocket. 'Please, get your cigarettes out. I'll not tell if you don't.' He removed the screw top and, turning the tube upside down, let the single Havana fall into his palm. 'Better open the window a bit, Bill.' Wafting a match back and forth across the cigar, he let the smoke drift from his lips.

'I take it you work for the government?' said Valerie, accepting a light from the colonel's dying match.

'Kind of,' said Simonds quickly. 'We're not a bunch of gangsters.'

'Yes,' said Thompson. 'All a bit cloak and dagger, I know, but we're definitely on the side of the angels.'

'And I'm supposed to jump in and give my country a leg-up, am I?' She drew on her cigarette and then, realising she didn't want it, looked around the room for somewhere to put it out. Seeing nothing suitable, she held it between her fingers like a used tissue.

'I live in a country that sells anything that's worth ten pence to the highest foreign bidder. Throws everything you can think of down the drain, all to fund the latest politically correct piece of garbage.' She stood and flicked the unwanted cigarette from the window. 'All the car industry gone, ICI gone, Roundtree McIntosh, Pilkington's, every precious and worthwhile company let go abroad.' Her knuckles whitened as she gripped the chair back. 'They blew every penny of Marshall aid on keeping a world presence and let all our industries go down the sewer. And where is the North Sea revenue? Gone. Wasted. And you want me to dive into my undies drawer and pull out my Union Jack knickers?'

She sat down again and looked at them both in disbelief. 'Dear God,' she said through clenched teeth, 'some ruddy hope.'

Again, Thompson cut in as Simonds was about to say something. 'Hold on, Bill. Just take a look at what we have here in front of us. You're looking at that most rare of creatures.' He got up and handed a card to Valerie. 'Can you come to this address tomorrow? Nine o'clock, okay?' He took her hand. 'Nice to have met you, Valerie. Oh, by the way, as I presume you're going to sleep on it, also consider this: your cut going from point seven five per cent to three.'

She wanted to ask how he knew of her arrangements with Southern and East but kept quiet.

***

To the edge of Trafalgar Square, Valerie stood outside the modest doorway, "Art Records" etched into the surface of a small brass plaque. She tapped Thompson's card on her fingers and turned it face up. *Colonel R. Thompson. British Museum. Fine Art and Antiquities. Records Dept.*

The oak door glided easily as Valerie turned the replacement alloy knob.

'Good morning, Miss.' To one side, almost hidden behind a large vase of lilies, a grey-haired woman in a tight-fitting, pink cardigan got to her feet from behind the desk. 'Would it be Miss Stone?' Before Valerie could reply, the woman carried on in a soft voice. 'Right on time. The colonel is expecting you. It's in the basement, I'm afraid.' She held a hand out towards the side of the small reception area. 'Down the stairs, along to your right. There is a sign on the door.'

As soon as she reached the last step, the carpet ran out. She followed the concrete passageway past four steel doors to the last one, that had the department name on a green composite plate. Again, a heavy-looking door opened easily and she entered a modern office. Two desks sat on an olive carpet, a man behind one desk, the other empty.

'Good morning.' Leaving his work, he got to his feet. He was young, about her age, and looked every inch the college graduate who, glittering with Oxbridge firsts, had been guided into the Civil Service. Before coming around to Valerie's side of the desk, he pressed a switch next to his computer terminal. 'Miss Stone is here, Colonel.' He continued his way round and ushered her through a thick oak door.

'You and the lady at the front door seem to be expecting me...' With slightly raised eyebrows, Valerie held on to the young man's gaze.

'Dennis, Miss Stone. Just call me Dennis,' he said, holding the door.

'Come in.' Thompson was sat behind an elaborately tooled, leather-topped Georgian desk. A smaller one to the side, plush chairs and a rich red carpet all contributed towards the feel of comfortable opulence. Small alcoves contained classically clothed statues of one sort or another, and the walls were decorated with impressive paintings, both contemporary and antiquarian. Highly polished dog irons sat either side of a wide fireplace. The whole room was larger than would be needed for just an office. It made her think of the Reform Club, not that she'd ever set foot in it. All this was accompanied by a steady whirring in the background.

'One of the perks of being in the same building as the arts,' he said, noticing Valerie's roving eye. 'Only drawback is having this bloody air-conditioning going twenty-four hours.' He took a bottle of water and half-filled a tumbler. 'Bloody canned air plays havoc with my chest.' Tapping at his ribs, he took a sip.

'Surprised you wanted me to come, after what I said yesterday.'

Thompson looked at the young man. 'Well, Dennis, you have the file on Miss Stone.' The young man pulled out a chair, sat at the smaller table and opened a folder.

'I have my own file?' said Valerie with slight surprise.

Dennis peeled off a few pages. 'Oh, just a few things, need to make sure we know with whom we are dealing. Then, of course, we've kept an eye on you since you started on this case. Down on the Exe with the fishermen and bringing *The Sun Dancer* back to the Medway with the younger one.'

'Okay, so why am I here, apart from my own curiosity?'

'Yes,' said Thompson, 'where to start?'

'Well, there's nothing in here,' said Dennis, patting the file with a flat palm, 'but…'

'Yes,' said Thompson, 'but… There's always a but.'

'I think we can, sir, especially after what you told me about yesterday's meeting.'

'Yes, I think so too,' said Thompson. 'Well, Valerie, straight in at the deep end, if you'll excuse the pun. The body on Weymouth beach was not, or we're pretty certain was not, Alan Preston.' He opened the highly polished box on his desk and selected a cigar.

'PC not worked its way into the basement then?' said Valerie, pulling a pack of cigarettes from her jacket.

'No,' said Thompson, reaching across with a lit match. 'That's the beauty of working here. No one's going to charge in and drag us off to Camp Delta.' A smile of satisfaction illuminated his face as the thick smoke was pulled towards the extractor.

'The body found at Weymouth was not Preston?' she repeated quizzically. 'Seems you disregard DNA as you do the law on smoking. And his personal assistant, I presume you've had a word with her?'

'No, I'm afraid not,' said Dennis, waving a hand across his mouth while pushing his chair away from the smoke. 'She seems to have disappeared just after signing the papers. Not been heard of since.'

'DNA? It's either right or it's not.' Valerie looked at each man in turn.

Thompson rolled his cigar between thumb and forefinger. 'That's easy,' he said. 'You find the lab technician, shove a pile of fifties and a blood sample under his nose, and tell him you know where he and his family live.'

'I'm afraid we're dealing with people that are going to get what they want and are not all that fussy about the way they get it,' said Dennis. 'It's the way of the world.'

'Okay,' said Valerie, 'what's it about?'

Thompson tapped a forefinger on the table. 'Let's start with Alan Preston's possible location.' Valerie nodded and he carried on. 'If he's alive, and we think he is, he's anywhere he wants to damn well be: South America, West Indies, Hong Kong, South Africa.' He shrugged his shoulders. 'Where is not as important as why.'

'Yes, I suppose,' said Valerie. 'Okay, why? And who was on the beach?'

'Yes, let's go to who was on the beach,' said Dennis. 'Almost certain it was Clive Trent.'

'Trent... okay, and where does Clive Trent fit into all this?'

Dennis took a file from a drawer in the small desk, removed the top page and handed it to Valerie. 'One of us,' he said as Valerie looked at the official photo attached to the details.

'We think, or rather, we know,' said Thompson, 'it's to do with bringing undesirables into the country. They have various side-lines, but at the moment it's the trafficking of these rather nasty pieces of work.'

Valerie pushed a finger across her furrowed brow. 'They're coming in from all over the place, even rowing across the ruddy channel,' she said. 'You're not going to tell me this is just an economic migrant scam; all this trouble and expensive transport, they'd be losing money on the deal. A grand would get you in without going to all this messing around, for Christ's sake.' Valerie put the sheet of paper on the desk and looked at the two men. 'This is a lot bigger than you're letting on. And if you think I'm going to be the next body on the beach, you can think again. Anyway, why make a claim on Preston's insurance? It just draws attention.'

'Not making a claim might have drawn even more attention, that's, of course, if your new boyfriend knows what's going on. He might be just an innocent putting in a claim, when the bad boys would rather he kept quiet.'

For the moment, Valerie pushed the thought of David Preston being involved to the back of her mind. It was unlikely, she thought; very unlikely, she hoped.

'Well, it's been lovely meeting you,' she said, getting to her feet, 'but I think I'll get back to planet earth.'

'We have no one else, Valerie,' said Thompson, fixing her with a glowering stare. 'You're on the inside, or as much as we have on the inside. We need you. We can't send in anyone else. Not again. And, as you so eloquently put it, time to pull on your Union Jack knickers.'

'What for? This lot in Westminster, you kidding? The left is no better than Marxists and the others are somewhere to the right of Genghis Khan. They even use a Spanish bank. Where's their patriotism? Why should I care when the government doesn't?'

'No, no, let her go.'

Dennis got out of the way as Valerie moved to the door.

Thompson pulled a file across the desk and took out his pen. 'You have my card if you change your mind,' he said without raising his eyes.

***

It was just ten-thirty the next morning.

'Her Majesty's Revenue and Customs.' The man flicked at the plastic ID attached to the lapel of his grey suit as he bypassed Jane and approached Valerie's desk. 'We need to see you about your failure to submit a VAT return.'

'What?' said Valerie getting to her feet. 'Return? What are you talking about?'

'VAT.'

Dressed by Laura Ashley, a woman followed holding a tan briefcase under her arm. Dyed black hair was pulled tightly back from high cheekbones. The smile was thin, as were the lips that were heavy with lipstick. 'Seems like you've been a little economical with the truth.' Eyes that matched her hair swept around the office as she dropped a single sheet of paper on Valerie's desk.

A cold sweat froze on Valerie's spine. 'You're kidding?' she said. 'We're not registered, don't turn over enough.'

'Not what we've heard.' The woman sat behind Jane's desk, opened the drawers and, inclining her head, gave the contents a sideward glance. 'We think you've been a naughty girl. Making up VAT registration numbers just to bump up your accounts. Yes?' Pulling out files and placing them on the desktop, she smiled.

'Have to take all this lot back to the office,' said the man as he looked around the shelving heavy with boxed files. 'See if we can make sense of it all.'

In his mid-fifties, Valerie guessed him about the same age as the woman. Being out on the road towards the end of their careers, they had both probably been overlooked at several promotion opportunities.

Valerie went to her jacket hanging on the back of the toilet door and pulled out Thompson's card. Taking her phone, she punched in his number and walked outside the office. 'Okay,' she said as he answered, 'call the goons off. I'll come in and see you.'

'Valerie, lovely to hear from you.' She could imagine Thompson's smile as his plan fell into place. 'What goons, my dear? What's the problem?'

'You bloody well know. The VAT are all over me like a badly fitting suit. Get them out of my soddin' office.'

'Valerie, Valerie,' he said, 'I don't know what you're talking about.'

'The hell you don't. The VAT. Her Majesty's Revenue and bloody Customs, come in here like the Waffen SS, as well you know.'

'Valerie, calm down. What do you think I can do?'

'I want them out of here. I get the message.' She switched the phone off and stormed back in. 'I'll nail that manipulating sod to the wall,' she said, throwing the phone onto the desk.

The man, rather startled, took a pile of files to the waiting car, as the woman flicked open a notepad. 'Valerie Stone,' she said. 'That's right, isn't it?'

'Yes,' said Valerie, 'of course. And who put the finger on me? As if I didn't know.'

'And it's you here, and who else? Who do you employ?'

'Only a secretary,' she said, nodding across to a Jane, who was making an effort to look both confused and innocent.

'Just employed? Not a partner?'

'Just employed.'

Valerie was quite sure she knew what was going on and threw out anything that might keep them in the office while Thompson made his phone call. 'Bet the bastard keeps the number on autodial.' The woman raised her eyebrows, but Valerie carried on. 'What happens next? Do you know how long this is going to take?'

'We'll have this lot out quite quickly.' The woman had the smug expression of someone who was used to being in control. 'Don't worry.'

'No, I mean how long when you get it all back to your office? Before I get the books back?'

'Oh, usually you get put on the end of a queue, but we'll make a special effort to get your case sorted. Should hear from us in a couple of months. No need to worry until then. After that? Well... then it's oh-dear time.'

'Oh-dear time?' said Valerie. 'Love your job, don't you? Can't make it out in the big bad world, so get to dish it out as a civil servant.'

'Come on, Miss Stone, don't be a poor loser. You win some, you lose some. Or in your case, it's you lose some, you lose some more.'

The man came back, interrupting the conversation. 'Have to take your phone too.' Keeping his chin on the next pile of files, he held out a free hand.

'Hell's teeth, how am I supposed—'

Valerie was cut short by a phone playing a stupid tune in one of the woman's baggy pockets. Taking it out, the woman made her way onto the street.

'We'll soon have it all out,' the man said. 'Have you a box?'

'There's nothing in there,' said Valerie as he opened the drawer in her desk.

'Leave it,' said the woman walking back in. 'And bring the rest back.'

'What? I've just taken it all out. What's the idea? Why?'

'Because I told you to.'

'But this is crazy – she's about as bang to rights as you can get.'

'Bring it all back.' The patronising smile was replaced by a scowl. 'The bitch is fireproof.'

Mystified, Jane watched the files moving back in the opposite direction and, with arms folded, moved to Valerie's side. 'What was all that about?' she asked through the corner of her mouth.

'Friends in high places.' Valerie rubbed her chin and inspected the ceiling before adding quietly, 'Or rather, conniving bastards in high places.'

***

'Come on then,' Valerie pushed Dennis back into his chair and barged into Thompson's office, 'let's have it. How do you think you're going to get away with this?'

'Valerie. Good morning.' With elbows on the chair arms and a ruler between each index finger, Thompson swivelled back and forth. 'Going to get away with what?'

'Well, I'm not reporting fairies at the bottom of my garden!' Valerie's face flushed as she leant on the colonel's desk. 'Her Majesty's Revenue and Customs, what do you think!'

'They made a mistake, and I was just glad we could sort it out.' Thompson leant back and threw the ruler onto the desk. 'We're like that down here – a friend calls for help and we come running.'

'Just a coincidence then, was it?' Narrowing eyes and clenched fists accompanied the torrent. 'I turn you down and walk straight into Gunfight at the OK Corral.'

'Valerie,' he said quietly, 'can we start from where we are now? We would like your assistance. We have one of ours dead and you're the only one that can help.'

Quietly following her in, Dennis adjusted his jacket. 'Please, Miss Stone. We're trying to keep the country safe.'

'Oh, all for the government, is it?' The glare in her eyes didn't diminish. 'That's a bloody laugh. There's not one of them in that place fit to clean the boots of the bag lady in Piccadilly. There was only one good person ever got into Westminster.'

Thompson pushed back in the chair, expelling a short snort before adding dryly, 'And even he didn't get the job finished.'

'Then for the people,' said Dennis, trying to soothe the situation.'Do it for the people.'

'That's a misused word if ever there was one. The People's Revolution, The People's Republic. Get to the top and send all you can get your blood-drenched hands on over to Zurich.'

Thompson attempted to pull her back from this sudden outburst of indignation.'Valerie, Valerie. We are not a banana republic. Please, let's talk sensibly.'

'I noticed you didn't mention honesty.' With arms folded, she flung herself into a chair.

'I presume you're in?' Thompson nodded to Dennis.

'Like you're giving me a choice. God knows what else you've got up your sleeve if I say no.'

'Just stand in front of the wall,' said Dennis, picking up a digital Nikon.'The bit with no paintings.'

Knowing what was coming, Valerie arranged a passport expression.'Do I get to hold up my hand and swear allegiance to Her Majesty?'

Thompson smiled as Dennis left the room. 'Not in your case, probably not appropriate.'

'What do I get on my ID?' she said, sitting back down. 'MI5? Special Branch? Metropolitan Police?'

'No, no,' said Thompson,'we're not connected to any other department.'

'So who are you? Who's your boss?'

'There's no one above us. No one knows who we are; nobody knows we're here.' Thompson stood up and leant on the desk.'We are, what shall I say, a small department cleaning up where others can't or won't tread. MI5, Secret Service, not even the Prime Minister knows of us.'

'Okay,' said Valerie slowly. 'No one knows of you… so how do you exist? Who are you responsible to? What about money?'

'Right. A little history lesson. Between the wars, a general meeting of senior civil servants was coming to a close. There's no records, so we're not sure exactly when; somewhere around nineteen thirty-five or -six perhaps. Anyway, that's neither here nor there. While they were putting the papers away, one of them asked about some villain the authorities could do nothing about or didn't want to do anything about. So, as the story goes, they sat back down and had a bit of a natter. Three weeks later the department was formed and the villain disappeared. These senior people oversee vast, mind-blowing budgets. They each siphon off a minute amount and put it into our account. A contact in banking circles keeps it all quiet.'

'Someone gets rubbed out just on your say-so? Very democratic.'

'It was not just anyone, Valerie. Don't forget, back then fascism was turning into more than just a little threat. This country had a lot of problems and there was a great danger of democracy, if not coming off the rails, then becoming a little wobbly. Someone had to step in.'

'Let Mosley get on with it then?'

'He was easy. Well under control. He was so wrapped up in self-importance he couldn't tell our operatives from a hole in the ground. The other one was much more dangerous. And before you ask, no, I'm not going to tell you who it was.'

'And if I don't play, then what?'

'I know you, Valerie. As far as your allegiance is concerned, I know you through and through. At the moment you think we're a load of...' He let the words trail away as they sat in silence for a few seconds.

'Just sign this.' Dennis breezed back into the room, waving a piece of paper.

'As well as my retainer, I'll need Jane's pay. I'm not dumping her.'

'No, of course not. We'll make sure you get enough to keep her on, and you'll not have to worry about finding that monthly payment for a while,' said Thompson. 'And you can get your rent up to date,' he added quietly.

'What do you know of that?' said Valerie. 'Just how much about me do you know?'

'We know all about you, Valerie, but don't worry, it's none of our or anyone else's business. It stays in the family, on the confidential file. I'm the only one with access.'

'Mmm,' she said, while being quite sure that trust with this man went one way. 'So, Colonel, I think it's about time you tell me what's happening. What was Preston up to and why is your man dead?'

'Why Trent is dead is simple,' said Thompson, opening a bottle of mineral water. 'He was getting close and they found out.'

'And before you think I'm going to be next on the chopping block, you can think again.' Valerie pulled out a pack of Disque Bleu and held it up. 'May I?'

'Sure, carry on,' he said. 'As I said before, you're on the inside, so I don't think there's any chance of that, unless your new boyfriend is in on it too. And in any case, just tell him you've concluded your investigation.'

'More or less have,' she replied, drawing down a lungful of smoke. 'But let's have the payoff.'

'Preston was controlling the business of bringing into the country anything with money attached,' said Thompson. 'But lately they started branching out, bigger risks, but with big, very big, rewards.'

'Not drugs then?' said Valerie.

'No, not this time. They've started to put the country at risk.' Thompson took another sip of water then ran his finger thoughtfully around the glass. 'And we don't like that. Or should I say, we're not going to put up with that. Idiots shoving crap into their arm is one thing; the police and other services can take care of that. But we don't like it when someone crosses our country, especially when they've been born here, subjects of Her Majesty.' Squinting sideways, he started rummaging through a draw. 'Or should I say, where you're concerned, Valerie, citizens of the UK. Ah,' he said, producing a lemon, 'knew it was here somewhere.' He took a small penknife to the yellow fruit and dropped a slice into a glass.

'Yeah, citizen will do,' she said, taking an interest in what the colonel was doing.

Thompson removed a file from a nearby cabinet, held it up for a second, then dropped it onto his desk. 'The minister, Callum McCain.'

'The guy in the car accident a few months ago?' said Valerie. 'Left the road and went straight into a concrete pillar?'

'That's the one,' he said, opening the folder and handing it to Valerie. 'Killed outright.' He unscrewed the top from a bottle of mineral water and poured it over the lemon.

'Well?' She thumbed through the few pages until she came to the summary. 'Murdered.' The final half a page gave a little more detail, but that was the conclusion at the bottom. 'Overseas connection. What does that mean, as if I didn't know? It feels like a big truck is coming around the bend and is aimed straight at me.'

'Not the usual run of MP, I think you'll agree,' said Thompson. 'A little more upstanding, yes?'

'Okay, yes,' she said, remembering his honourable crusades, 'slightly above the rest.'

'He had more or less concluded an investigation into a foreign power's involvement into supplying highly sophisticated arms to people we would rather keep away from these types of weapons. He went into an overhead bridge support, and all the files disappeared.'

'What the hell's it got to do with Preston, and your man?' Valerie asked, pushing the file back across the desk.

'We're almost certain the killer was brought in and taken back out by *Sun Dancer*. An expert of the highest calibre. Almost made it look like an accident.' Thompson got up as Dennis came back in the room. 'Your ID, I think.'

Dennis handed the laminated card to Valerie. 'Folded this way,' he said, removing it from the cover, 'you are a chief inspector; highest rank we could give you without it looking a little silly. Don't worry, it will check out.'

'And folded the other way?' she said, noticing the double side.

'It's meaningless code to anyone not familiar with an undercover department.'

'Which is most people,' she said.

'Yes, that's right, but senior officers seeing that will know you are in—'

'Spooks Are Us,' cut in Valerie.

'No... That you are in the service of Her Majesty, undercover, and must not be hindered in any way. Also, they must give any assistance you call for. There is also a security pass in there.' He pointed to a laminated blue card. 'It clears you up to... Well, let's say it clears you for as far as you'll need to go.'

'So, if I'm caught on the M25 doing a hundred and twenty, all I have to do is...?'

Looking exasperated, Thompson put a couple of fingers to his temple. 'No, Valerie, it's not been issued for you to evade motoring misdemeanours.'

Stroking the cards, she smiled. 'But it will work?'

'Yes,' said Thompson wearily. 'It will get you out of just about anything. But, luckily, the chances of doing a hundred and twenty on the M25 are pretty slim.'

Valerie folded the ID back into its cover and slipped it into her inside pocket. 'So now I'm *one of us*, what are my instructions, Colonel?' She momentarily swung her eyes to the ceiling. 'Good grief. *One of us*.'

'You just need to keep an eye on things. Your boyfriend might be quite innocent, but he's about all we have. As we pointed out, you're on the inside. You might try the laboratory where the DNA was confirmed. And what about the fishermen?'

'Fisherman,' said Valerie, stressing the singular. 'Pretty sure the older one knows nothing. Put a bit of pressure on Ben but got the minimum back. Not sure if he's just a lackey or in a lot deeper. By the way, what happens if we find Alan Preston? Drag him back home screaming and kicking?'

'That's if we're allowed to,' said Dennis. 'Depends how friendly the country he's escaped to is. If not…' He left the rest of his thoughts unsaid.

'Dear God,' said Valerie, now realising just why this unknown department was so "unknown". 'The long arm of revenge.'

'Oh,' said Thompson, 'not sure it will come to that. Don't want our overseas friends finding a body where it shouldn't be. Two Alan Prestons ending up face down in the sand would look rather like a clearance sale.'

Valerie smiled at the macabre remark. 'By the way, what you said about McCain… almost looked like an accident?'

'Another quick cremation, but don't think they would have found anything; there was nothing to find. It was the car. We still have it.'

'Been tampered with?'

'No, that would have been too easy to spot. This man was very clever. There's a crease down the off side where it shouldn't be.'

'That's a bit thin,' said Valerie, pulling out another cigarette. 'He'd driven into a concrete pillar – there'd be all kinds of damage. And all on top of a crumpled mess.'

'Yes, of course,' said Thompson, reaching across with a lit match, 'but nowadays we have computers.'

'And clever programs,' said Dennis, turning a screen around.

Valerie watched for the next five minutes as one scenario after another was sent across the screen.

'Only one conclusion,' said Dennis, closing the program. 'Something large and heavy pushed the car off the road at the exact point—'

'He was approaching the pillar,' said Valerie, blowing a perfect smoke ring. 'But what about paint from the other vehicle? There'd be paint somewhere.'

Thompson gently swung his chair from side to side. 'A few fibres, something like carpet underlay. And those could have come from anywhere, even blown up from the road.'

'For crying out loud,' said Valerie, 'you just attach some underlay along the side of your lorry and off you go! He's a clever sod, I'll give him that. And removing files?'

'Alan Preston was head of a computer company,' said Thompson.

'Or find some hacker and ply him with fifties,' said Dennis. 'The computer world and security is just a joke. Any kid in his bedroom could get into most things, never mind an expert with a wad of money shoved under his nose.'

'Another thing,' said Thompson. 'In circles that count, McCain was going to be a future prime minister. And although we're aware of your views on politicians—'

'Yes, I know,' interrupted Valerie, 'as they go, he was pretty near the top.'

'Since the war, he was one of the best...' Valerie noticed

Thompson getting agitated, 'and he was a friend. So from a personal viewpoint I don't take very kindly to what's happened. I want this... sorry, we want this sorting out.'

'You two are not short in the brain department,' said Valerie. 'I think you're way ahead of why this happened, and weapon trading is just a screen, yes? Some foreign power did not want a Prime Minister McCain.'

A momentary glance was exchanged between Dennis and Thompson, but little else, and for a few seconds the three of them sat in silence.

'Weapon trading is bad enough,' said Thompson slowly. 'But we're not putting up with anyone telling us how to run our country.'

'Right.' Valerie ground out the single word before getting to her feet.

'Your assessment was correct,' said Dennis, looking again at his boss.

'Bloody well knew you were, Valerie,' said Thompson. 'All along, since we first met. Bloody well knew you were.'

'Oh yes,' she said, 'you knew what?'

'You're patriotic. Only someone that loves their country would complain so vehemently about it being sold out and torn apart.'

She turned as Dennis held the door open. 'By the way,' she said, nodding to a modern painting behind the colonel, 'Jackson Pollock never signed his name upside down in the top left-hand corner.'

FIFTEEN

THE ILLUMINATED DOORBELL FLICKERED AS VALERIE released the button and looked around. The house was a pleasant, modern dwelling and stood among its equally pleasant and modern neighbours on a tastefully well-planned estate. Apart from the occasional child's toy, all was neat and tidy. Inside her pocket she revolved the warrant card between her fingers and thought about introducing herself as a police officer for the first time.

As the door opened, Valerie loosened her fingers from around the card. Two young children flanked a man who was straining to hold on to a black Labrador.

'Mr Hardy? The name's Stone, Valerie Stone. Might I have a word? I've been retained by Southern and East. I'm just putting the final couple of pages together about Alan Preston.'

The man in his early thirties, with a shock of ginger hair accompanied by an equal shock to his beard, pushed one of the children inside and told the other to follow with the dog.

'What can I tell you?' He hesitated, furtively scanning the road. 'I did the autopsy and put a report in, same as any other body that comes my way.' Signifying this was a conversation that was going nowhere, he pulled the door behind him and stood on the step.

'Can we go inside? I just want to fill in a few blanks, that's all. Something to give the insurance company.'

'I can't tell you anything.' Standing firmly in front of the door, Hardy clenched his teeth. 'Now go, before I call the police.'

Valerie faltered for a moment, unsure of how to proceed now that she had foolishly decided against the guise of an official. 'Who was it that got to you?'

'What the hell are you talking about?' Blood flushed around his cheeks as he became aggressive. 'I did my job. Full stop. Now get out of here!'

'Robbie, I can call you Robbie, yes?' She attempted to connect with unresponsive eyes as he kept looking around. 'This refusing to come clean, refusing any help, and believe me, you need help… you're putting yourself and family in great danger.' He continued to check the street, looking anywhere but directly at Valerie. 'And if you think they're keeping you under supervision, then think on this: they're probably watching you now, so you might as well ask me in.'

He moved back, pushed at the door and waved her in. 'On the left.'

Valerie sat on a soft corded settee and waited for a fidgeting Hardy to settle down on the matching chair. 'Don't worry. If you tell me what happened, I'll make sure you and your family will be safe.'

'Oh yeah.' He managed a strangled, sarcastic laugh. 'How are you going to do that?'

'You let me worry about that. Your concern is telling the truth.'

'There's nothing to tell. Or almost nothing,' he added quietly. 'This woman came here.'

'What, here? Your house?'

He nodded and went to a nearby cabinet. 'You want one?' he said, sliding the flexible door to one side. 'Only Scotch, I'm afraid.'

'No, I'm fine,' said Valerie with a negligible shake of the head.

He poured out near half a tumbler of Tesco's own brand, then added a splash of soda. 'Told me there was a body arriving at the mortuary that evening.' He swilled down half of the whisky and, shaking, sat back down. 'She gave me a bottle with a couple of swabs inside. Said there would be a DNA test request, as well as the standard autopsy, and that I was to use the sample on the swabs for the result.'

'That was it?'

'Yes. She looked around at the photos of my wife and children, even picked one up and said what a nice family I had.' He finished off the drink and, coughing slightly, held the back of a hand to his mouth. 'She didn't have to say another thing; I knew exactly what she was talking about. Then she got up, threw a large envelope on my lap and walked out. Never heard from her before or since.'

The first whisky had done nothing to steady his trembling hands as he took the bottle by the neck and poured another. 'And now I've put my family in danger. What am I going to do, run off down the road with a kid under each arm and a screaming wife following on behind? Why the hell did you come here? All you've done is screw things up, and anyway, who the bloody hell are you? Working for the insurance company my bloody left foot. Sell jokes on the side when you can't fuck up people's lives, do you?'

'It's all right.' Valerie tried to soothe his agitation. 'Don't worry.'

'What the hell do you mean, don't worry?!' he said, getting angry again. 'What the bloody hell can you do about it? I might as well put a gun to my kids' heads!'

Valerie pulled the mobile from her pocket and retrieved the recently stored number. 'Dennis? It's Valerie. We need some transport at Hardy's house.' Hardy sat back down with his, now third, drink and listened as Valerie reeled off the information. 'Presume we have a safe house?' She nodded while making positive murmurings. 'Oh, and a ruddy big dog,' she added before ending the call and looking at the now half-cut Hardy. 'Better get a couple of cases packed, they'll be here in an hour.'

He still looked worried, so she added, 'It's safer this way, believe me. Not sure even keeping your mouth shut would have been of any help. We're dealing with ruthless people. If they decide they'd be better off with you no longer around…' Preferring to let her remarks sink in, she left the rest unsaid.

Hardy stumbled to his feet. 'Thanks a fucking bunch.'

Valerie wondered if it was a particularly low threshold to alcohol or just plain terror as he put out a hand to balance himself.

'Get your family together,' she said quietly.

'Who are you?' said Hardy, leaving the room.

'Right now? I'm your guardian angel.'

***

The impressive, but deserted, detached house stood in its own grounds of about an acre. 'Must have been well paid,' Valerie mused as she stood on the gravel drive. 'And more than just a secretary.'

The woman that identified Preston's body was about the only line of investigation Valerie could think of. And if there was going to be anything to find, a start at her house would be as good as anywhere. She looked around, noting the alarm box under the eaves. There was a chance to get in unseen, so she took a Swiss army knife from her pocket and slid the sash window catch to one side. Then she opened the window enough to set the alarm off, before pulling it back down and pushing the catch back in place. The side of the house lit up by a pulsating light set in the alarm box. She turned and slowly walked into the garden, sat behind a large elm, and lit a cigarette.

Forty minutes and two cigarettes later, a white security van crunched along the drive towards the house.

'A pound will get you ten it's another bleedin' false alarm.' An overweight man eased himself from the passenger seat.

'Good job it's your turn then, ain't it?'

The guard let himself in while cigarette smoke from the driver's side curled out of the van window. Five minutes later he pulled the front door shut, before testing it with his shoulder. 'Nowt, I've re-set the panel.'

Valerie looked at her watch as the van disappeared down the drive. She gave it twenty minutes before releasing the window catch again. She had to do it three times, in all, before the guard came out and told his mate that he couldn't find a fault and that it would have to wait until the morning.

'I've closed it all down, can't be doin' with coming backwards and forwards all bloody night.'

After watching the van's lights fade along the road, Valerie checked the indicator on the box above her head and entered. As there was now little chance of anyone interrupting a search, Valerie switched on the lights and looked around the impressive room. 'Money,' she said quietly, 'and plenty of it. No wonder everything in this enquiry gets nowhere if everyone is on megabucks.'

Pulling open desk drawers and skimming through papers seemed to reveal little more than domestic receipts. Before looking over the rest of the house, she switched on the desk computer and left it going through its start-up routine. Moving from room to room, it crossed Valerie's mind that, exactly the same as the yacht, everywhere was clean and tidy to the point of obsession.

There's going to be nothing on here, she thought, pulling out her mobile on returning to the computer. 'Jane, sorry to phone so late. Got a computer here that's probably been wiped clean, but we'd better have a look. Talk me through copying it all down.'

'Got a memory stick?'

'Sorry, not on me. No—'

Jane cut her short. 'Well, you can't copy it onto thin air.'

Telling her to wait, Valerie went back into the drawers. 'Probably need more than one if there's lots on it,' Jane added. 'Like a bloody handful.'

'Five,' said Valerie, lining them up on the desk.

Without a clue what she was doing, Valerie followed Jane's instructions and, with just the occasional 'okay', they were finished in under an hour.

'What the hell happened to the good old days?' she said, looking at the USB sticks. 'Lobbing a house brick through H Samuel's high-street window.'

SIXTEEN

Valerie looked over Jane's shoulder. 'Well?'

'Give me a chance, let the dog see the bleedin' rabbit.'

'Thought you'd have had it done by now. You've been at it since eight.'

'Do you mind? It takes the forensic bogies ages to break into deleted files.'

'Christ.' Valerie went across to her desk and slumped into the chair. 'What do we do in the meantime?'

'I said it takes the fuzz ages. But me...' She made a show of deft fingers diving into a pool of computer keys. 'Not all my expertise was learnt on my back.'

Absentmindedly, Valerie started playing a losing game of cat's cradle with an elastic band. 'No, I'm quite sure...' She stopped and threw the band back into the drawer. 'Sorry, I'm putting you off.'

'It's okay,' said Jane, 'we're both female, I can multitask same as you. What were you going to say?'

'What did you think about when... you know?' Jane's

fingers didn't hesitate in their dexterous journey across the keys.

'Not very original in your questions, are you? I seem to remember you asking me that before, back in the bad old days when we were exchanging traumatic experiences.'

'Yeah, I remember.' Valerie pulled out a cigarette and raised her eyebrows towards Jane.

'Go on then,' Jane replied, looking towards the "No Smoking in These Premises" sign. 'Just blow it the other bloody way. That's one vice I've never had to deal with.' She watched momentarily as Valerie slid the top on the Zippo. 'Should be "No Smoking on These Premises", shouldn't it?' she said, emphasising the *on*.

'Suppose,' said Valerie, making an effort to blow smoke over her shoulder. 'But getting back to what I said. All I got from you then was "oh, you know".'

'Right, I see, you want an in-depth view of "How to Be a Hooker". Well, I suppose if I was paying tax on the money, I should have been thinking of England.'

Valerie coughed a laugh on the next lungful of smoke. 'And?'

'Well, if you're going to give the inadequate bastard his money's worth, you just have to moan and compliment him in all the right places. Especially when he... you know.'

'Yeah, I know,' said Valerie. 'But that's not what you're thinking about, is it? That's just doing the job to the best of your ability... for want of a better expression.'

'Thinking about?' Jane stopped typing and looked over the monitor. 'Jesus, you wanting to descend into my soul?'

'Sorry,' said Valerie, 'none of my damn business.'

'No, no. If anyone's got a right to know, it's you. Still have been swimming around in the sewer if you hadn't come along. Best thing I ever did, fall into your doorway.'

A thoughtful gaze crossed Jane's face. 'I tried to keep my mind clean. Sounds daft, I know. But somewhere inside there's a place no one can touch, all private. I'd go there and hide. Like sitting by a stream in the spring sunshine. Then all the moaning and groaning is automatic. I got very good at it. I could be seeing to this deficient and his every need, and be sitting by my little piece of water. Stupid sod would be thinking I was smiling at the size of his prick. But I'd be smiling at the little ripples catching the sunlight.' Not even remotely able to put herself in the same position, Valerie said nothing. 'No one that hasn't been there could ever understand. Don't worry, don't mind telling you.' Then, smiling, she added, 'I had a priest once. Well, more than once actually.'

As if dragged from a deep well, Valerie's mood switched instantly. 'What!' She laughed. 'You can't be serious?'

'Bloody right, he used to call it his weekly cleansing.'

'Never!' Valerie screamed. 'This is a joke, yes?'

'No way, sure as I'm a demon typist. Straight up.' Like a perfectly paired duet, they broke into uncontrollable giggling. 'And he could too,' said Jane, trying to regain control. 'Stand, I mean.'

'Christ almighty,' said Valerie as the tears rolled down her cheeks. 'That's one struck from the list of hundred things to do before you die.'

'Sometimes didn't remove his collar.'

Concerned that she'd choke on the next lungful of smoke, Valerie pushed the cigarette into an ashtray hidden in the desk drawer, while Jane looked over her computer screen and grinned.

'Oh no,' said Valerie, chivvying Jane along, 'I'm not buying that one.'

'It's bloody true. True as I'm waiting for this bus,' said Jane, still typing. 'After the first couple of times, he brought a black habit with him.'

'Dear God in heaven. For him or you? And more to the point, where did he get it?'

Again, Jane looked mischievously over the screen. 'Don't know, but he had us both in it,' she whispered. 'I charged extra, of course.' She sat back up and looked serious. 'I wasn't risking everlasting hell and damnation for a flat fee.'

Valerie took two cans of Coke from the drawer and handed one over. 'And how did he square this with his Christian calling?'

'Like I said, he thought it a kind of cleansing. He said if I wanted cleansing I'd go to church, so he came to me. Kind of makes sense, doesn't it?'

'Hmm,' said Valerie, pulling the ring and tossing it in the bin. 'Think he'd have a hard time getting that one past his bishop. Is there anything you wouldn't do, you know, off limits?'

'Apart from the obvious?' Jane looked down, examining her fingernails. 'Never let them kiss me. Ever.'

'What! Sex from here to Christmas and no kissing?'

'If you've never been there, then you wouldn't understand. Kissing is for someone special, it's intimate. Secrets told with the lips. Not for no bloody money. No,' she added thoughtfully, 'definitely not for sale.' Momentarily she looked at the wall with unfocused eyes. 'Here, put that into your laptop.' She tossed a USB across. 'Four to go,' she added quietly.

Valerie could almost hear the USB laughing as she searched through old business files. 'Hope you can come up with better than this.'

'I can only find what's there,' said Jane.

'Yeah, I know, I know. But I think our new masters are expecting a little more than tax-dodging.'

'Oh, I don't know,' said Jane, 'that's how they got Al Capone.'

'Yeah, but he was alive. At least he was when they caught him. Didn't he die of—?'

'Yes,' said Jane, shuddering, 'he bloody did. Yuk.'

Valerie's mobile suddenly stopped the supposition.

'They got to him,' said Thompson. 'He's shut up as tight as a clam. If there was more to come, he's not telling.'

Valerie furrowed her brow. 'Got to the safe house?'

'No,' said Thompson, 'his mobile. Stupid idiot that was looking after them forgot to take it away.'

'You've got to be kidding.' One-handed, Valerie took a cigarette and slowly tapped it on the desk. 'Thought you had better than that in the department.'

'We do,' said Thompson. 'He was still protesting his innocence as Simonds kicked him down the street. He's back on the beat, or wherever he was found.'

'But they're safe?' she asked.

'For now, yes. But you'll have to get it sorted before they can go home.'

'Let him keep the money, Colonel.'

She ended the call just as Jane threw another USB across. 'Not sure that one's any different from the first,' said Jane.

'What about getting pregnant and things?' asked Valerie, forgetting her cigarette as she looked through the files.

'And things?' said Jane. 'Well, you know about "things", you hoicked me off to the clinic. Funnily enough that was the only time I needed to go. I insisted on condoms, but one must have slipped or got damaged. Thank Christ it was just the clap and nothing worse.'

'Jesus,' said Valerie, 'it's a dangerous bloody game.'

'You're telling me.'

Requesting silence, Jane held up a hand and buried herself in the next load of files. Occasionally making notes, she quietly mumbled to herself for the next fifteen minutes, then sat back and took a sip from the can of Coke. 'Got pregnant once. Not when I was on the game. It was just before Vinnie got his claws into me.'

'Blimey, you must have been young?'

'Yeah,' said Jane, smiling innocently. 'Sweet sixteen and never been kissed. Nor nothing else neither.'

'Well?'

'You remember me telling you about that Scottish lad?'

'Andrew something or other,' said Valerie, 'used to work at Asda.'

'That's him, Andy. Still does. Climbed up the ladder. Assistant to something or other he is now. Well, I'd only been going out with him for a few weeks and popped in on my way home from school.' She blew her cheeks out and wriggled her nose at the screen. 'He was working on the fish counter, very smart he looked in his white coat.' She stopped and smiled again.

'And?' said Valerie. 'If you're going to reminisce, do it out loud.'

'Oh, yes. Well… we'd been very close to doing it once or twice, but never quite made it… you know, never got over the finishing line. I think we should both have had L plates. It was my first time and I'm damn sure it was his too. There had been lots of fumbling in his mum's front room, but little else.' She paused, looking a little vacant.

'Jane?'

'Oh.' She jumped before continuing. 'Yes. It was quiet when I went in and we both made a grab at each other. Then he shoved me through into the storeroom. It wasn't very romantic being pressed up against cases of frozen cod fillets, but we must have been building up a head of steam for too long. No resistance left, as it were. Me knickers came off and his trousers dropped around his ankles then away we went.

Of course, I'd got romantic thoughts of crisp white sheets and Chanel Number Five. Instead I came out with a sore you-know-what and smelling like a Grimsby trawler. Anyway, next thing I knew I was in the club. Me mum went absolutely bleedin' spare. Dragged me off screaming and kicking to have a termination.'

'Cripes,' said Valerie, 'all that must have come as something of a shock.'

'You're friggin' well telling me! I only went for a tin of spaghetti hoops.'

'Didn't your mum give you a girl-to-girl talk when you were young, you know?'

'Suppose your mum did?'

'Yeah, she was quite good. A bit embarrassing, but at least I knew what was coming around the corner.'

'Know what mine said?' Valerie shook her head. 'When I was about twelve, me mum looked me straight in the eye and said, "Don't you go bringing no trouble round here. Men are only after one thing."'

'And that was it?'

'Yeah. I ask you… just made me take a firmer grip of me tube of Smarties.'

'No tax?' said Valerie.

'What is… or isn't?' Jane frowned at the change of subject.

'Being on the game. Tax-free?'

'You thinking of changing profession?'

'Hardly. Haven't got the balls.'

'Yes,' Jane stroked a pencil across the side of her head and looked up thoughtfully, 'got to have them if you're going down that street. But some of them pay tax. Even know of one that's VAT-registered.'

'Get out of town. VAT-registered? That would be one inspection I'd like to see.'

'Sure, they put themselves down in the service industry. Escorts. Some title themselves as consultants. Some clients even ask for a VAT receipt, put it through the books.'

'And I thought I was sailing close to the wind.'

'When you come to work, you get off the bus by the park and walk through to the next stop? Nice ten minutes and quicker than waiting for the next bus where you got off. Yes?'

'Yeah, sure, pleasant ten minutes.'

'Sometimes there's a tall, elegant woman, about your age, looks like she stepped off the pages of *Vogue*. Usually walking a pair of Dalmatians, yes?'

'Er, yes, I've noticed her a couple of times. Looks like some model that's married a minor royal. Black fur coat, hair piled up on top?'

'Yeah, that's right, but the fur's faux. Very conscientious,' said Jane. 'She's one.'

'Behave yourself, no way. She's elegant with a capital E.'

'Her and I think three, maybe two, others share a place overlooking the lake down there. Don't get between her sheets unless you got serious moolah. No pimps, no madams, they just employ a big tough guy to look after them. He gets a straight ten per cent and they get safety. Ex-boxer. Apparently he's part of some strong-arm business; you want protection and they provide it.'

'Like a kind of Ruffians R Us.'

'Yeah.' Not breaking concentration, Jane grinned. 'Like a kind of Ruffians R Us. I did hear of a punter who got a little nasty and he had to step in. Out through the front door and didn't stop bouncing till he hit the opposite curb.'

'And no refund?'

'Yeah,' said Jane. 'No friggin' trousers neither.'

'We're wasting our time,' said Valerie, pulling another USB from her laptop.

'Oh, I don't know.' Jane's deft fingers continued to dance across the keys. 'We've had a nice chat.'

'Put them in a bag when you've finished. I'll take them round to the department, see if that mob can make anything out of it all.'

Jane looked slightly aggrieved at the thought anyone else could uncover hidden information where she could not.

SEVENTEEN

IT WAS SUCH A SMALL THING THAT WAS STILL BOTHERING her, almost insignificant, so Valerie once again put it to the back of her mind. And once again she was drifting along in a fuzzy cloud of indecision. When it happened, it was as sudden as it was brutal.

The warbling of the houseboat phone usually annoyed, but, unable to re-set the tone, she was still putting up with it as the master of a whining puppy might.

'Miss Stone?' The voice of a girl on the line was familiar.

'Jane? What's wrong? You sound upset.'

'It's not Jane. It's Flo, Jane's sister, we met once.'

'Oh yes,' she said, but was unable to start with any niceties; Flo abruptly interrupted.

'Jane's been…' She stopped.

Valerie heard a shuddering intake of breath and swung her legs from the settee and stood up. 'What? Accident? Where is she?'

'She's in hospital.'

Jamming the phone to her ear with her shoulder, Valerie pulled her jacket on the other shoulder while listening. 'Okay, okay. I'm on my way.'

Taxis were not her usual mode of transport, but she sprinted into the road, flagging the first one down. She danced out of the way as it swerved.

'I've got a fare, you stupid bitch, get out the way!' The taxi driver leant out of the window, waving his arm around before raising two defiant fingers. 'Trying to get yourself killed? Yer bleedin' idiot.'

The rank across the road being empty, she ran around to the corner café and put her head inside. 'Need a taxi, any drivers in here?'

At a far table, three men looked at each other. 'Mine, I think.' One of them gulped down the remains of a mug of tea. 'Where to, Miss?' Pulling on his jacket, he made for the door, jamming an iced bun between his teeth.

'The Lister Hospital.'

Valerie followed the driver to a small pull-in behind the café. Obviously used to speaking with a bun in his mouth, the driver pulled the rear door open and ushered Valerie in. 'Okay, bit of a hurry, are we?'

As the driver got behind the wheel, Valerie pushed her warrant card through the partition. 'Don't worry about leaving any flashing cameras behind.'

'Oh boy,' the driver rubbed his hands together before grabbing the wheel, 'a mercy dash.'

A young constable stuck out his hand as the taxi skidded to a halt at the second set of lights. 'Okay, Fangio,' he said, reaching for his notepad, 'who set your trousers on fire?'

'There's one of yours in the back.' The driver nodded over his shoulder. 'Got to get to the hospital.'

The constable made an attempt at a salute as Valerie

pushed her card against the glass, then, jumping into the middle of the junction, he halted the traffic. 'Okay, ma'am.' He repeated the salute while waving the taxi through. The traffic at the next set of lights was halted as they miraculously picked up a police outrider on his motor bike.

'Must have radioed through to his mate,' the driver yelled. 'Never had this much fun with me clothes on.'

By the time they had reached the end of the road and were flying round Trafalgar Square, blue lights and sirens had joined in the excitement.

'Bloody hell,' the driver said, 'wait till I tell me missus. All we need now is some Van Halen blasting out.'

Arriving outside the hospital, Valerie took her wallet out.

'No, no,' said the driver, 'have this one on me, Inspector.'

She rolled up a couple of notes and pushed them into his hand. 'As you forgot to put the meter down, shove it in your pocket.' Then, turning to the mounted policeman, she said, 'Make sure he hasn't been booked by any eager beaver.'

The familiar clinical, clean smell wafted around as Valerie pushed at the door and looked over to the desk. 'Employee of mine been brought in,' she said before reeling off Jane's details. With a racing mind, she was only half-listening as the click-clack of high heels approached from behind.

'Miss Stone.' Jane's sister pushed a tear away from red eyes. 'I don't know what's happened to her. She's in a terrible mess.'

'Accident?' asked Valerie, giving Flo a hug. 'Can we go and see her?'

'Twenty minutes… a doctor is with her now. I could do with something to drink.'

Valerie gave Flo's hand a squeeze and went over to the Royal Voluntary Service counter. 'Tea, coffee?' she asked, looking back over her shoulder.

'Coffee's fine.'

'Two?' The woman behind the servery was tall, slim and well dressed. 'Would that be with milk?' The smile was well practised, warm but slight. Valerie supposed she had given the expression a lot of thought. A positive welcome, but not something that might offend anyone who was under strain. Although around sixty, she revealed near-perfect teeth and, as far as could be seen, they looked to be her own.

'Yes, milk,' said Valerie, getting the nod from Flo.

'Sugar's on the side.' The woman pushed her purple shawl back across her shoulder and pointed to a small table.

'Did they tell you anything?' said Valerie, stirring her coffee. She tapped the plastic stick on the side of the cup.

Flo shook her head. 'I got a call and came as quick as I could.' They both moved their legs to one side as a nurse came trotting down the corridor.

'Busy place.' Valerie, unsure of what to say now they were just waiting, was glad of anything to pass comment on.

Attempting a smile, Flo nodded. 'Yes.'

A doctor, followed by another nurse, briskly walked by as flashing blue lights reflected through the main entrance. Two medics, crashing a trolley through the entrance doors, disappeared down a side corridor. With the distraction over, Valerie went back to peering into her cup, and Flo with fingering her broach.

Valerie eased her head back against the wall. 'Will they give us a shout when we can see her, or…?'

'Not sure.' Flo looked at her watch, then started tapping her heels on the floor. 'Give them another fifteen minutes and we'll go in any case.'

Valerie watched the last minute tick by and got to her feet. 'Come on,' she patted Flo's shoulder, 'lead on.'

Flo pushed the door of a private room at the ward's

entrance. 'She's in here. The consultant said she needs quiet; the more she sleeps the better.'

'You'll get nothing out of her.' The nurse they met was one of the many from Africa that were preventing the NHS from falling into the abyss. 'Sedated,' she added, looking at Valerie as if she held her personally responsible. She pushed at her short sleeves while continuing with an evil eye. 'You know anything about what's happened here?' she said between tight lips. This nurse was obviously from the detective side of the "administering angel department". Thinking that she had more than met her match, Valerie said nothing. 'Well?'

The nurse relented slightly when Valerie asked if she would be all right. 'Ruptured spleen, two broken fingers, and she's been bleeding internally. But yes, she should be all right.' The nurse might have eased up a little, but she still kept up the quizzing. 'Who did it? Do you know?'

'It wasn't an accident?'

'Accident my fat arse. She's been worked over good and proper.'

'Then no, I don't know who did it,' said Valerie. 'But I'm bloody well going to find out.'

Over the next thirty minutes, first the nurse left and then Flo got up.

'Better get back,' she said, 'I have to catch up with the kids, they'll be out of school soon.'

'Sure,' said Valerie. 'I'll hang around for a while.'

Sat in the corner, she watched the monitor relay Jane's condition. Like her personality and spirit, the beat of the cardiac line was firm and regular, just fluctuating by the odd digit. She was wearing only a short nightdress and, as the room was warm and comfortable, there were no bedsheets covering her. Valerie looked at the bruises on her left leg and butterfly stitches holding a gash together on the other. Neighbouring broken fingers were bound together with a small metal splint. Looking at her face, it was now obvious that it was no accident. She had been beaten to within an inch of her life. Who and why would have to wait until Jane came back from the induced, peaceful rest.

Valerie had little idea of how long she had sat there, but her backside was getting numb. She got up and stretched before going out to find a coffee.

It was getting late, so all the food and drink outlets in the hospital were shut. Towards the end of the corridor she found a vending machine and fed in enough for a bar of Fruit and Nut, and coffee. She leant on the machine and tore the wrapping from the chocolate bar. Breaking a small piece from the block, she chewed thoughtfully and watched a nurse approaching along the passageway. As she drew nearer, cloudy recognition began to unfold and her mind went hurtling back to the last time they had met, four years ago.

'Valerie?' The nurse approached with outstretched arms. 'It is you.' They embraced for a few seconds before the nurse stood back, holding on to Valerie's shoulders. 'What on earth are you doing here?'

'Hello, Gillian.' Glad to see a friendly face, Valerie brushed her hair back as the nurse dropped her hands. 'Yes, long time.'

Gillian pushed a coin into the vending machine. 'And how have you been?' she asked, catching a can of Pepsi as it tumbled from the flap.

'Oh, you know, getting by.'

'But you've moved on, yes?'

'Well, look at you.' Avoiding the question, Valerie pointed to her dark uniform. 'Promotion?'

'Nurse practitioner.' She smiled. 'On the up. Engaged too.'

'Oh, that's wonderful.' Valerie gave the nurse's hand a squeeze. 'Hope he's good enough for you.'

'He sure is, about as near to Prince Charming as you can get.' She took a sip from the can and tried again. 'You've moved on?'

Valerie put the chocolate onto a side table and looked into her coffee. 'Guess I'm just a hopeless case. But you helped. By God, you helped more than you will ever know.'

Gillian put a hand under Valerie's chin and gently lifted her face until their eyes met. 'He's still…?'

'Yep,' said Valerie, 'still in the same place. Go in every week.'

'Oh, for Christ's sake, Valerie.' Gillian spoke quietly, almost a whisper. 'You have to let go, you…' She stopped as the tears started to glisten in Valerie's eyes. 'Sorry, sorry, nothing to do with me.'

Valerie shrugged her shoulders. 'As much to do with you as anyone else. I'd have jumped from one of the Seven Sisters long ago if it wasn't for you.'

'You want to come in and see me again?'

'Got something much more important than me at the moment,' said Valerie. 'Run my own business now, and my secretary has been beaten up.' She motioned with her coffee to the nearby room. 'She's in a right mess. Jesus, is there a fire escape around here? I need a bloody fag.'

Gillian led the way to an emergency side door. 'I'll have one too,' she said. 'Unless you're still on those bloody French things.'

'Sorry,' Valerie produced the blue and white pack, 'only these.'

'Oh, go on then.' Gillian pulled one from the wrapper and accepted the offered light. 'Bloody hell.' She blew out smoke while giving the cigarette a quizzical look. 'I'm trying to give up, so I suppose I could buy this crap. Bit drastic, though, and bloody expensive from what I remember.'

'Steady on,' said Valerie, recovering a little humour, 'you're talking about my best friends.'

'Ha,' said Gillian, 'thought that was your car. Don't tell me you've sold that black and chrome petrol guzzler?'

'No, not likely.' Valerie blew a long, steady stream of smoke into the still night air. 'If that goes then everything else will have gone before it. Fags included.'

'What about your secretary then? How did she wind up in here?'

'Don't know. Got a call from her sister and came down to find her in a hell of a mess. She's been involved with some real dregs of society before, so if her past has come back and bitten her in the backside...' She shrugged her shoulders. 'I don't know. But it seems the most likely explanation.'

'Secretaries getting beat up... what kind of business you in?' Gillian didn't take another draw on her cigarette, instead just looked at it between her fingers. 'Don't suppose it's a perfume shop.'

Valerie smiled and, leaning on the escape rail, stared out into the night sky. 'Private investigator.'

'Good grief. Just couldn't be anything ordinary, could it?'

'Oh, I don't know. Get a lot of humdrum stuff. Not every day I come back to this kind of bloody mess.' She took a last drag on the cigarette and flicked it into the darkness.

After looking at the unfinished one in her hand, Gillian also threw hers away. 'Best place for them,' she said, peering into the darkness.

***

With one thing and another and keeping Dennis up to date, it wasn't until the next evening that Valerie was able to get back to the hospital. She dropped the large box of Ferrero Rocher and *Hello!* magazine onto the bedside table and looked at the card attached to a bouquet of flowers.

'How the hell did he know?' she said under her breath while looking at David Preston's signature. She pulled her phone out, then put it away as someone came in.

'She's a lot better.' The nurse from the previous evening plumped Jane's pillows. 'Even mumbled a few words and had a drink of water. Think she'll sleep for the rest of the night. Might be making a bit of sense tomorrow.'

'That's good,' said Valerie. 'Police been in?'

'Yes, they've been. Had a look, made a few notes and went. What you going to do now?'

'I'll stay a while.'

The nurse picked up a dish containing a discarded syringe. 'As you please,' she said curtly, leaving Valerie to her solitary vigil.

She sat for maybe an hour before rising to stretch her legs. Opposite Jane's door was the ward's general office. Two nurses were chatting away over their coffee. The talking drifted around like white noise, not entering Valerie's brain until two words stung like a trapped wasp.

'What?!' she said, pushing in and confronting the two young women.

Startled, the two shot glances as Valerie entered. 'Pardon?' said one.

'What you just said. What did you say?'

'Just talking,' said the other nurse.

'Yes, but you said something. What was it?'

'We were just talking about the girl you've been visiting. She came around for a few minutes and started talking. The usual rubbish when someone's been out for a while, you know.'

'No, I don't know,' said Valerie, raising her voice. 'What did she say?'

'No need to get excited.' The first nurse put her mug on the side. 'She was talking a load of gibberish.'

'Yes, but you said something.' Valerie, wanting to make sure of what she heard, did not attempt any prompt. 'What did you say? Just before I came in, what was it?'

'Your friend Jane,' replied the girl calmly, 'she came around for ten minutes or so, had a drink of water. She was a bit incoherent. Muttered things like not going to work for Vinnie. Something about car insurance. Just silly things, a butterfly and a rose. Things get jumbled up when…'

The girl's words hung in the air as Valerie flew into Jane's side ward and grabbed her jacket.

***

The Beggars Hat was, more or less, what Vinnie used as a headquarters. Valerie burst in demanding to know where he was. The barman looked like he hadn't moved from the spot since she was last in the place.

'Where's who?' he said, rubbing a soiled cloth around a glass.

'Vinnie, who else?' she said, looking around. 'Where is the bastard?'

'Oh, Vinnie.' Holding the glass to the light, he revolved it a couple of times before replacing it on a sticky shelf. 'He's away for a few days, er, filming. Down Eastbourne somewhere, I think.'

Valerie put her hands on the counter and leant across. 'Where?' she demanded. 'Never mind "Eastbourne somewhere".' With practised agility, the barman moved away from Valerie's grabbing hand. She went to the end of the counter and flung open the trap. 'Where?' she repeated, cornering him between the bottled beers and a dusty jar of pickled eggs.

'Fanny, Fanny!' Straining to the side, he shouted through to the back, 'Where's Vinnie staying?'

'No bloody idea,' a woman's voice barked from the darkness. 'But he's back tomorrow.'

Valerie let go of his grubby collar and pushed him back, before storming out.

A man on the end bar stool didn't look up from his *Daily Mirror*. 'Guess she'll be back,' he said quietly.

***

The colonel was not in the office when Valerie walked in.

'Then it will have to be you,' she said, telling Dennis of what had happened. 'I'm afraid you're going to have to go onto the back boiler for a couple of days while I get Jane's problem sorted. There's a lunatic on the loose out there, and I'm not leaving her in the middle of a bloody war zone.'

'No, of course not, Miss Stone. But as we don't know what's happening, we'd better give you some help.'

'Don't need anyone,' said Valerie stubbornly. 'I prefer to be on my own. Then no one's going to let me down.'

'No, no,' he said, pressing the intercom on his desk, 'not that kind of help. Besides, I don't think we've anyone on your wavelength.'

'Sir.' The man's appearance confirmed that the colonel was not the only military personnel on the payroll.

'Take Miss Stone down to the range please, Sergeant.' Then, turning to Valerie, he said, 'Peterson will get you up to speed.'

'Let's see what we can do for you, Miss,' said the sergeant, leading the way down another corridor. 'It's Johnny, by the way. Just call me Johnny.'

He had the crown and stripes of a staff sergeant attached to his olive-green shirt, and walked with the confident stride of an experienced soldier. His haircut was the type started each morning with a razor on his chin and didn't stop until every centimetre of his head was close-cropped.

'Here we are,' he said, standing to one side of a steel door, 'my office.' He ushered her into a glassed gallery of perhaps ten metres that overlooked a deserted indoor shooting range, then took keys to a double-locked, metal cupboard and looked at Valerie before taking three pistols from one of the shelves. 'Let's get you sorted. Nothing to worry about, they're quite safe.' Valerie nodded as the sergeant went over to a small steel door let into the opposite wall. 'Keep the shells separate.'

Pointing her to the first range, he put the pistols and ammunition on the back table. 'Now then, just a few—'

Valerie cut him short. 'I was in America for about a year and belonged to a club. They're Glocks, yes?'

'That's right, all Glock nine millimetre. The nineteen's standard military issue. What did you use in the States?'

'Used the thirty-four,' she said, looking at the table.

'A good competition gun, but a little big for us.' He picked up a couple of ear defenders and handed a pair to Valerie. Then, checking one of the pistols was empty, he handed it over. Pulling the slider back and forth, Valerie checked the gun again. 'How did you get on?' he asked, pushing six bullets into a clip before passing it across. 'In the States, I mean?'

'Oh, managed to hit what I was aiming at now and again.'

Pointing the gun to the floor, she nodded down-range. 'They've been our allies since nineteen forty-five.'

'The target?' queried the sergeant. 'The charging Nazi hasn't changed in years. We call that one the figure twelve target. See the one on the other range, the same guy but crawling towards you? That's the figure eleven.' He held an open hand down-range and adjusted his ear protection. 'Shall we?'

'What distance are we at?'

'We're on the maximum for an indoor range, thirty metres.'

Unfazed, Valerie cocked the gun and fired into the centre of the target, grouping all six rounds into a circle of about twelve inches.

'Not sure I can teach you much about how to shoot,' he said, taking the gun and replacing it with another.

'Came second in a couple of competitions.'

'Only second?'

'Yeah, we had a real Annie Oakley in the club. When she stepped onto the range, it was who's going to be best of the rest. She couldn't make it to one meeting, but I still came second. Someone else I could usually beat finished top. Over-confident, I guess. Went home and kicked the cat. Figuratively speaking, of course.'

After watching her using each gun in turn, he dropped his ear defenders onto the bench. 'You shoot well with all of them, but I think the smaller forty-three is best suited. It's the same as the others, no safety, as such. So no embarrassing moments. You can drop it and it won't...' he stopped for a moment, 'shouldn't,' he stressed, 'go off. And the slim grip fits well into—'

Valerie opened her hand and looked at her palm. 'You think I should have a girlie gun?'

He stood back a couple of paces and stroked his chin. 'We have to think how you're going to carry it unnoticed, and that one's the smallest. Only six in the mag. You can keep one in the chamber if you want. Still a nine mil, though, plenty of punch.' He took a plastic package from a cupboard and pulled out a small belt holster. 'There's that one that you can attach to your belt and put it over your, um...'

'It's okay, Johnny, you're allowed to say bum. What else have you got?'

'Shoulder?' he said, producing another holster.

Valerie removed her jacket and stretched the expandable support across her back. Letting the gun pocket nestle under her left arm, she held out a hand. 'May I?' Pointing it at the floor and pulling at the slider a couple of times, the sergeant handed over the small Glock and Valerie pushed it home. Then, putting on her jacket, she looked around. 'Pity there's no mirror.'

'Can't see a thing,' he said. 'Feel okay?'

'Sure. Shall I wear it or is it going to cash and wrap? Only kidding, Johnny,' she said in response to his tight lips and raised eyebrows.

'I'll find you in the colonel's office,' he said, taking the gun and holster back. 'I'll get it packed up.'

Valerie was having a coffee when Johnny came in. He took a plastic card from the top of two packages and handed it over. 'Licence,' he said. 'Make sure you carry it with your other ID.'

'Sure,' she said, putting it away.

'I mean it,' he said, 'with your other cards.' He watched as she opened her wallet and slipped it into the vacant holder next to the security pass.

'Sorry, Johnny, didn't mean to be flippant. I know it's serious.' She put out her hands to take the boxes, but he drew them away.

'I'm coming to your place,' he said, 'as you can't go charging off to draw your weapon anywhere. I've got to put a cabinet in for you.'

'Okay, soldier,' she said, getting up, 'let's go. Anything I can carry?'

'My box of tools,' he nodded towards the door, 'in the corridor.'

***

Valerie shouted from the galley, 'Milk, sugar?'

'Yeah, both, three sugars.'

She walked through to where the sergeant was bolting the cabinet into a secluded corner and slid the mug towards him.

'Bad for you, too much sugar.' She leant on the doorjamb, cradling her own mug.

'You're kidding.' He stopped drilling and took a sip of the coffee. 'I run five miles every morning. Burn it off in the first few hundred yards.'

'Don't just work for the colonel then? You're a regular as well?'

'Special attachment, official secrets and all that.' He finished the holes then slid bolts into each one. 'What about you?' he asked, taking a spanner to each fixing in turn.

'Fell into it. I was minding my own bloody business when they descended and stitched me up good and proper.'

'That sounds about right.' The sergeant got up and opened the box.

'Blimey, Johnny, it's got a nickel top. You got me a girlie gun.'

'Thought you'd like it.' He put a choice of two holsters into the cabinet before holding up the Glock. 'One thing, Miss. You point this at someone and pull the trigger, you'll kill them. Respect it at all times. There might come a day when you have someone's life in your hands. Don't abuse it... But,' he added slowly, 'when the chips are down and you're up against it, don't mess about... Empty it into his chest.'

He put the gun away, locked the door and handed her the keys. 'Well, it's yours now.' He took a slip of paper from a folder and handed it over with a pen. 'You just need to sign for it.' He gave her a small box of ammunition and told her to hide it somewhere separate from the gun. With a deliberate flourish, Valerie put her name to the receipt.

'Here's hoping it stays where it is,' she said, handing the chit back. 'Johnny, can I ask you something?'

'I think I can guess what,' he said. 'It's amazing how many people ask when they find out what I do. I was just old enough for the Gulf. Second time around, of course.' He stopped and sat on a nearby stool. 'It's a job. You and the rest of the country ask me to do it. It's not just my job but duty, if you like. I swore allegiance to the Queen and that includes you, too. It's funny when you think of some other countries, a lot of them in fact. The army for them seems to be some sort of gangster alliance. If you don't like the ones running the country and fancy having a go yourself, then…' He shrugged his shoulders. 'Goes for money too. They can't grasp that they are there to guard the country, not take it for every bloody bean they can lay their thieving hands on. We're not like that. Like I said, we swear allegiance. Difference is we mean it. And if you, that is the government, say go, we go. We don't argue, don't even think about it, we go.'

Shifting around on the stool, he stretched his back. 'I did a count up when we crossed into Iraq. I was just eighteen and was the thirteenth British soldier across the border. There was an encampment-cum-convoy on the other side, Iraqi soldiers, you know. We wiped out sixty transports and killed a hundred and twenty men. And all in the first two or three hours. Talk about a baptism of fire. And no, before you ask, not scared, too full of adrenalin for that. Before you go, yes, frightened as hell, but not during.'

He looked out the window towards the bridge, where the streetlights reflected yellow on the river. 'Read quite a bit about conflicts, old ones, Second World War. Apparently they gave the guys uppers, you know, speed, on D-Day, keep them going. If they wanted it, of course. If I'd have been on speed, I think I'd have carried on to Baghdad, with all the extra I was generating myself. Captured Saddam all on me own.'

'Think I'm starting to look on working for the department in a different light,' said Valerie, swilling the last of her coffee.

'If it's really not for you, go and tell them. They might have applied pressure to join, but they don't see it through.'

'You sure?' she said, thinking of the customs visit. 'Anyway, about what you were saying.'

'Not going to let me go with only half a story,' he said.

'No, sorry, if you don't want to tell me, I understand. It can be very private.'

'That's okay. Me dad calls me abnormally normal. I can put it in a box when we come home. I'm lucky. Some of the guys go off-centre in a big way. The only people I take it out on are idiot bloody motorists.'

He looked back out at the light dancing on the water. 'They flew us into Cyprus afterwards. For forty-eight hours, you know, to calm down. And get pissed. Most of us flew back with a bloody hangover, then had to put our bags over our shoulders and smile. But it don't help some of them. Back at camp, my mate lost it, caused all kinds of trouble. One night he got hold of one of those BB guns and ran around shouting his head off. Trouble is the gun looked like a real one. They had the MPs out, civvie cops, the bloody lot. He's out the army now. Eighteen stone and no bloody job, just sits and stares at the TV all day. Enough to make you weep.'

'Christ, what happened?'

'Happened to both of us. We were the same age and halfway across the desert when we come across this village. Some kids had been playing with unexploded ordinance. We were given black bin liners and told to go and clean it up. Me mate was never the same again. I wake up screaming about it sometimes.

'Anyway, we got to the Tigress Valley when it finished. We were on a peacekeeping watch, playing football with the natives, generally having a good time. We had this young lad, he'd have been around ten years old, used to run errands for us and generally hang around. Kind of a mascot. Well, some of the villagers were real old school and weren't going to put up with that. We found him hanging in a tree one morning.

'My mate went absolutely bloody apeshit. Grabbed an SA 80 and charged into the village, bayonet and all. We got to him just in time. Hostilities had only been over a week and he was about to singlehandedly kick it off all over again.' Looking at Valerie he patted his chest pockets. 'Need to get outside for a smoke.'

'Here.' She threw her Zippo across. 'Don't know what you'd call it, but you've landed in the opposite of a smoke-free zone.'

'Thanks.' Putting a cigarette between his lips, he offered the open pack.

Valerie shook her head and headed into the main cabin. 'Drink? There's Scotch or Southern Comfort. If you want a mixer it's in the tap.'

'Scotch,' he said, watching her light up a Disque Bleu. 'Ice?'

'In the kitchen. Fridge on the left.' She slid down into an easy chair and held out her glass. 'Thanks,' she said as the ice splashed into the aromatic bourbon. 'Wife and kids?'

'Kids and ex-wife. She couldn't stick the tours.' He took a couple of sips from the heavy tumbler. 'Did five in seven years. She just snapped.'

'Wanted a nine-to-fiver, did she?'

'Not her fault; she didn't go off with another man. Just couldn't stand the strain. Six months at a time wondering if the father of your kids is coming back. Some just can't take it. I'd go on tour and she would weigh nine and a half stone.

Come back, she was seven and a half. Lives with her parents, children and all. Still no other man as far as I know. The stupid thing is, the position I'm in now, I won't get deployed again.'

'Well, get back together,' said Valerie. 'The reason for breaking up has gone.'

'Yeah, I know,' he said wearily. 'But the spark has gone. You've got to have the spark.'

'Yes,' said Valerie, vacantly staring into a lifeless television. 'Or get rid of it.'

They drank on for another hour before the sergeant said, 'Have to get a taxi, neither of us can drive now.'

Valerie got up and pointed to the guest cabin. 'In there. Sheets not been changed since my secretary used it, but I think you'll survive.'

'What happened to you?' Johnny said, getting to his feet.

'Shows, does it?'

'Takes one to know one.'

'Maybe tell you another time,' she said, shutting her bedroom door.

EIGHTEEN

THE ANGER HAD BEEN SUPPRESSED FOR THE LAST twenty-four hours but now, on her way back to the Beggars Hat, it began surging around her brain like burning coals. Revenge is best served cold, but when Valerie walked through the door it had turned into spitting hot fat.

Men made up the majority of maybe twenty customers in the bar, but they all faded into a fuzzy haze as the figure of Vinnie, bent over a young blonde, came sharply into focus.

'You bastard!' Valerie howled, launching herself at his hunched back. Pulling him around by his hair, she started beating him about the face before bringing her knee abruptly into his groin. Then, grabbing his collar, she savagely punched his nose. There were many abuses running through her head, but all that screamed around the room was, 'You bastard,' over and over.

'Get off, get off, you crazy bitch!' With arms crossed in front of his face, Vinnie defended himself. He managed to pull away for a second. Swinging a punch, he caught Valerie on the ear; that sent her sprawling to the floor. At first unaware of the ringing in her ear, she got to her feet and renewed her attack. 'Someone get this fucking cow off me!' shouted Vinnie, falling into the corner, his hands back in front of his face again. A strong arm came between the two of them, and she came face to face with Charlie.

'It was you!' she choked as the scream tore from the back of her throat. 'Beat up a little girl not even half your size! How much did this arsehole pay you?' She struck out at him and winced as her bruised knuckle hit his chin. She started again with the only words that would leave her mouth as she beat his chest: 'You bastard, you bastard, you worthless bastard!'

'Grab her.' At Charlie's command, two men held her tightly, locking both of her arms. 'Now, what's this all about?'

She squirmed while trying to bite one of the vicelike hands. 'You know! You stinking piece of crap!'

Vinnie staggered to his feet and struck the helpless Valerie across the face, then whimpered as Charlie grabbed his arm. 'Leave her alone,' his deep voice rumbled, demanding instant obedience. 'If you don't,' he added with a smile, 'I'll get the boys to let her go.' He pointed to a chair. A compliant Vinnie, wiping blood from his lip, cowered into the corner.

'Well?' said Charlie, dancing back from an attempted kick. 'I think I know what this is all about, but let's hear your side. Without the abuse,' he said as Valerie poured out more vitriol.

'You know,' she repeated, attempting to get loose.

'Take her over there,' he nodded to the table he'd been sitting at, 'let her cool down.' He again smiled. 'And for Christ's sake don't let her go.'

He accepted a large drink, leant his back to the bar and looked at Valerie. 'Drink?' She had stopped her futile struggling but, looking away, still managed a defiant expression. 'Anyone know what she drinks?' said Charlie, looking around.

From among the blank stares and silence, Valerie acquiesced, 'Southern Comfort. Ice.' For the first time since she'd walked in, her voice became near normal. 'In a clean glass,' she added as Charlie turned to the bar.

Charlie sat opposite Valerie and pushed the drink across. 'Can they let you go?' Getting no reply, he motioned them away. 'From the beginning.' He delicately took a small sip of his bourbon.

'Tell you what you already know?' Valerie looked at her drink then swallowed it in one. She coughed as the large amount of Southern Comfort caught the back of her throat. 'Suppose I'm next?'

'Okay, okay,' said Charlie, 'I see it's going to be one of them conversations, so I'll tell you. Your friend Jane... She comes in here to meet someone, had a Coke and went. Me and the boys went out a few minutes later, had a wander along the river, going down to the Warf Inn. Had a bit of business to see to. So, we comes around by them old cast-iron bollards and there's this hell of a rumpus going on. Your Jane's right in the middle of it. Two real heroes giving her a right seeing to.'

Valerie waved her glass at the barman for another, then turned to Charlie. 'Who was it?'

Charlie shrugged his shoulders. 'We sent one into the river and was going to ask the other a couple of questions, when Old Bill comes around the corner. They gets an ambulance for Jane and takes the other one off to the station. I was just trying to comfort her while we waited, you know, just holding her in me arms. Poor little cow.'

'Bloody hell,' said Valerie, 'that's why.'

Charlie took the two fresh drinks and put them on the table. 'That's why what?'

'That thing on your neck. Apparently, Jane was muttering all kinds of nonsense, including a "butterfly and rose". She slumped back in the seat and looked Charlie in the eye. 'Sorry.'

'That's all right, had worse.' He stroked the back of a large fist across his chin. 'Just can't remember where or when. You pack quite a punch…'

'Valerie, it's Valerie.' She flicked her fingers a couple of times. 'Sod it.'

'What's that?'

'That Vinnie. Broke my bloody fingernail.'

Charlie gave a light scratch to his forehead and smiled. 'Well, I didn't beat her up.' He nodded across the room. 'And your friend over there didn't do it.'

'Yes,' said Valerie. 'So who? And, more to the point, why? Sex attack?'

'Naw,' said Charlie. 'She had all her clothes on and they were beating her up, not, you know.' He finished his drink and stood up, patting his pockets. 'I need a fag. Come on, I'll show you where we came across her.'

'Don't suppose you've got a nail file?'

The man on the bar stool folded his *Daily Mirror* as Charlie and Valerie left. 'Said she'd be back.'

***

Valerie watched a straining tug pull large gravel barges upstream, as Charlie lit first her cigarette and then his own.

'Have to give these up one day.' He put the matches away while blowing smoke above his head. 'Me girlfriend don't like the way the nicotine stains the old moustache.'

'Yeah, I know what she means.' Walking backwards a few steps, Valerie took in the handsome growth. 'Don't see many like that.'

He took a finger to each end in turn, giving it a curl. 'Just along here,' he said, pointing at the bollards. 'Kicked one over the edge. Think he must have swum to the other side.' He stopped for a second and looked across the water. 'Or went under. The other's in the nick.'

Valerie took her phone out as they each selected a bollard and sat down. 'Dennis, sorry about the bother. Can you find out something and call me back?' She reeled the details off before putting the phone away, then watched the tug and barges disappear around the bend.

'Me dad was a river man,' said Charlie, breaking the quiet moment. 'Used to work the barges along here and further down… back in the days when we were more than just a bloody museum. Jesus, you look around and there's nowt left; it's all cafés, takeaways and the ruddy service industry. We don't make a bleedin' thing anymore.' Valerie laughed and took in another lungful of smoke. 'Okay,' said Charlie, 'I'll buy it. What's so funny?'

'You, Charlie. You're in the service industry.' She laughed again as Charlie joined in.

'Never thought about it like that before.'

Seeing that there was nothing more than tobacco on offer, the one or two seagulls that had landed a few yards away flew off in search of better pickings. Valerie searched her pockets for something as the gulls were replaced by a bold robin. 'Sorry,' she said, holding out a flat palm, 'nothing.'

Slowly and quietly, Charlie pulled at the loose grass around one of the bollards. He had almost circumnavigated the iron lump when a small grub fell from the dry soil. 'Here you go,' he said, throwing it across. The robin jumped nearer to Charlie then hopped back, keeping his eye on the two of them all the time. After a couple of abortive expeditions, he finally made it to the grub then flew just two or three yards away to enjoy it. 'Brave little sod,' said Charlie. 'Ain't afraid of nowt.'

'Yeah, he's got balls,' said Valerie as her phone rang. She nodded as Dennis passed on the information. 'About par for the course,' she said, switching it off. 'No details of anyone taken to a police station for attacking Jane.'

'Well, they sure looked like bogies,' said Charlie.

'What, big feet?' Valerie dropped her cigarette onto the pathway and ground it in with her heel. 'Anyone on the take around here?'

'They're a pretty straight lot on this manor,' he said. 'But it's not a given, of course. I'll get the guys to ask around.'

Holding out her hand, Valerie got to her feet. 'Thanks, Charlie.'

'No problem.' His handshake was not what Valerie expected. Although he covered her hand with his, it was gentle.

'Sorry about, you know.'

'That's okay,' he said, stroking his chin. 'Let me know if you want a job.'

'Sure.' She turned and walked off down the towpath. 'Tell Vinnie sorry.'

NINETEEN

'Didn't call before,' said Preston over the phone, 'thought you'd be a bit tied up after what happened.' With a key in one hand and shopping in the other, Valerie held the phone to an ear with her shoulder as she stepped from the gangplank.

'How did you know? And the flowers?'

'Kenny heard something from someone who heard from someone else, you know. And when it turned out to be the secretary of a lady detective, well, that was it. Just had to be you.'

'I see. Think I'll hand the business over to you. I'll go lie on a beach.'

'You can come and lie on my beach any time.'

'Tempting, and before you ask, I can't.'

'Can't what?'

'Dinner, lunch, tea. Not even breakfast, I'm afraid. I need to find the son of a bitch that's responsible for doing this to Jane.'

'Well, we can meet up for lunch, just an hour while you catch your breath?' He carried on quickly before Valerie could interrupt. 'How about a quick picnic tomorrow? Where can I pick you up?'

'Okay. I suppose you know where my office is by now. Call around, I'll be there.'

The next morning, Valerie rang the Beggars Hat.

'Who's calling at this bleedin' godforsaken time? Jesus, I got a pub to run, I don't do nine in the friggin' morning.'

'Need to get in touch with Charlie. You got his number?'

'Charlie? Charlie bloody who? Who do you think I am, 118?'

'You know who Charlie is. He's in most nights, was in last night. We had a slight fracas.'

'Oh Jesus, it's you. Don't know. Now piss off.'

'Come on, course you know,' said Valerie, supping a coffee with her free hand. 'Or do you want the next call I make to be to the health authorities?'

'Shit, you ever get fed up with causing friggin' mayhem? Wait.' The line went silent for a minute until the barman came back and rattled off a number. 'Now take a hike. And by the way, you're fucking barred.'

'Cripes,' said Valerie, punching in Charlie's number, 'that's one off my bucket list. Never been barred from a municipal tip before.'

Valerie made several attempts to call Charlie, each one resulting in being put through to his answerphone. She sat for a couple of minutes, doodling what few thoughts she could be certain of on a piece of paper, when her phone rang.

'It's Thompson. Hardy's disappeared. Family and all.'

'Oh, for Christ's sake,' she said. 'Doesn't he know he's safer where he is? I don't know what some people carry in their head, but it sure ain't brains. Any ideas, or is that it, vanished?'

'At the moment, yes,' said Thompson. 'His protection went up to check this morning and they were gone. I'll get a few feelers out, but I don't think he's taken them to his aunt Nellie's.'

'Hope not,' said Valerie, revolving a pack of cigarettes around the table. 'Whoever it is won't be long getting around the obvious places, before realising they're at a safe house.' She ended the call. 'Or not at a safe house, to be precise,' she added quietly.

As she studied the few things she had written down, the phone rang again. 'It's Charlie, got your number logged on me phone. Who is it?'

'Sorry, Charlie, it's Valerie. Got your number from our friend at the Beggars Hat.'

'Jesus, bet you were popular.'

'Hope you don't mind. Did you find anything out?'

'Not sure, I think we have someone on the take… or rather, someone under someone's thumb. Beginning to think a lot of this is run on fear. Nasty.'

'Can we meet, Charlie?'

'Sure, how about our bollards?'

***

Charlie was sitting on one of the bollards, throwing crumbs into the grass.

'Look,' he said quietly, 'our friend's back.'

'Hello, Charlie.' Walking up slowly, Valerie looked over his shoulder. 'A bit of a softy for your line of work, aren't you?' She followed as he got up and started along the riverbank.

'Leave him to his breakfast.' They walked in silence for a few seconds before Charlie spoke again. 'What makes you think I'm some kind of bandit?'

'Not sure you are, Charlie. Know what Vinnie called you? The Lone Ranger. By the way, how is he?'

'Who, Vinnie? He's fine, couple of cuts and bruises, but fine.' He stopped and looked across to a pleasure boat making its way upstream. 'Who the bloody hell are you, Valerie? Or should I say, who are you working for?'

'Right at the moment, Charlie... Right at the moment, I'm not sure. But the money keeps dropping into the bank.'

'You know what I think?' he said. 'I think you're not allowed to tell me, that's what I think. Anyway, crooked cops. There is someone, a middle officer. But as I said before, he may be receiving a payoff, probably is, but I think he's frightened. Someone with a lot of muscle is on top of this. And I'll tell you something else, I'd watch my back if I was you.'

'Oh, why?'

What Charlie said next made an icy-cold finger stroke her spine before descending the back of each leg. 'It wasn't Jane they were after. That was a mistake. They thought it was you. That's what I think.' Charlie handed over a small white card.

'What's this?'

'You'll find him there this evening, written it on the back.'

'Jamison, an inspector. High enough to pull a few strings,' she said, tapping the card on her fingers before turning it over. *C W Frances Security and personal advisor*, it read on the reverse, with contact details. 'Blimey, Charlie, I am disappointed. Thought it would have said "Have Gun Will Travel". Or at least "Muscles R Us".'

'What's that bloody Vinnie been telling you? This place is full of scum, Valerie, all of them wanting a shortcut to the folding stuff. We help when you're too small or weak to fight for yourself, simple as that. I ain't no gangster, no way. Me mum didn't bring up no thugs.'

'Fair enough, Charlie.' She slid the business card into her wallet. 'I'd better get going. Got a lunch date.'

'You owe me one,' he said.

'Sure thing, Charlie.' She pushed her hands into her jacket pockets and turned away down the towpath. 'Sure thing.'

***

'Bloody hell, this is good.' Valerie looked out from the clifftop as she put the chilled glass to her lips. 'All this and Chablis too.'

Having asked about Jane, Preston stretched out a hand and lightly stroked Valerie's shoulder. 'Off to Antigua in a couple of months. I've got a place overlooking English Harbour. Probably stay until next year. How about it?'

She lay back on the thick wool rug. 'Bit sudden.'

'Don't you ever get tired of playing hard to get?' He sat hunched, sipping at his glass.

Valerie rolled onto her stomach and looked up. 'How long have we...?' She stopped for a moment. 'I was going to say how long have we known each other, but we don't, do we? Know each other, I mean. Been out on a few dates and into bed once.'

'Jesus.' Preston flicked a chip of flint amongst the grass. 'I don't believe in love at first sight, it's bloody stupid. But waking up and seeing your head on the pillow, I came as close as one can get.'

'And that's it?' She stood up and wandered towards the cliff edge, glass in hand. 'Sex.'

Following, Preston took hold of her hand. 'No, it bloody wasn't. And you know it.'

Valerie kept looking out to sea. She was not sure of much at that moment. But one thing she was sure of: she was not flying off across the Atlantic on such a short acquaintance. 'Let's just keep it as it is, yes?'

'Sure.'

***

'Look who's back from the edge.' Holding a kidney dish, the nurse kept the door open with her back.

Jane, propped up on a pile of pillows, was using a straw to drink mineral water through bruised lips. Gingerly withdrawing her mouth, she managed a croaky, 'Hi.'

'Hell's teeth, Jane, you gave me a bloody fright.' Valerie bent down and gave her a kiss then the lightest of caresses, but it still brought a deep-down groan. 'Oh, Christ.' She pulled back and dropped the latest reality magazines on the side table. 'Sorry.'

With the two broken fingers, Jane beckoned her back. 'Should have brought a liquidiser.' She attempted to point at the Ferrero Rocher.

'Kept that for the bastards that put you in here,' said Valerie.

The choking laugh was followed by groans and a tightening face. 'Shut up, boss,' Jane whispered between clenched teeth. 'Any more of this and I'll have to get you barred.'

'Bloody hell, twice in one day, must be some kind of record.'

'Eh?'

'Nothing, nothing.' Pulling a nearby chair to the bedside, Valerie gave a dismissive shake of her head. 'Anything you can tell me?'

'Big, both of them. Bloody big. Could have scared me off with a look, didn't have to go to all this bleedin' trouble.'

Valerie held the straw to Jane's lips as she started coughing again. 'I'll do the jokes,' said Valerie, 'you stick to descriptions.'

'Peculiar.' Her throat easing a little, she grinned. 'One was dressed like something out of that Michael Douglas film, you know, striped shirt, wide flashy braces. This guy's were bright red with yellow birds.'

'Really?' said Valerie. 'How about the other?'

'Suit, black I think, not sure – he was the one holding me from behind.'

'Real brave lads,' said Valerie, pinching a Ferrero Rocher. 'Anyway, that one should be easy to identify.' She tossed the gold wrapper into the waste basket. 'Just so long it's not his beating-up-small-girls uniform,' she added quietly.

Valerie stayed for a couple of hours. Before leaving, she phoned Charlie. 'I think we need a guard on Jane. Don't want to call in the police in case we get a bent one. If you can spare someone? Needs to be twenty-four hours or there's no point. Make out a proper invoice and I'll make sure you get paid.'

Valerie waited outside Jane's room for perhaps twenty minutes until a slim but well-built man of about six foot two came along the corridor, his patent leather crocodile shoes marking out long, measured steps. The pure white shirt cuffs, revealed at the sleeve ends of his neatly cut grey suit, were fastened with opal links that matched the tie pin on his blue silk tie. His eyes were soft brown, and the slight smile revealed perfect white teeth.

'Miss Stone?' His voice was sweet, dark and thick, like the molasses of his native Barbados. 'I'm Winston. Charlie sent me.'

Valerie pushed at the door. 'Meet Jane,' she said, ushering him in. 'Only leave her to hand over to someone else.' On raising his eyebrows, she added, 'There's a shower and toilet through the door in the corner.'

'Okay.' He approached the bed and put a large but gentle

hand on Jane's shoulder. 'Now don't you worry no more, Miss Jane, Winston's here.'

Seeing Jane's face relax, Valerie slipped quietly from the room as something very private and very intimate silently passed between the two strangers.

TWENTY

In spite of brown parcel tape securing the two cracks in the glass panel, it still rattled as Valerie knocked on the faded blue doorframe. The flat was part of a dreary concrete complex. Graffiti covered the walkways that connected three flat-roofed constructions. The part-tarmac, part-mud parking area at the foot of the compound had several vehicles up on breeze blocks, the occasional new car indicating where that particular tenant's priorities lay.

Along the open corridor, split and untied black bin liners spilt rotting contents into a communal gutter. Broken toys, long abandoned in the grime, were scattered around. *Architects got praise for this heap of garbage*, thought Valerie. *They should have been made to live in one, or thrown from the top of the highest.* She shook oily water from one of her trainers.

Balancing a strawberry yogurt and plastic spoon in one hand, a short-sleeved man pulled back the door. 'Yes?'

Valerie moved away as he thrust himself forward. 'Inspector Jamison?'

'Well?'

'Can I come in? Have a word?'

'About?'

Thinking that she would only get the door shut in her face with a general enquiry, she pulled out her security pass. 'Inside would be better.'

'Jesus Christ and chief constables,' he tutted, 'it's the bloody Girl Guides.' Stepping aside, he motioned her into the lounge.

The paintwork had long lost its gloss in the gloomy room and was now a pale yellow. Wallpaper showed oblongs of dust where pictures had been removed. The odd piece of matching furniture sat on a carpet that had not been vacuumed for several weeks. If this man was on the take, it was not being spent here.

Moving a basket of underwear and socks to the ironing board, she brushed the chair with the back of her hand and sat down. 'Maid's day off?'

'No. Wife and kids' day off. Bleedin' permanent.' He moved a couple of ornaments along the mantelpiece and put his yogurt down. 'What do you want?'

'Few nights ago, your lads pulled someone at the scene of a beating down by the river. Where is he?'

'Why, what's it got to do with you? Your mob let Queen and country sleep at night. What's a second-rate sex attack doing on your desk?'

'Where is he?'

'Don't know,' he said, taking a bottle from the side and pouring two glasses. 'I'll just get some ice.' Valerie shook her head. 'Tea?'

'Coffee if you have some, milk, no sugar.'

He returned a few minutes later, handed a mug to Valerie and took a mouthful of the whisky. 'Good stuff. Small distillery on the Western Isles, got a couple of bottles when I was up there last year. Very smooth. We had the guy in custody for just an hour when a couple from the Yard breezed in and took him away. That's all I know. They just flashed their cards and that was that. Special Branch.'

'We'll check,' said Valerie, getting to her feet and finishing the coffee. 'If you're straight then I'm sorry for disturbing you.' She started to hand the mug back, but her fingertips went numb and it slipped from her grip, while colour drained from the surroundings. Staggering back, a black curtain descended and she fell to the floor.

***

A pain between the eyes was the first thing she became aware of, then a dim lightbulb, dangling from the ceiling, came into focus. Unresponsive limbs refused any command, but she managed to raise a head that felt full of lead.

Why time should be so important she wasn't sure, but there was only a pale shadow around her wrist; the watch was gone. Motionless, she let her eyes take in the surroundings. The ceiling was low, no more than a couple of metres. The walls discoloured and cracked, an odd patch disclosing the old distemper. It was obvious that, as bad as the flat complex was, she was no longer there.

The only sound, as she let her head fall back, was the creaking of rusty springs. Her dry tongue tentatively moved around her mouth. She closed her lips and attempted to breathe slowly through her nose. After about a minute, she managed to produce enough saliva to swallow. In an effort to stop the rising panic, she first, very gently, managed to wiggle the fingers on her right hand, then her left. One foot after the other responded to her mental commands, each circle of movement getting larger. Then with relief she was able to flex each knee. Her brain started to clear as she flicked feeling into her left arm, becoming conscious of a chain around her right wrist.

After about fifteen minutes, she managed to turn and sit up. As her eyes became accustomed to the light, she could see that she was on an old single, iron bed. A table, with peeling veneer, and chair were nearby. To their side was a bucket and lid, together with a few sheets of toilet paper. As there was no window, she supposed the small room to be a cellar. A tantalising bottle of what looked like water, and a plastic glass, sat on the table.

She stood up and took a few tentative steps but, because of the length of chain that had been attached to the wall, could not reach the door. She stretched for the handle but was not even close. Sitting back down on the bed, her dry mouth refused to let her eyes leave the bottle of water.

She sat there reassuring herself that, as she was not face down in a ditch, whoever was responsible for her imprisonment had other things on their mind. She also reasoned that in order to soften her up, she would not see them for at least twenty-four hours. That only left one problem to work on in the meantime: was the water drinkable? It seemed common sense that there was nothing wrong with it, but the primitive desire of survival made her sit back and look away.

Trying to keep some sense of time is difficult. Anyone deprived of daylight changing to night, let alone no watch, is quickly days out. Like being lost in the desert, trying to get out just ends up in a circle back to finding the footsteps that started the journey. On top of that, how long had she been unconscious?

Pulling the blankets over the bed, she managed to sleep. It could have been ten hours; it could have been one. With her mouth full of thick saliva, it was probably several, but that could just have been lack of water. After making use of the bucket, she flopped back onto the bed, waiting for the appearance she was sure would come soon. Meanwhile, she tried to slip the manacle from her wrist. It had been bolted rather than locked on, leaving a small but definite gap. If she could get hold of some soap, and if the pain was not... The door opened.

A man in his early twenties came in and put a plate of gammon and fried eggs on the table. From what she could guess and her complaining stomach, she thought it early evening. He looked at the water, took off the top and drank a small amount, before cutting a piece of gammon and putting it into his mouth. He then went to the door, picked up a clean bucket and replaced the one by Valerie's bed. It was over in less than a minute.

The man left no knife or fork, but even eating with her fingers, the thick gammon was gone in seconds. Licking at the last dribbles of egg, Valerie then washed the salty taste away with the cold water.

So as to try and keep some sense of how time was passing, she took the manacle and marked the wall. She judged it twelve hours before the man reappeared.

'Wait. Please.' She held his eye as he handed her a plastic bowl of stew. 'I need some Tampax.' Only raising his eyebrows, the man still said nothing. 'Time of the month. I'm not wanting to smoke them.' Immediately regretting the wisecrack, she gave a weak smile. Although the man said nothing, Valerie continued, 'And I'll need some soap and a little water, please.'

After the meal, she wiped her hands on the blanket and longed for a shower. The request would be futile, so she pushed the thought aside.

On the next visit, Valerie got the Tampax. The soap was the prized item, but not wanting any evidence of the tampons not being used, she was pleased when he also dropped disposal bags on the bed.

It was while experimenting with the soap and shackle that Valerie started to wonder how long this was going to go on. Just how clever were her jailers, apart from being sharper than she had been? She was aware that a comfortable feeling had started to drip into her brain. Were they drugging her? Or was this how prisoners, left to their own devices, began to feel? Suddenly, in the middle of this meditation, the manacle slipped from her wrist.

Not knowing what was on the other side of the door or how many guards were there, she pushed the shackle back into position, which hurt a lot more than its removal. Lying back on the bed, the pain and anguish gave way to fitful sleep.

Then there was a moment when she thought the situation had been something her overactive brain had come up with. A gentle sensation smoothed her face, then travelled down to a willing breast. But stirring, the beginning of a smile fell away as she became aware of the cold dampness. She was not in a warm apartment, stretching out to a desired lover.

'What the hell?' She twisted round as the thoughtful caressing of her breast turned to a painful squeeze. 'Bastard!' She pulled away as the colourful braces came into focus. 'This the way you get your thrills? You friggin' pervert.'

The squeeze was replaced by a sharp slap across the face. 'Come on, you fucking tart, don't make out you're not getting all sweaty,' he said, reaching to the top of her thighs.

'Not for you, you bloody creep.' She struck out, throwing the chain around his neck. 'Now get your filthy hands off me or I'll reduce your windpipe to a pulp.'

Gripping the chain, he moved his head to one side, choking for breath. 'Okay, okay.'

'What the bloody hell's going on?' The young man had returned with a fresh bucket. 'You know what Jenny said, keep your bleedin' hands off.'

'Thanks.' Valerie scraped the chain over her attacker's head and, with a flexed knee, sent him across the room.

He wiped blood from his cheek with the back of his hand, swore and pointed a finger across the room. 'Another time, girl. You and me ain't finished.'

'You stupid prick,' she heard the young one's hushed voice as the footsteps faded along the corridor, 'only Jenny dishes it out. Carry on like that and you'll follow the others.'

Alone again, she leant back against the grubby wall. Bloody hell, what was wrong with Gillian's idea? Surround herself with Giorgio Armani and Christian Dior. From where she sat now, a little perfume shop was definitely preferable. She was musing about who was responsible for her incarceration and if she'd ever met them, when the door opened.

'You fallen into something you can't get out of?' Valerie said, trying to catch his eye as the young man returned and placed a lamp on the table. 'I know someone else like you. Call the police and I'll do what I can. Carry on like this and you'll finish up in a skip, staring at the stars.'

A woman walked in. 'Trying to corrupt one of my boys?' she said, stopping by the table. 'Well, Miss Stone, what are we going to do with you?' She motioned the young man away. 'You're getting to be a bit of a pain in the backside. We're here trying to do a little business and you keep shoving your nose in.' She switched on the light, preventing Valerie from seeing who else had quietly shuffled in. 'Let's start with what department,' the woman continued. 'MI5?'

Holding allegiance to none but herself, a way out was Valerie's only thought. Squinting at the glaring light, she shrugged her shoulders. 'I'm just a private investigator. Just doing some work for an insurance company.'

'Do me a favour,' said the woman, throwing Valerie's ID onto her lap. 'Those did not drop out of a packet of cornflakes.'

'They're just something I got printed up. Most people don't know what an official ID looks like. Gets me no end of information in my work.' Gambling that the woman wouldn't know a true warrant or security pass from a counterfeit, Valerie tried a straight bluff. 'Have a close look. All of them are fakes; real ones have a luminous blue stripe down the side.' She threw in the false description in a matter-of-fact voice.

The woman's eyes narrowed as she crossed the short distance and picked the ID back up. 'Don't get cute with us, Valerie.'

Her querying expression gave Valerie a little hope as the woman went back behind the lights, where a few soft whispers were exchanged. 'There's no way out,' she said returning. A strike across Valerie's face was sharp and unexpected. She threw the cards back down. 'The hand you're holding is crap.'

The searing pain, made worse by the large ring on the woman's finger, drove the little spirit Valerie had into a black pit.

'It's true, honestly.' Managing to keep her growing dread under control, Valerie licked the blood from her lip. 'What do you want me to say? I'm just caught up in something I know nothing about. I was asked to look into the insurance claim on Alan Preston's life. I'm just trying to spin the expenses out. Just a body on the beach, and every day I can add is more in my account. That's all there is to it.'

The woman disappeared behind the lights again, but all Valerie could hear were low murmurings. Resisting the urge to be sick, she swallowed hard, the bile burning the back of her throat. She rose unsteadily to her feet, trying to ease the panic. She was immediately confronted by the two men who, with a steel grip, held her securely while the woman struck out with a piece of garden hose across the back of her thighs. It was as excruciating as it was sudden.

'Any ideas come to mind?' she said, taking a breath before nodding at the two men. One of them ripped the sweat-drenched T-shirt from Valerie's back as the man with the braces stepped from the shadows and handed the woman a cigarette. She drew deeply, clearly enjoying the nicotine and Valerie's dread, before blowing the smoke towards the ceiling. 'You've been running around the south coast like bloody Wonder Woman, causing us no end of fucking trouble. Now we'd like to know what you've found out, and no shit about a bloody insurance company.'

Somewhere in the house, Valerie could hear music. It must have been playing for a while, but only now did she become conscious of it. Beethoven.

The frantic cry was dragged from deep inside as jagged pain shot through her arm. A violent twist sent a bent wrist up between protruding shoulder blades, mixing fear with the agonising torture. At first she thought it broken or dislocated, but as it was released the pain eased.

With the diminishing pain returned the music. The Emperor Concerto. The particular Beethoven skill of making the piano notes seem to bounce, mixed with Valerie's terror, left a surreal emotion she could not define.

The woman drew in another lungful of smoke as the two men turned Valerie around, the hose flashing across her back, extracting a violent scream that rebounded from the walls. Begging for respite, she felt the cigarette burn into her tender skin lower down.

'Well? Any ideas or is it tits next, before we move on to the more interesting parts?' The woman smiled as she produced a Stanley knife. 'You choose, my dear. Burn them off, or would you prefer something a little sharper?'

Valerie twisted from side to side as electrifying bolts of terror shot through her brain. The nightmare of pain and death reached down and gripped her pulsating body as she realised they knew all about her. What information might have satisfied them she couldn't retrieve, as her racked brain refused to work, the roller coaster of panic descending into a black tunnel.

A bell rang from somewhere above them.

'Fuck!' The woman ground the cigarette into the floor with her heel. 'Who the bloody hell is that?' With blood pumping crimson streaks through her cheeks, she flung an obscenity at Valerie before striking her across the face. 'Who the bloody hell is that?' She looked around at the blank expressions. 'Out!' she screamed at the two men. 'Get upstairs. Out!' She took a final kick at Valerie, picked up the ID and followed the men out of the cellar.

It was either now or her mutilated body was going over the nearest cliff. She caked her wrist in soap and savagely yanked her hand free of the manacle. Holding her wrist, the door gave way to a hard shove and she stumbled through into the corridor. 'Stupid bastards.' Feverishly looking around for a weapon, she grabbed her jacket and picked up the hose end. 'Useless,' she said, throwing it into a corner.

One way led to a small flight of steps; the other ended in a coal store. Turning, she pulled the door shut behind her, then opted for the coal store. There was a little light visible from the trapdoor above the coal shoot. Deciding against looking for a light switch, she remained still for a minute, letting her eyes adjust to the low light. Stumbling towards the crack of light, lumps of coal fell to the floor, but no one came.

Fortunately, the bolt to the trap was on the inside and slid back without too much effort. Scrambling out, Valerie fell to the grass and lay looking at the stars. There were lights on in the house, but she could hear no voices, no noise. Although futile, she brushed herself down as she got to her feet and moved behind some rhododendrons. A quick glance back, as she kept off the gravel drive, confirmed it was the same house that she had broken into before.

With no money, no phone and looking utterly dishevelled, Valerie put her thumb out when a safe distance from the house. Two cars passed before a small lorry pulled up. Leaning over, the driver opened the nearside door. 'Dear God in heaven!' He pushed to keep the door open, then held out a helping hand.

'Had a bit of an accident,' said Valerie, scrambling into the cab. 'Remind me, where are we?'

The driver pulled off his flat cap and switched on an overhead light. 'Bit of an accident!'

To get a look at herself, Valerie pulled the large door mirror towards her. 'See what you mean.'

The driver looked at the blood showing below her jacket as she leant over. 'Think we'd better get you to a hospital.'

'No, I'm fine. Where am I?' she repeated, wanting confirmation she was where she thought she was.

'Just past Guildford on the A3.' Valerie pushed the mirror back into position and gingerly eased herself into the seat. 'If you can take me into London, I've a boat on the Thames.'

'That's not a problem, Miss. But I do think you need medical attention.'

'If you can drop me off… I'll pay, of course. You don't have anything to drink, do you?' The driver pointed to a bottle of water as he slipped the lorry into gear and re-joined the traffic. Valerie unscrewed the top and took a gulp of the lemon-flavoured drink. 'I'm okay, honestly. Just been in a bit of a scrape. You don't have to worry.' She pulled a piece of paper from the dash and, grabbing a pencil from behind the driver's ear, started to write. 'My office,' she said. 'Get in touch and I'll give you something for your trouble. What's your name?'

'Mike,' said the driver.

During the next half hour, Valerie only opened her eyes to direct the driver to the bridge along from the houseboat. 'Thanks, Mike.' She eased herself onto the road. 'Don't forget, get in touch. And thanks for not asking,' she said as he drove off.

***

Ignoring the mirror, Valerie walked straight into the steaming shower cubical. She squeezed at the large tube of shower gel, throwing it over the top of the screen only when empty. After carefully sponging and rinsing for half an hour, avoiding her lower back as much as possible, she allowed herself a look in the mirror. Several seconds passed before she swore a pledge to the tortured image.

After towelling down, she sorted through clean jeans and T-shirts, unlocked the gun cabinet, and pulled the holster over her shoulders. She cringed as it rubbed against the burns. The ammunition clip checked, she banged it home with the palm of her hand and put the gun into the holster.

The Jaguar was locked away in Nigel's garage, so she walked to the main road and hailed a taxi.

'Blimey, Miss, that's going to be a bit pricey.'

'Leave the flag up and I'll give you cash.'

The driver pulled his hand back from the meter. 'Okay, but it's still going to cost.'

'It's not a problem, just extra for you as it's out so far.'

The driver joined the A3 and headed for Guildford. Forty minutes later, Valerie pressed a chunk of twenty-pound notes into his hand and thanked him.

'That's okay, Miss.' He ducked his head through the window and gazed at the driveway. 'Just the one way?' he said, looking at the money.

'Yeah,' said Valerie. 'Just the one way.'

There were many things tumbling around a slowly clearing brain. But thinking back to the terrifying imprisonment, only one thing remained. Everything else dissolved into insignificance as she walked between bushes and shrubs to the side of the house.

Hearing laughter as she entered the house, she vaguely wondered why the men should still be there. They had obviously not checked the cellar. Her trainers made no sound along the hallway towards what sounded like a card game.

Playing poker around a table floating with money and beer, men sat accepting cards thrown by the dealer.

'Hope you're not going to bet that,' said Valerie, nodding towards her watch.

As if frozen by a photographer's command, the room was motionless as they all looked up at Valerie standing in the doorway.

'What the fuck?' On the far side, the man with the braces threw his cards onto the table. 'Has no one been down to the cellar since Jenny left?'

'Just waiting till she got back, were you?' Valerie pushed the door to with her heel. 'Going to pick up where you left off?'

'Well, look who got all cleaned up for us, lads.' The man to her left moved his chair back. 'Time for a different kind o' party, I think.'

"Braces" asked who would like to be first, just as Valerie drew the Glock from beneath her jacket. 'I'll have my watch first.' The order was calm and measured.

Nervously releasing the clasp, the man with the Rolex took it from his wrist.

'What you doing, man?' The unshaven male opposite snorted as he bared his teeth. 'Even if it's real, she ain't going to use it.'

In the small room the noise was deafening as Valerie squeezed the trigger, sending a round into the centre of the table. Money and cards flew in all directions.

'Shit!' The man with the watch threw it across.

'That will do for starters,' said Valerie, slipping it into her pocket. 'Now my phone, wallet and ID.'

'What makes you think you're going to get away with this, you stupid bitch?'

'You, just keep quiet.' Concentrating on the loud one with the braces, Valerie did not waver from her demands. 'I'd like my things back… please.'

Used to being in charge, he was reluctant to back down. 'You stupid fucking cow. You're dead, you know that? You're fucking dead.'

'My things,' she repeated. 'And you with the mouth, keep it closed.'

'Or what?' Getting to his feet, he leant on the table. 'Come on, what? You—'

The Glock barked again and he fell to the floor, grasping his thigh. 'My things,' she said quietly as he gasped for breath.

'You bitch, you fucking bitch!' he shrieked. 'I'll bleed to death.'

'I don't think so,' she said in the same straight monotone. 'My wallet, phone and ID.'

The quietest of the four, the one who'd brought her food, stood up slowly. 'Think they're in the d-desk, b-by the window,' he stammered. 'Shall I?' Valerie nodded and let him pass in front on his way to retrieving her things.

'Stupid fucker,' said the one on the floor still grasping his leg, 'why didn't you grab her as you went past? Prick.'

'He's still got his brains,' said Valerie, 'something you won't have if you don't shut your face.'

'Who you kidding? Kill one of us and you'd go down for thirty years.'

'My ID,' said Valerie. 'I lied, it's real. Killing you would be no more than an inconvenience. I'd have to spend half an hour at my desk with a pen and sheet of A4.'

He pulled a handkerchief from his pocket and pressed it to the seeping blood. 'I'm in pain here.'

'I'll get you an aspirin.' She took the ID and wallet and told the "sensible one" to phone for an ambulance. 'Right, cars out there. Keys, please.'

When the young man had finished calling an ambulance, he pulled out his own keys and carefully put them on the table with the other two and Valerie's mobile.

'All of you over by the window.' She stood back slightly, pocketed the keys and let them pass before looking back at the one on the floor. 'And you, sunshine, let's have your keys. Ooo, Beemer, nice,' she said, catching the keys attached to a BMW fob.

'That's an M5, you bitch. Put one mark on it and I'll kill you.'

'Don't worry, I'll make sure I park it well away from anything else.'

***

Blue lights flashing and siren wailing, the ambulance sped past as Valerie drove off towards the city. Guessing Gillian would still be working the same shift pattern, she pulled into a side street next to the hospital. She removed the holster and gun and locked them in the BMW's glovebox. It took just a few minutes for reception to locate Gillian and give directions to her office.

'Hi.' Gillian half-turned and stood up. 'Come for a chat?' She leant on the desk and gestured to a tub chair.

'No,' said Valerie, removing her jacket then peeling off the blood-stained T-shirt. 'I'm hoping you can help with this.' She turned her back towards her friend.

Gillian stepped back, holding a hand to her mouth. She directed Valerie to the treatment table and pulled on a pair of latex gloves. 'Lie face down. Jesus Christ, they're cigarette burns. Oh, for God's sake, Valerie. Stay there.' Gillian put her head outside the door. 'Nurse, quick, burns medication.' The urgent tone of Gillian's cry brought a nurse quickly, pushing a trolley.

'She's been beaten as well.' Gripped by forceps, the nurse passed over a swab.

'Not too worried about that,' said Gillian, 'but some of these burns are deep. Go and get Mr Leech.'

The adrenalin was now subsiding, bringing Valerie back into the real world that she'd left a few days before.

'Going to tell me what happened?' said Gillian, trying to clean some of the outer injuries. Tears glistened as Valerie flinched at each touch. Then, as if dropped into a bath of ice, she started shaking.

A few minutes later Mr Leech followed the nurse in and, after a few seconds, pronounced Valerie to be in shock. 'Get some warmth into this room.' The grey-haired physician pulled on gloves and began running his fingers around the burns. 'Sorry, lassie, this is going to hurt, I'm afraid.' Through the pain, Valerie attempted a smile at the thick, soothing Scottish accent. But she said nothing.

After an hour of careful cleaning and gentle application of gauze to each burn, Mr Leech straightened up and stretched his back. 'No bikinis for the next twelve months,' he said, 'but given time they will all but disappear. I'm not sure we shouldn't be calling the police.'

Momentarily unaware she had on neither T-shirt or bra, Valerie swung her feet around and pulled her ID from her pocket. 'Okay,' he said, removing his gloves and throwing them into the nearby bin, 'hang around for a few hours, make sure you're all right. If you need anything, call.'

Gillian passed a woollen top across, along with a couple of tablets. 'You going to tell me?'

'What, and get you involved? I don't think so. Let's just say there're one or two people out there that I seem to have rubbed up the wrong way.' Valerie took the offered water and washed the tablets down. 'Painkillers?'

Rattling a bottle, Gillian nodded. 'Some more in there if you need them.'

Although managing to get Valerie to stay for a couple of hours, Gillian got no further than cups of coffee.

As the dawn light began glowing through the office window, Valerie looked at her watch. 'Better get going. Got a car out there gathering tickets.'

'Oh dear, it's a bit expensive around here. I'm afraid it's going to cost you.'

Valerie set off down the corridor. 'Oh, I don't know. I've a feeling it's going to get a lot more expensive before this morning's out.'

The fresher air outside the room, along with the painkillers, perked Valerie up as she trotted down the stairwell. She peeled the ticket from the windscreen, tossed it onto the passenger seat and set off towards the south coast. Because of the personalised registration, it wasn't possible to tell the age but, by the mileage and smell of leather, the car was only weeks old.

Navigating the A and B roads towards Beachy Head, it felt as if the engine and gearbox had been filled with thick Jersey cream instead of oil. She pulled up at the cliff-top hotel and walked into the restaurant, which was all but empty. With tartan carpets, hard varnished tables and exposed stone walls, it was a typical chain hotel.

Although advertising late breakfast, only one waiter took any notice of Valerie; the rest scurried about getting ready for the lunchtime trade. She took a window table that looked out on the BMW, since the Glock was still in the glovebox. She didn't fancy explaining that, if the car was taken.

'Damn shame.' She took another mouthful of the fluffy scrambled eggs, along with two more painkillers, all the time keeping an eye on the deep red M5.'All those extras, it must be all of a hundred and twenty-thousand pounds.'

'Madam?' The waiter at her side inclined his head slightly.

'Oh, just mumbling to myself,' she said quickly.'Shame not being able to share such a lovely breakfast with someone.'

'Oh, thank you, madam, I'll let Chef know. Always a pleasure to serve an appreciative customer.'

'Can you get me a taxi?' she asked the receptionist on her way out. 'Fifteen minutes should about do it. Take me to the station.'

'Madam?' The girl looked at her enquiringly.

'Taxi?' Valerie smiled.'Please.'

The receptionist looked over her shoulder towards the M5, and then back to Valerie.'A taxi… madam?'

'Please,' said Valerie, exiting the main door. 'Fifteen minutes.'

Still retaining a quizzical look, the girl picked up the phone.'Certainly, madam.'

Valerie drove away from the gaze of the reception window, pushed the Glock into the holster, stretched it around her back and zipped up her jacket.

Cruising a few hundred yards along the high coast road, she turned off onto the thinly grassed cliff-top. The M5 sat on a narrow strip of land that bent down to the sharp drop, the engine idling in neutral. She took a small USB from her pocket, put it into the hi-fi system and lit a cigarette. With "Wheels on Fire" pouring from the speakers Valerie released the handbrake and walked back to the hotel.

TWENTY-ONE

'WE THINK THERE'S SOMETHING GOING DOWN IN THE next few days,' said Dennis as Valerie walked into the arts department.

'You're getting into modern word speak, aren't you?' she said. 'Something going down. I'm sure you weren't taught that at Harrow. More likely Latin.'

'Yes,' said Dennis, 'Latin. And Rugby, actually.'

'So, what's to do?'

'You need to meet up with your boyfriend.'

Valerie, unsure of who to trust anymore, queried the suggestion.

'We've had a little whisper from the east,' Dennis continued. 'We think that's where our last joker came from, and he could be on the move again. Our contact is as sure as he can be.'

'And you think David could be the one in charge?'

'Don't know, but—'

'Oh, good bloody grief, what are you turning me into, Dennis? An assassinating hooker?'

'You don't have to go that far, do you?'

Valerie watched as he nervously pulled his shirt collar away from his neck. 'And what do you suggest? Sorry, David, but you're going to have to put it away, I think I've left the iron on?' She followed him into the inner office and looked around. 'By the way, where's the colonel?'

'Liaising with the other big noises. They're all getting a bit edgy. The last thing we want is someone else going the way of McCain. I'll be more in charge here for a while.'

'You're the man now, are you, Dennis? *Le grand fromage.*'

'Suppose.'

Valerie thought it sweet that the young man, who'd had all this responsibility dumped on him, blushed. 'Better start by calling me Valerie... Chief. And if I ever come out the other side of this in one piece, it's going to cost.'

'Taken as read, Miss... Valerie.'

'By the way, I need to draw some more ammunition.'

'Crikey,' said Dennis. 'You been using that thing already?'

'Don't worry, just had to teach some guys the meaning of rubbing me up the wrong way. No one's hurt... much.'

He sat back in the boss's chair, pushing a pencil from side to side between his two index fingers. 'If it all gets a bit, you know—'

'Heavy is the word I think you're looking for, Dennis.' With the colonel out of the office, she went no further than just fingering the cigarette packet in her pocket. 'And I think it's gone beyond heavy.'

Dennis pressed the button on his desk. 'Sergeant, a box of nine millimetre, please.'

A few minutes later, Simonds came in. 'Sergeant's on the range.' He handed over a cream and red box with 9mm stamped at each end. 'Heard you'd had to use it,' he said, producing a receipt. Seeing the slight surprise on Valerie's face, he added, 'We hear the dramatic down my end of the building long before it filters down the official wire.'

'Better fill Dennis in then,' she said. 'He seems to know nothing about it. By the way, he deserved it.'

***

The only way to play it was low-key, which meant not contacting Preston; it was better to wait for his call. And that was about as far as any deliberation went. She didn't even want to think about how to keep her injuries from him, whether he was responsible directly, indirectly or not at all. All that became academic when he called and she agreed to meet up across the Thames from Westminster.

Arms folded on the embankment parapet; Valerie looked across the water. 'Did you ever meet your brother's assistant?'

'Jenny Lawson? Just the once, or maybe twice. Alan ran that side without much input from me. Like I said, much of my time was spent out of the country.'

'What was she like?'

'Oh, mid-thirties, I suppose. Brunette. Your height and weight.' He put his foot on the low stone ledge, twisting it from side to side. 'But as to her personality, I don't know really. Why, what's this all about?'

'We can't find her. Or at least...' she stopped and, taking careful aim at the Houses of Parliament, flicked a pebble from the top of the wall, 'the insurance company can't find her. You may be in for a bit of a wait.'

'Not worried about that, but I would like you to answer a question.'

'Okay, if I can.'

'Who are you really working for?' Before she could say anything, he continued, 'It's not just Southern and East, is it?'

'I'm working for the insurance company,' she replied innocently. 'They just keep adding more and more questions. Some of them stupid, like asking the same thing two different ways. There's just got to be some middle-management jerk in there justifying their salary. I don't mind, I've got them paying me a retainer.' Following the pebble with a half-finished cigarette, she watched it drop into the water as the last few words drifted away on a stream of exhaled smoke.

'You don't trust me, Valerie.'

She turned around and stroked his cheek. 'I wouldn't get into bed with anyone I didn't trust.'

'Fair enough.'

'Blimey, Dennis, I'm beginning to think you fancy me,' she said, answering her mobile. Her frivolous joking tailed off as she listened to what he had to say. 'For Christ's sake, Dennis.' She nodded a couple of times and then said, 'Yes, I'll go now.'

She put the phone away and popped a Tic Tac into her mouth, momentarily moving it around her tongue before grinding it between her teeth. 'Sorry,' she said, pushing her parted lips onto Preston's. 'The call of trouble.'

'Tonight?'

Valerie stroked Preston's cheek and lingered over a goodbye kiss. 'I'll call.'

***

'Down the steps,' said the constable, looking at Valerie's security pass. 'Not a pretty sight.'

To the right, six railway lines, flanked by a battery of signals, disappeared under a bridge. Across the other side, tall, discoloured tenements, topped by satellite dishes, shrouded the scene with a dark shadow. The noise of shunting wagons echoed from the left where the rails vanished around a bend.

When she reached the bottom, another officer looked at her pass and called to a plainclothes man squatting next to a body skewed up beside the high sidewall. From above, a broken pipe dripped water onto the crumpled corpse.

'Lady here with a security pass, boss.'

The man got up, put his hands above his head and gently stretched his back. 'What?'

'Lady here; she's carrying a blue card.'

The plainclothes officer gave one more twist of his neck. 'Getting too bloody old for this.' His grey hair was thinning, and although the face was deeply lined, Valerie put him at no more than fifty. 'What the hell do you lot want with this? The guy's been hit by a train.'

Valerie stepped around the victim's legs and looked into the grey, lifeless face of Hardy. 'How long's he been dead, anyone know?'

'Doctor's gone,' he said, waving a couple of men forward with a stretcher. 'He reckons early hours of the morning, but we'll know more when he's taken to the mortuary. Anyway, what do you want with him?'

'Oh, nothing special. Just a couple of loose ends.'

'I'm Watkins, by the way,' he said, taking a cheroot from a leather case. 'DI Watkins.' He lit the miniature cigar and held out his hand.

'Stone,' said Valerie taking his firm handshake. 'Valerie Stone.'

Standing to one side, they watched the two stretcher-bearers struggle back to road level.

'You can't tell me any more?' said Watkins, looking around the trackside. 'Or won't?'

'I presume there'll be a preliminary look at the body when they get it back. I'll call round, if that's okay?'

'Sure, sure,' he said, seemingly used to getting brushed off, 'give us a couple of hours.'

***

There was a marked drop in temperature as Valerie walked into the autopsy room.

'Come and look at this,' said Watkins, waving her towards Hardy's body. He pointed at bruising across the shins and arms. Valerie stepped aside as the mortician started to remove blood from around the face, while his assistant measured and copied down the lengths of the bruises and gashes. 'And this,' said Watkins.

Valerie flinched as she looked at the cluster of what looked like cigarette burns on his groin and penis. She said nothing.

Watkins turned, leaning his backside on the table, and looked directly at Valerie. 'Don't get them on the local commuter run.' Folding his arms, he kept his eyes locked on hers.

'What killed him?' she asked, deflecting his question.

'Well, it wasn't the six-fifteen to Potters Bar... was it, Miss Valerie Stone?'

Valerie could tell his brain was whirring along, gathering information. He was clever. But, she wondered, was he straight? She had no idea of who she could trust and, although she thought it unlikely, that included David Preston.

'No, it wasn't the train,' she echoed quietly.

'Are you going to tell me what's going on? Or are we going to go along playing independent blind man's bluff?'

She wanted help from someone and the inspector seemed of the old school. Was he old-school straight? Or old-school had enough of long hours and low pay?

She was saved from a decision when a shout came from the other room. 'Tea in here if anyone's interested.'

Valerie studied the inspector's quizzical face as she sipped at a chipped Arsenal mug. 'I know of someone else with similar bruising and burns. Not in the same place,' she added hurriedly, 'but similar.'

'And this person, dead?'

'No, not dead, but most likely would have been if...' Trying to weigh him up, she scrutinised the experienced face. He wasn't tall, barely her height. Maybe a stone overweight, but no more. He wore unfashionable round glasses. The little shrimp of a moustache, below a bulbous nose, looked as if it may scamper off at any moment. In shapeless trousers and checked sports coat, he was dressed like a favourite uncle. The drip of egg yolk on his tie had been vigorously scraped, but the shadow remained. Although pleasant, his aftershave was inexpensive. She noted the basic Seiko on his wrist and moved over to the window.

'Tell me...' She held the mug between two hands while pointing a forefinger. 'Cars out there, which one is yours?'

'What?' he said incredulously. 'Car?' The last thing he needed was frivolous chitchat.

'Humour me. Which of the cars in the car park is yours?'

Watkins swung his eyes to the ceiling as he went over. 'Bloody car... that one.' He pointed to an old silver Ford Focus. 'Jesus,' he muttered, 'car.'

'You got an office here, somewhere private?'

'Yes, I've got the use of one. Why?'

'Lead on, Macduff.'

She followed him down a short corridor and into an office cluttered with filing cabinets, boxes and, in one corner, a single table and chair.

'Now what's this all about?' He leant on the table as Valerie dropped the door latch and handed him her jacket.

'For Christ's sake, steady on,' he said as she peeled off her T-shirt. 'What the bloody hell are you doing? I'm a married... Oh my sweet Lord,' he said as she turned her back. 'Oh, my good God.'

After pulling the top back on, she pushed her hair into place and held out her hand. 'Jacket.'

Watkins handed it over and sat down. 'Jesus, I've a daughter your age.'

'Hope she's got a steadier job than mine.'

'Okay, Miss Stone, or may I call—'

'Yes, of course. Valerie.'

'So where to now?'

'We could go to the only place I know that's connected with this business.' Valerie opened the door as Watkins stood up. 'You got one or two officers you can trust?'

'Trust? Oh, bloody marvellous. We've got rotten apples in the barrel, have we?'

'I know of one, and where there's one...'

'Yes, I've got some good ones.'

The inspector grimaced when Valerie asked if they were authorised to carry firearms. 'Jesus, we really are in the Secret Service. What are you, MI5?'

* * *

'I'll be your oppo,' said Valerie as they approached the familiar house. 'Not sure we'll find anything, but you're the professional.' She quickly showed her security pass, which may as well have been gibberish for all the elderly woman knew. 'Stone,' she said, 'Sergeant Stone. This is Inspector Watkins. May we come in?'

From her first faltering words, it was clear the woman was totally clueless as to what had been happening. 'How can I help?' Not questioning their right or reason to enter, she hung on to the door as they swept in.

'May we have a look around?' Watkins glanced down the hallway. 'There have been a number of break-ins. Expensive places like this. We're trying to catch them, of course, but in the meantime we might be able to give some advice. Are you the owner?'

'No, no,' she stammered, 'my husband and I are from a house-sitting agency. We only arrived a few hours ago.'

'Don't suppose you can get me one of those warrant cards?' asked Watkins as they left the old lady in the lounge with her husband.

'What, security?'

Steadying himself on the iron rail, he followed Valerie into the cellar. 'Thinking more of commissioner.'

Valerie thought the inspector talented, but he was independent and had likely stepped on too many toes to climb further up the ladder. He was stuck and would stay at the same rank until he retired.

'See what I can do.'

Trying to rid herself of the memory, she rubbed the backs of her hands as Watkins held the door into the room in which she'd been kept. It was brilliant white, the smell of paint heavy in the air from redecoration in the last twenty-four hours.

'Just like a couple of other places I've seen,' she said, telling him of the boat and abandoned fort that had been scrupulously cleaned. Moving from room to room only revealed the same. The house was spotless. Even the carpet and table in the cards room had been replaced.

Watkins sent the two constables around the grounds. Offering a cheroot, he listened to Valerie tell him everything since Rosemary Benson had walked into the office.

'You know what I think?' he said when she'd finished. 'I think you've been hung out to dry.' She raised her eyebrows. 'Oh, not by the insurance company, but by whoever it is that has their claws into you. They lost a man on the inside and you dropped into their lap. Manna from bloody heaven. Who's got you, MI5? Special Branch?' Her only reply was a noncommittal shrug of the shoulders. 'It doesn't matter.' He blew un-inhaled smoke to one side as he watched Valerie draw deep into her lungs. 'Whatever part of the haunted house has you in its grip, they're all the same. By the way, I don't think Preston is in on it. He's had too many chances to throw you beneath the bus.'

'I was hoping someone else would be thinking the same as me—'

'Claude, it's Claude.' Seeing her amused look, he smiled. 'I know, I know. There can be some devious stunts performed when families get together at the font.'

'Suits you.'

'Any more quips like that and you can work the rest out on your own.' He dropped his cheroot to the ground as Valerie smiled at hers and kept smoking. 'You're the bait to tempt out the sharks. And we're not just talking bent coppers.'

'Think I worked that one out for myself. Trouble is, we've got two dead and, not counting me, another beaten within an inch of her life.'

'Stakes are high, Valerie.'

The two officers returned, shaking their heads. 'Nothing, boss.'

A moment later Valerie's phone rang. It was Preston asking to see her. 'I'm tied up at the moment,' she told him, but he was insistent, almost fraught. 'Sorry Claude, got to fly.'

***

She was once again escorted up to the penthouse apartment overlooking the Thames. But this time she did manage a smile and quick "thank you" before Robins, pressing the button, disappeared below.

Preston's "sorry to call you away" and Valerie's "this had better be good" got mixed together as she walked in.

He handed her a large tumbler of ice smothered in Southern Comfort. 'Think you're going to need that.' He took a drink of his scotch and pushed his lips together.

Valerie sank into one of the wonderful leather chairs and let her head flop back as she closed her eyes. Wanting a few seconds to herself, she held up a hand while going through the ritual of washing the amber liquor around her mouth before letting it trickle down her throat.

'Okay,' she said as the glow spread through her chest, 'I can see the apartment's not on fire.'

Taking the seat opposite, Preston leant forward, his elbows on the armrests, and, as if afraid someone might hear, whispered, 'Had a phone call.' Not sure of how to proceed, he got up and walked to the balcony.

Remaining seated, Valerie said nothing, watching the thick liquid as she swirled it around. 'Who the hell are you, Valerie?' A perplexed anger flushed his face. 'And I don't mean a minor innocent investigating an insurance claim.'

Draining her glass, she followed him to the balcony. 'Suppose you tell me what has happened,' she said, taking out a cigarette. Nodding his approval, she flicked the Zippo and inhaled. After the small Davidoffs, the smoke failed to give the same satisfaction.

'Someone phoned and told me to call off my new girlfriend… that is if I didn't want to see her floating down the Thames.'

'Bit late for that,' she murmured, blowing smoke out into the evening air.

'What?'

Dismissively, Valerie shook her head. 'Nothing, nothing, just muttering. Take no notice. Mention me by name?'

'Oh, no,' he said sarcastically. 'Got girlfriends everywhere, running all over the south coast and getting their secretaries beaten up. Everyday occurrence.' Once again, he lowered his voice as he ground out the rest. 'Course they mentioned your bloody name. What the hell's going on?'

'What else?'

'Oh,' he said, going back inside and pouring another drink, 'pulling the roof down on top of us isn't enough? You want to go all out for the bloody jackpot?'

Trying to keep this new side of Preston calm, she continued quietly, 'Tell me what else.'

'The call was on my personal mobile. There's no more than a dozen people got the number. Only close friends, one or two business contacts, that's it. Only people I want to talk with.'

She smiled. 'Is that the number I've got? Am I one of the chosen few?'

'Course you are... arrogant bloody cow.'

'Come on, what else? Everything you can remember.'

'It was short. Told me, no, ordered me to stop you doing whatever it is you are doing.'

'Did they say what?'

'No, they were as bloody aggravating as you. Not a bloody thing, just stop. Bugger off to paradise and set up home with me.' He managed a half-grin while offering Valerie a refill. 'Must say I agree with that bit.' She shook her head, looking around for somewhere to put her cigarette. 'Said they knew where your office was. Knew the car you drive. Curiously didn't mention where you hang your hat. But I don't suppose many do. And that includes me.'

'And the killer punch, David? What else?'

Preston spoke slowly and deliberately. 'I told you I'd only met her a couple of times, so I can't be sure, but it sounded like Alan's assistant… I know it doesn't make sense. The thing is, you're in something rather nasty right up to your pretty little neck. What are we going to do?'

'We?'

'Yes, we. You're telling me nothing, but I'm mixed up in this, one way or another… whatever it is.'

'Think I'd better get going.' She dropped her cigarette into the only ashtray and selected a bottle of mineral water from the fridge. 'May I?'

'I'm coming with you.'

'That's very sweet, David,' she softly stroked his cheek, 'but I don't even know where yet.'

He disappeared into the bedroom before hastily returning with a backpack. 'I'm coming with you,' he repeated firmly.

'Okay, okay, but like I said, I don't know where.'

'My place in Poole.'

'They know you, they know where your house is,' said Valerie.

'Okay, I'll drive while you look up a self-catering cottage somewhere; should be plenty at the moment, schools aren't on holiday.'

'My place first, need to pick up a few things.'

As well as toiletries and a few clothes from the houseboat, she wrapped the Glock and ammunition in a towel before stuffing them into the bottom of a grip.

One night in the car was not a problem but wanting to keep her injuries from Preston for the two nights at the cottage, Valerie gave him the usual excuse by patting her abdomen and saying, 'Sorry, cramp, time of the month, I'm afraid.'

On the fourth day she left a short note on the kitchen table apologising for taking the Golf and slipped off into the early-morning light.

TWENTY-TWO

NOT WANTING TO SPEAK WITH ANYONE, ESPECIALLY Preston, Valerie left her mobile off on the journey down to the river. Ben was the best chance, probably the only chance, of tracking down Jenny Lawson.

One or two small black clouds were low on the horizon as the little VW drew up next to the harbour master's office. Along past the main jetties, seagulls waited patiently at *Fresh Dawn*'s empty berth, the odd one gliding around on the rising breeze.

'Back in a couple of hours,' the harbour master said in answer to Valerie's query. 'They radioed in a while back. Got a good catch on board according to Dan.'

Pushing her hands deep into her pockets, Valerie left the office and wandered along the estuary embankment. A boat, a little smaller than *Fresh Dawn*, nudged alongside, and a young man around Ben's age jumped from the foredeck with the bow line and threw it over the nearest post. Then, bracing his foot against a bollard, he drew the stern in with the other warp.

Lighting the cigarette that had been dangling between his lips, he made his way up the newly placed gangplank.

'Let's go.' He clapped his hands enthusiastically. 'I've got a pint and girl waiting in the Harbour Arms.'

Valerie shouted across before he could disappear below, 'Ben and Dan on the way?'

The young man turned, pulling in a lungful of smoke. 'Not far behind. That's probably them.' He pointed to a smudge on the horizon, then put the cigarette back between his lips.

Valerie thanked him and looked out at the steadily rising sea.

Churning water at the river mouth turned the sea into froth, then, released on the wind, it rolled up the river in large chunks. She took out a pack of Wrigley's Spearmint, raised her collar and pulled the zip high on her jacket as occasional gusts ruffled her hair. The rising tide caused spray and foam to be whipped along the harbour, encouraging Valerie to move back towards an alcove in the wall behind.

Looking out to sea again, the sun was lower in the sky and *Fresh Dawn* had turned from a far-off smudge into something that belonged on the sea. The boat in front of her had dropped several boxes of cod onto the quayside, plus two valuable turbot. Again, the young man clapped encouragement as a small, rusty van came along and picked up the catch. A few minutes later, Valerie was on her own.

'Like waiting for Omar Sharif to arrive on his ruddy camel,' she said as the waiting eventually came to an end.

Although clearly surprised, Ben managed a smile as he threw a rope for her to catch. While helping to secure the boat, she ignored the questioning of why she was there.

Dan appeared from the hold and dropped a battered wooden box onto the deck. 'Hello, beautiful. Look at that, box full of gold.' Their claws secured by red bands, large lobsters were piled on top of each other.

'Few quid's worth there, Dan.'

He pulled another box from below the deck, dropped it at her feet and jammed an unlit pipe between his teeth. 'I'll say, and more below. Found one in most pots. Can't remember a better day.'

For the next half hour, Valerie helped unload before Dan drove the heavily laden Land Rover away across the car park.

A hard edge had replaced Ben's light-hearted manner as he washed his hands under the dockside tap. 'Out for a daytrip, is it?'

'Oh, you know, Ben, just come around for a visit. A quiet chat.'

'A quiet chat?' he said as Valerie rinsed her hands and accepted the worn towel, before they both walked slowly along, Ben kicking the odd pebble into the water.

'I can help you,' she said, breaking the short silence, 'but only if you help me. If you don't then you won't be going fishing for a bloody long time.'

'Oh yeah?' He managed to conceal a sneer, but the contempt was clear.

'Ben, for Christ's sake, wake up.' She stopped in front of him, blocking his way. 'I've just left the body of a guy tortured to death and then dumped like a piece of garbage. The one on the beach… that was no bloody accident either.'

'Course it was.'

'No way, Ben. You're mixed up with a right load of bastards. Money and power is the god, nothing else. They use fear like a fuel, bloody high octane at that. They'll sell their so-called friends, anyone they've paid off, even the country's security. And if you think they'll look after you, you'd better well think again. You want to know my theory?' Before he could say anything, she continued, 'I think the poor sod on the beach was held over the back of *Sun Dancer* while the prop was still turning. There's also a girl in hospital lucky not to have joined the dead ones, plus,' she said quietly, 'another was tortured and warned off.'

Ben retreated from the tough persona he'd tried to hold on to. 'I only supplied dope, and maybe some Columbian marching powder. That's it. I don't know nothing about no fucking murders.'

'Smuggling?'

'Okay, okay, I was given some packages to take up to London, but that's it, honest to God.'

'So, you knew Preston?'

Ben hung his head and looked at the ground. 'Yes.'

'Alan Preston? What about his brother, David?'

'Once or twice, when we was racing. He said thanks after the races, but that's all. We all lined up as he shook our hands. Don't think he knows me from Adam.'

'Jenny Lawson?'

'Not out racing, that was serious, strictly men. But otherwise, always around Alan Preston.'

'Was she the one who told you it wasn't Preston on the beach?'

Looking like a poor innocent caught up in something way above his head, Ben nodded. 'Yeah, she called. I had to go and pick Alan Preston up. Took him along to her place.'

'Where is he, abroad?' She raised her voice in an effort to get through. 'Ben, for crying out loud, I'll do all I can to help. Otherwise you're looking at drug dealing, conspiracy to murder, helping to pervert the course of justice, treason and Christ knows what. The judge will send you down for thirty years, and instead of time off for good behaviour he'll probably put in an option to extend. You'll be an old man if you ever get out, and your mother will be long dead of a broken heart.'

Ben shook his head. 'They thought it risky to go overseas too soon. Let the dust settle. He's got obscene amounts of money; he could hide away for ever.'

'Best bet, Ben?'

'Her place.'

Valerie shook her head. 'No, they've bailed out of there.'

'Where's the wheels?' said Ben as they got to the car park.

'Friend's.' Valerie pointed to the dark blue Golf. 'Mine's locked up.'

'I suppose I'd better find a cave or I'll be the next one on the beach... and not licking no bloody ice-cream neither.' He paused, clenching his fists in frustration. 'Christ, Mum! Coming here you've put me mum in danger!'

'Steady, steady,' said Valerie, putting a hand on his arm. 'They're cruel and ruthless. They're not stupid. They know you won't have told her anything. They'll go nowhere near her; it would draw attention with no return.'

'How did you guess I was mixed up with them?'

'Oh, something Dan said, but don't go blowing off at him; he was just making conversation. Besides, I knew you were involved before, or rather, guessed. Something quite innocuous.'

'What?'

'On the back of the yacht, its name: *Sun Dancer*. You called it the same as David Preston: *The Sun Dancer*.'

'You're kidding, that's bloody stupid.'

'Yeah, I know, stupid, but it stuck in my mind.' Valerie stood there as another penny, or maybe only half a penny, dropped. 'Oh, sweet Jesus. Claude was right, I've been hung out to dry. Come on, Ben, where are they likely to be? I'll do all I can.' He was on the point of saying something, so she carried on with the only ammunition she had: 'Think of your mother.'

'Tomorrow,' said Ben, 'Preston and Jenny, er, Lawson.' More frightened than reticent, he stopped. Valerie took out the packet of Wrigley's and handed him a piece. Thinking it better to let him give up the information without further threats, she kept quiet while peeling the wrapper from her own stick of gum. 'Bringing in one, or maybe two, tomorrow. They're being dropped off at the fort and Lawson is doing the pick-up.'

'What kind of time?'

'One in the morning, when it's quiet and still enough darkness left to come ashore unnoticed.'

'You involved?'

Ben shook his head. 'No. I just run around when they're ashore, get anything they need… bottles of scotch usually.'

'Right, time to earn some brownie points, might even keep you out of the slammer. Come with me and we'll follow them to wherever they're holed up. It's all right,' she said, reacting to the dread on his face, 'we'll keep our distance.'

TWENTY-THREE

Resigned to his fate, Ben's expression had hardened.

'Glass is dropping,' he said as they walked along the harbour side towards *Fresh Dawn*. Beyond the river mouth, wave tops were starting to break.

'Won't stop your friends,' she replied, throwing her grip on deck.

Below in the small crew cabin, Valerie pulled on a sweater, glad that she had also brought the small belt holster along with the Glock. She pushed it into the small of her back. Then, balancing two mugs on a tray, she came back up into the wheelhouse.

'Coffee?' Ben pressed the starters and nodded to the chart table, before going on deck and releasing the mooring ropes.

Holding the top of the doorjamb, he swung back into the wheelhouse and picked up a mug in one hand while easing *Fresh Dawn* out into the river with the other. The light drizzle had now given way to a steadier fall as he silently sipped at the coffee.

'How long?' said Valerie, lighting up a cigarette.

Ben looked at his watch. 'We'll be there by midnight. I was hoping we could hide amongst a few other boats out fishing, but with this weather we're on our own.'

Valerie followed his eyes to the radar screen. The coast and river mouth echoed a green return. But out to sea there was nothing.

'We don't have to be on top of it, do we?' she said. 'We've got your box of tricks. We just sit off a mile or two, then follow them in.'

'And how do we follow them when ashore?'

'Me. Not you. You can drop me ashore then take the boat back; I've got transport sorted.'

Valerie had been in touch with Claude. He was waiting with a few trusted officers, roughly where she thought they would likely land. She could fine-tune the final position by mobile as things developed. Ben kept to saying as little as possible.

'Don't worry,' said Valerie, 'I've got some help.'

Rounding Portland Bill, the force of the building easterly storm broke over *Fresh Dawn*'s bow.

'Cripes!' Valerie instinctively ducked as the spray hit the wheelhouse. 'Wasn't expecting that.'

'Kept us in Lyme Bay as much as possible, but we had to come out sooner or later.' He jammed his foot against the wheel housing as a large wave hit the side. 'Currents all over the place here.'

'Wind over tide, yes?'

'Yeah, that's it. Makes a right mess of the sea state. Like we're in a bloody washing machine.' Spinning the wheel, Ben kept *Fresh Dawn* between the troughs. 'We'll be out of the tide race in a few minutes, but I can't do anything about the wind.'

The pushing and pulling gave way to regular crashing of waves over the foredeck as they rode up and down the increasingly large waves.

'Thank God for that,' said Valerie, 'anything's better than not knowing which way it's going to throw you.' She braced herself into a more comfortable position and lit another Disque Bleu. Ben concentrated on keeping the little boat on course through a wind that was climbing rapidly.

'You ever going to give those up?'

'Not today.'

She looked out through the spinning Kent Clearview screen, but only the bow was visible, then blackness. Splintered glass suddenly flew across the cabin as a rogue wave hit the side of *Fresh Dawn*. Water rolled along the deck and poured into the cabin. They lurched into the following trough and the wheel was ripped from Ben's grip.

'Life jackets on that side and some towelling over there.' Ben pointed behind her as he regained control. 'Grab anything you can and shove it in the bloody hole.'

Slipping on the flooded floor, Valerie crashed against the side. Then, on hands and knees, she pulled the locker door down. Two yellow jackets, along with rags and a towel, stopped the worst. She took a sodden cigarette from between her lips.

'Keep the bloody sea where it belongs.' She hit the bent window frame with a heavy spanner, then wedged herself in the engine room hatchway and pulled a disintegrated pack of Disque Bleu from her pocket. 'Hell.' Rubbing bits of tobacco and paper from her hands, she lobbed the remains down the steps.

After an hour of being thrown around, Ben slowed the engines to tick over and put the bow head on into the now-storm-force winds.

'That's it,' he said, pointing to the instrument binnacle. Valerie looked at the black screen illuminated only by a green flash as each rotation of the radar sweep pinpointed the fort.

Around one-fifteen, Valerie pointed to the screen as a blip approached the fort. 'That's them coming in with the drop-off, I presume.'

'That's it,' said Ben. 'They won't be there together in this kind of weather, too dangerous. They'll drop them off and go. We've about fifteen minutes before they come and pick them up. They'll have been in touch by radio and watching on radar. Just hope that when they see our contact, they'll think it's just some brainless idiot out fishing.'

Valerie watched as another boat came from the shore side of the screen, before phoning Claude. She gave him the position from where it had seemingly departed, then hung up.

Ben was down using the toilet as the blip moved off course.

'Why are they doing that?' she asked as he returned.

'Christ,' Ben spat out with real venom. He swung the wheel around, opening the throttles. Although hard against the stops, he kept pushing at the chrome levers. The *Fresh Dawn* was a good boat with powerful engines, but they were built for low-end grunt, not speed. 'Bollocks. Why did I ever get fucking mixed up with you?'

The blip on the radar came down, closing the distance between them at an alarming rate. 'Should've gone off into hiding, stupid bugger that I am.' He looked across at Valerie as the big ex-navy gunboat came out of the filthy weather. 'We're dead, Valerie. We're both fucking dead.'

Towering above them, the grey boat slewed up to their port side, spewing cooling water from the large exhaust outlets on the stern. The roar of powerful engines, giving out their own violent message, was momentarily overpowered by a loudspeaker.

'Well, well, Miss Stone, out for an evening's fishing, are we?' The voice was distorted through the ancient Tannoy but was instantly recognisable. On board was the woman that had been wielding the cigarette with such perverse pleasure.

Four men jumped onto the small fishing boat and entered the wheelhouse. Two of them, holding handguns, soon had Valerie and Ben stumbling onto the other boat.

'Take it into the channel and sink it,' the woman yelled through the window of the small, enclosed command bridge. 'I'll send someone out to pick you up when we get to the fort.' She pulled the window shut and yanked on the lock as Valerie and Ben were kicked inside. 'Don't give up easily, do you!' The woman brushed raindrops and sea spray from her sleeve. 'The fort,' she said to the man at the helm. 'Can't waste time on shit like this.'

Valerie's Glock rubbed temptingly into her back. But with two pistols pointed at them, pulling it out would only result in both herself and Ben ending up on the wrong side of any disagreement.

The high, derelict structure was soon towering above them.

'After you,' said the woman as they stood on deck next to the rusting ladder. Ben nervously climbed, followed by Valerie. Halfway up, a large wave broke, sending heavy spray across. Valerie almost lost her grip. 'Might as well get acclimatised,' said the woman peering into the blackness, 'you'll be down there soon.'

They were pushed, pulled and kicked into the first tower where two men were waiting. Both were around thirty years of age, unshaven and, to Valerie's eyes, eastern European.

'What's all this?' The accent was definitely not from the west. Slavic, maybe.

'Nothing,' said the woman, waving an automatic pistol around, 'just come across a couple of cross-channel swimmers.

Thought we'd give them a little rest before they resume their journey.'

'Not until I've had a little word,' said the man, now minus his braces, entering with a little help from a walking stick.

'Not my lucky day,' said Valerie.

'Now that's an understatement if ever I heard one,' he said, before striking her across the face.

The woman took hold of his wrist as he went to hit her again. 'Not now, Max. Later. Tie them up. And you,' she said to one of the gun-hands, 'take our two eastern friends to the boat. Get them a scotch, make them comfortable.'

Hobbling around, Max searched them both and threw Valerie's gun to the floor. Taking cable ties, he bound their wrists and ankles.

'Try to soap your way out of that,' he said, pulling the last one tight.

'You've just got to be Jenny Lawson,' said Valerie.

The woman picked up the Glock. 'That's right. And you're…' She stopped for a moment. 'Bet you wouldn't have said yes to the colonel if you'd known that you'd be dead in a couple of weeks, would you? Swap for Her Majesty's Customs and Excise right now, wouldn't you?'

Working out just what was happening further up the chain, Valerie nodded. 'Think I'd have been better off chasing bad debts and divorces.'

Lawson put Valerie's things onto a step, next to a sawn-off shotgun and some brown packages. Then, turning to Ben, she pulled him to his feet. 'Now, you've been a silly boy, haven't you, Ben? Very silly. You've been paid well, but it seems loyalty isn't one of your strong points.' Sweat building on the back of his neck, Ben could only mouth a few incoherent words.

'Leave him,' said Valerie. 'This is all my doing, nothing to do with Ben. All this is way above his head. He fell into something that he'd no idea about. He's an innocent in a nasty world. Now let him go, he'll say nothing.'

'Of course he's going to say nothing,' said Lawson, picking up a green plastic can. She unscrewed the top and poured the contents over Ben. Choking petrol fumes filled the concrete chamber. 'Now just how much do you hate me, Valerie? On a scale of one to ten, somewhere around eleven I should think.' She took the Glock, pulled out the clip and removed all the ammunition. Then, checking to see it was empty, put one round back into the breach. 'Cut her hands free.'

'What for?' said Max, raising his stick. 'They're both going for a swim.'

There was undiluted menace in her voice when she spoke again. 'Cut her loose.'

Releasing his grip on the stick, he took a knife and cut the cable tie. Lawson took Valerie's lighter and, standing on a higher step, held it above Ben's head. 'How much do you hate me, Valerie?' She looked across to Max and handed him the Glock. 'Give it to her,' she said, flicking the lighter into life. 'There's one in there, Valerie, no tricks, one in the slide ready to go. You can shoot me if you want.' A light crackle accompanied a small flare above Ben's head as the flame caught the rising fumes. 'But if you do then our friend goes up in smoke.'

Valerie took hold of the pistol. 'Okay, let him go,' she said. 'What the hell do you want?'

'Nothing you can give me, Valerie. I just want to know how much you hate me.'

Valerie lowered the gun to her side. 'Whatever. I'll do what you want,' she said. 'Just put that bloody lighter away.'

'Oh no,' said Lawson, 'you don't get off that easily. Ben goes up in smoke whatever happens.' Whimpering, Ben screwed up his eyes.

'What do you want?'

'Shoot me,' said Lawson, 'and I drop the lighter. Don't shoot me, give the gun back to Max, and I drop the lighter. Thought it was obvious what you have to do.'

'Come on,' said Valerie, 'say what you want, must be something? Name it, it's yours. Time to get away? Anything you want, just put that lighter down. This is stupid.'

'I'm waiting, Valerie.' Lawson had to step back as the fumes danced around the flame. 'Shall we have a countdown?' A light smile accompanied her childish singsong words. 'Three, two—'

Valerie raised the gun quickly and shot Ben straight between the eyes. He did not jolt back, nor did he spin around. Like a puppet having its strings cut, he dropped to the floor.

'If I ever get out of this, there's nowhere to hide. Nowhere.' She threw the gun into a corner as Lawson closed the Zippo.

Max put another cable tie around Valerie's wrists and pushed her to the floor as the boat returned.

'Get that shit cleared away, Max.' Lawson pointed her foot at Ben. 'And anything else here, throw it over. That goes for her too,' she said, motioning at Valerie. 'And make it bloody heavy. We don't want anything floating back up again. By the way, I don't much care if she's breathing or not when she goes in. I'll send the boat back.'

Even with his injured leg, Max had the place cleared in under an hour. Then he turned to Valerie. 'Think you owe me, girl.' He cut the tie around her ankles then slid the penknife back into his pocket. She didn't struggle as he loosened her belt. Instead, putting bound arms over his head, she drew him closer.

'No need to be in a hurry,' she said, giving him her open mouth. She felt his response through her jeans as she teasingly ran her tongue around his. Then, tenderly, she bit and nibbled before sucking his lower lip deep into her mouth. The scream ejected from his depths was harsh and sharp as Valerie clamped her teeth shut and jerked sideways. She spat the piece of flesh to the floor as blood spewed down his neck. The attempted response of foul language only resulted in unformed words tumbling from a hideous mouth as he grovelled on the concrete looking for the lost chunk.

'Bitch! Bitch!' The incoherent curse erupted with a strange disability.

With the plastic tie biting into her flesh, she went quickly to the corner and, opening the sawn-off, checked the chambers were loaded. Then, hitting the crawling Max under the chin with the butt, she buried the barrels into his groin before pulling the trigger.

The screams and gunshot mashed together as they echoed around the tower. With a stunned glare locked on his face, he slumped back against the wall.

Extracting the small knife from his pocket, she nicked herself a couple of times before managing to sever the cable binding her wrists.

'Reckon you have about half an hour before you bleed to death, Max.' He pushed a hand into the bloody mess between his legs as Valerie leant back against the wall. 'Now, you can tell me where they are going, and I'll call for an air ambulance,' she said, waving her mobile in front of his face. 'Or you can lie here in silence and wait for everlasting glory.'

Max had to speak slowly and deliberately to make himself understood.

'Okay, Max,' she said, holding her mobile. 'Thanks.' Although contorted by pain, he still managed a questioning expression. 'Ambulance?' Valerie tapped the phone lightly against her cheek. 'Sorry, Max, battery's dead.' She put it away and, picking up the Glock, made her way towards the walkway. 'Looks like you're going to have to amuse yourself singing soprano until the angels arrive… maybe.'

She made her way to the next tower. 'Blood and sand, what do I do with no phone?' She had about an hour to decide before the boat came back. Get on board and hide? Hide around the towers, probably in the water, until they gave up searching and left? Then what? With the weather still bad, it would likely be days before anyone would come near enough for her to get their attention.

Dawn was breaking when the boat returned. Although not good, the weather had eased. Valerie had decided to stay. She slipped into the water at the foot of the ladder and was soon shaking as the sea drained the heat from her body.

After the shouting had died and Max's body had been taken off, Valerie was near the stern of the boat where she noticed a small boarding ladder. Clinging to the wooden steps as the boat moved off, she concentrated on anything that would take her mind from the cold churning water and her aching muscles. One thing did pass through her mind: that Trent had been hung over the back of this boat, not *Sun Dancer*. The turning props just below were a constant reminder not to fall off.

After twenty minutes, the swirling wash diminished as the engines were throttled back. Valerie climbed up a rung and, seeing land close by, jumped back away from the stern. Shaking with cold, she struck off to the nearby headland.

Struggling over the rocks to a footpath, she realised that, once again, she was in a bloody mess and miles from anywhere. The worst of the storm had passed and reverted to an early-morning breeze, so she hung her jacket and jeans over a handy bush and lay back, letting the sun bring back some feeling.

***

Adrenalin that had been surging around her body for the last twelve hours drained away, only to be replaced by uncontrollable sobbing.

***

Total exhaustion forced a couple of hours' sleep. Only the nightmare of what had happened jolted her back. For a few minutes she lay on the sand. Tears ran freely, forming tiny pools on her lips. The muscles in her chest ached from the intense crying.

With her clothes now reasonably dry, she brushed herself down and put them on. 'Christ knows what I look like.'

'Looks fine from where I'm standing.' She turned to see a man, a rucksack on his back, leaning on a fishing rod.

'Daft question,' she said, pushing grubby fingers through her hair, 'where am I?'

'Seriously?'

'Seriously.' She nodded, climbing up to the path. 'Been a bit of a night.'

'Yarmouth.'

'Yarmouth! Bloody hell. Can't be.'

'Yarmouth, Isle of Wight.'

'Thank Christ for that. You going out or returning?'

'Returning,' he said, waving a string of mackerel.

Valerie held up her phone. 'Got to get this charged.'

'Okay, I'm just over the rise there. Looks like you could do with a cuppa as well.'

***

The fisherman's place had once been a pretty cottage. Now, with a modern whitewashed extension stained with algae, it was in a sorry state. Broken and slipped tiles sat above small windows sick with rot. It stood there unloved, waiting for the building industry's equivalent of Dignitas.

The man pushed at the composite door and ushered her in. The room was both kitchen and diner and in little better condition than outside. A chair croaked its resistance as he dragged it across the stone floor and offered it to Valerie.

Even though she had done her best to keep water out of the mobile, she was still surprised to see it light up when plugged into the mains with a borrowed charger.

'Hungry?' The man of about sixty held up the catch of fish.

'Not really a mackerel person, if I'm honest.'

'I've not much else, I'm afraid, not been shopping.' He held one up. 'It was swimming around a couple of hours ago.'

'So was I,' she murmured.

'Sorry?'

He started gutting the fish before throwing the first one into a pan of smoking hot butter. Receiving no answer, he carried on. 'I'll put plenty of lemon juice on. That will cut through the oiliness. And some parsley.'

The fish smelt good and she wanted to like them, but even with loads of lemon and a pile of parsley they did little more than stop the hunger.

'Better than I thought they would be,' she said, washing the taste away with a mug of tea.

With the phone still charging, Valerie called Claude to apologise for the shambles and asked if someone could pick her up.

'You get around a bit,' he said. 'No wonder we were twiddling our thumbs up some ruddy creek, if they were cruising into the Solent. I'll come myself.'

She felt rather guilty waving goodbye to the host whose name she did not even know. Especially after taking the last of his hot water for a shower.

TWENTY-FOUR

CLAUDE UNCONSCIOUSLY EASED HIS FOOT FROM THE accelerator as Valerie filled him in with the details of the night before. Just before reaching the ferry back to the mainland, he pulled over. The inspector kept a firm grip on the wheel as they both sat in silence for a while.

'Nothing you could do. It'll be with you for a long time, but you just have to keep remembering what I said. You had no choice.' He turned around and pulled her face to his. 'You had no bloody choice,' he ground out between clenched teeth. 'It had to be done.'

Tears ran down Valerie's cheeks as her shoulders started to shake. 'Thanks, Claude.'

She did not tell him where they could be found. With freezing hands, and muscles locked in cramp, she'd sworn a solemn oath while clinging to the stern of the high-speed launch. Not caring if she spent the rest of her life in Holloway, she'd see Lawson dead. But if Claude were there...

***

'Want a lift to the Exe?' she asked Preston on the phone.

'With you? Love to. But why the River Exe?'

'I'm afraid the Golf's down there collecting parking fines. I'm in the car park behind your apartment.'

'Well, hello, where've you been?' he said, appearing a few minutes later. He gave her a kiss and put his jacket behind the seats. 'I was beginning to wonder if I was ever going to get a ride in this.'

'Course you were,' she said, throwing him the keys before sliding into the passenger seat. 'Just remember, wrecking it's a capital offence.'

'Ruddy hell,' said Preston, carefully guiding the long bonnet across traffic lights, 'it's like trying to thread a bloody needle.'

'Stop before you put it into first,' she said as he crashed another gear. 'It's the original box and first has no synchro.'

'Beginning to find that out.'

He grew in confidence as they headed along the embankment, smoothing out each gear change with a double declutch.

'Jesus, just look at everyone. Can't take their eyes off.'

'Yes,' said Valerie, pushing her cigarette end into the ashtray, 'it never fails to turn heads.'

'Not sure what it is, you, the car, or both.' He gave her a quick glance. 'Of course, this time that's mixed with the men cursing me.'

Valerie made appropriate noises during the journey, but the major part of her brain was churning around like an unbalanced concrete mixer. Unable to keep it to herself, she asked Preston to pull in to a pub car park.

She sat at a garden table while he disappeared through French windows into the bar. Looking around the flowers and neatly clipped lawn, it was all a million miles away. All so peaceful, all so normal. Hard to imagine this was the same planet, let alone the same country that bred the filth she was chasing.

Setting off with two bottles of Pepsi, a man held the gate back for Preston.

'Hey, mate,' he said, putting the palm of his hand to Preston's chest, 'drop-dead good-looking woman, I can live with that. Just. And black beauty out there in the car park,' he nodded across to the Jag, 'I can live with that. But both! Now that's just bloody obscene.'

'Haven't got the one,' he murmured, 'and not too sure about the other.'

'What did he say?' asked Valerie as he sat down.

'Oh, just admiring the car. That's all.'

'I'm ninety-nine per cent sure Alan's not dead. And I'm just as sure he's at the top of something very dirty. I'm telling you only because I'm sure about you being straight.' She sat back, taking a sip of Pepsi while waiting for him to say something. Which he didn't do straight away.

He made several efforts to reply. 'When we first started...' He stopped and asked if she had a cigarette.

'You don't smoke,' she said.

'Used to, and need one now.'

'Sure?' He nodded and Valerie pushed a pack and Zippo across the table.

'When we were approached by the guy to help in his business... you remember me telling you?' She nodded, and after lighting the cigarette he carried on. 'Well, when he got into trouble... or to be more correct, when I thought he was in trouble...' He stopped and dropped the cigarette to the floor. 'What the hell are those?'

'An acquired taste.' She leant back, watching butterflies about their business on a nearby buddleia. 'But carry on. What about Alan?'

'Never told anyone. People told me, including the guy we lent the money to, but I didn't believe them. He was my brother and I trusted him. The rumours were that Alan cheated and threatened him out of his own company. I think he must have sensed that I wouldn't have anything to do with that sort of thing and got me away on overseas ventures. Straight, honestly, my side is straight.'

Valerie nodded. 'Well, if you're bent then everything else is off to hell in a handcart. Come on,' she said, 'let's go and get your wheels before those penalties get into four figures.'

***

Leaves blew around her ankles as Valerie stepped from the Jag. By the side of the harbour, the car park felt cold and remote, the little VW a forlorn object in the corner.

'You know where they are, don't you?' he said, looking at the bunch of tickets on the windscreen.

'Yup.' She helped him remove the notices and threw them onto the passenger seat. 'Sure do.'

'I'm coming with you.'

'No bloody way,' said Valerie firmly.

'Why? And don't say it's too dangerous.'

'That's very sweet, David, but I signed up for this. It's not your call.' She took his jacket from the car and put it on the Golf's bonnet, along with the keys. 'And besides, there's no way you're going to approve of what I have in mind.'

'You're going now, yes?'

Valerie nodded, taking a Disque Bleu from the pack. 'Right now.' She shaded both cigarette and lighter from the rising breeze. 'While my blood's on the boil.' The wind pulled at her hair and put a flush in her cheeks as the cigarette smoke flew across the car park.

'Then I'm coming. And no guff about I can't. That's a bloody good car you've got, Valerie, but you can't outrun the R.'

She wound up the curving road away from the coast, the little VW behind in faithful attendance. With little fuel, she pulled into a service station.

'I've enough petrol, I'll wait.' Preston folded his arms and leant on the car door. 'Besides, I wouldn't put it past you to fly off, leaving me at the desk with nothing more than a red face.' Going off to pay, Valerie mixed an innocent smile with a half-curtsy.

After an hour she turned off the headlights, and with a near full moon managed to follow a narrow, winding road up to a wooded knoll. The flickering stop lights shone in front of two stone pillars, before she slipped the car out of sight behind thick shrubbery. Guided by the Jag, Preston shut off the Golf's lights and quietly parked to the other side. The door closed with a smooth clunk as he gently pushed it with his knee.

'Okay, Modesty Blaze, what's next?'

'Good ruddy question.'

Below the small coppice, a narrow drive wound down to where a cottage sat in a shallow dell. Pale yellow light leaked from a couple of windows, and a little smoke lifted slowly from the chimney in the still air.

'Think we'd better go and have a look.' Before making their way down, Valerie made an excuse to go back to the Jag. 'Give me a sec. Just want something from the boot.'

Preston scowled as they walked towards the grassed area behind the cottage.

'Cheeky bloody sods.' Behind a couple of locked posts, his S-Class and Lamborghini were neatly parked side by side. Avoiding the pathway, Valerie walked quietly over the lawn to the back door.

'Think we're looking at something a little more serious than twocking.'

The kitchen was in darkness, except for a thin shaft of light coming from a half-open door leading off to another room. Valerie drew the Glock and told Preston to try the door.

'Christ almighty.' He swallowed hard at the sight of the pistol. 'What the bloody hell?'

'Now don't go all goody-goody on me. You're the one that wanted to come to the party.' With both hands she held the gun high to the side of her face. 'We're dealing with bastards that make the Krays look like the fucking Chuckle Brothers.'

'Don't like you swearing either.' Looking a little embarrassed, Preston scratched at the back of his head. 'Unless... You know, when...'

'Get your mind back on what we're doing and open the bloody door,' she hissed between clenched teeth. 'There's plenty of time for that later.'

The door swung easily but groaned from little-used hinges. Valerie swore under her breath as a querying remark came from the adjacent room. At the sound of movement, Valerie motioned Preston to one side.

The young man that had seemed a little more hesitant than the others when around the card table, came in.

Before he could say a word, Valerie grabbed him by his collar and shoved the Glock under his nose. 'Quiet,' she whispered, pushing him away from the door. 'You know me?' The young man nodded. 'So you know I'll use it.' The nodding became enthusiastic as his eyes bulged. 'Good boy.' She patted his cheek before twisting his collar again. 'How many of you?'

Valerie pushed him against a cabinet as a shout funnelled through from the other room. 'What's going on?'

'Tell him you're getting something to eat.' The young man relayed Valerie's instructions, adding that the wind had blown the door open. 'Clever boy,' she whispered as her strengthening grip made him choke. 'How many?'

'Four.' Unable to shrink back anymore, he raised himself on tiptoe. 'Three and me.'

'Where are they?' He hesitated and looked appealingly at Preston, but all he received in reply were shrugged shoulders. Valerie pulled the slide back on top of the pistol. 'Where?'

'Two through there, one upstairs, front bedroom.' He pointed a finger above his head.

Keeping the gun in his face, Valerie swung him around towards the door. 'Right, son. You tell whoever is in there that you're going out for some fresh air. Then you go, and you keep going until you're holding on to Mummy's apron. Don't look round and don't come back. If you do...'

'Sure, sure,' he said, before shouting back into the next room. Valerie pointed the gun towards the back door. 'You'll not see me again,' he said. Then, stumbling out into the night, he disappeared.

Exasperated, Preston glared.

'Don't worry, he'll be a mile over the hill in ten minutes.'

She edged towards the light and walked in.

'Say nothing,' she said, holding a finger to her lips. Along with Lawson, who sat stunned, with a scotch halfway to her lips, was Preston's chauffer. 'Please, finish your drink,' said Valerie quietly, 'you'll probably need it.'

Lawson calmly put the glass back on the table, then raised her eyebrows as Preston appeared.

'Kenny!' Betrayal and anger surged into clenched fists as he saw the chauffer.

'Sorry, David,' said Valerie, 'but it was you or him, and I had my money on our Kenny here.' Valerie leant back on a sideboard opposite the stairway and looked back to Lawson. 'Whoever's up there, call them down.'

'Of course. You seem to be holding aces this time.' The smile on Lawson's face had Valerie wondering if she knew of any other expression. 'Oh, Alan,' she said in a silly, singsong voice, 'come and look who's dropped in for a visit.'

The cottage was old and the footsteps from above were easily tracked through creaking boards towards the stair head.

'Visit? What the hell you talking about? No one's coming around for a visit.'

David Preston's face drained colour as first feet, then legs, then body and finally face of the recognised voice were revealed through the rustic railings.

'Bet this was the last person you thought you'd see,' said Lawson. 'Or wanted to,' she added dryly.

'Alan?' In disbelief, David Preston choked on his brother's name. The incredulous look on David Preston's face brought an instant retort from his brother.

'I'm afraid so, bro. Looks like you've found me out.'

'Stay over here.' Valerie pushed David back as he made to approach his brother.

'Good advice,' said Lawson coolly. 'I'm sure your new friend doesn't want you coming over to the dark side.' Valerie motioned her to sit back in the chair as she started to rise. 'No problem.' With the smile still firmly in place, she slid back down.

'All this time?' said David. 'Christ's sake, we didn't need this, Alan. We were great on our own.'

'You don't get the big money without bending things a little. Always were too honest, weren't you, David? Do you know...' He perched himself on a chair back and turned to Lawson. 'When we were kids, we found a five-pound note in a puddle. My honest brother here wanted to take it to the police station. I ask you, ain't going to get anywhere with scruples like that.'

'Well, what now?' said Lawson, trying to distract Valerie. 'How about a big wad dumping into an offshore account? You and David could go and live on your own private island. Somewhere warmer, West Indies, the Pacific even. Anything extra you want, just send an email, be in your account next day. You could raise little Valeries and Davids, swim in your own lagoon every morning.'

'All in all,' said Valerie, 'I think I'd rather see you dead.'

'Oh dear,' said Alan, 'not sure my upstanding brother would side with that. What about it, David, going to let Wonder Woman here blow us away?'

Unsure, David looked at his brother. 'She wouldn't do that.'

'Ha, there's a side to her you know nothing about, bro. That woman's one hard bitch.'

'Enough of this.' Valerie reached into an inside pocket. 'Time to call in the help.'

At the same time as Valerie took out her mobile, Lawson bent forward to pick up her glass. It was just a second, but for Kenny, sitting to the side, the small distraction was enough to bring a revolver up from beside his chair.

As before, the shot in a confined space was ear-piercing. Valerie gasped as the bullet tore through her sleeve, taking a small piece of flesh away and burying itself in the wall. She shouted at David to get down as she swung round and sent a reply into Kenny's chest just as he got a second shot off. In the confusion, Lawson sprang to her feet and ran, escaping through the front door.

Valerie raised her gun again, this time towards Alan Preston. 'Stay where you are.' Then, realising David was still on the floor, she tapped him with her shoe and was relieved when he groaned. 'You okay?'

'Bloody hell, Valerie.'

'You okay?' she repeated.

'Yeah, sure.' He staggered to his feet. 'Jesus, no I'm not.' Looking at the gash in his wrist, he fell into a chair. 'Need something to stop the bleeding.'

Keeping the gun trained on Alan, Valerie feverishly pulled drawers from the sideboard and grabbed some linen napkins.

'Here, unfasten your cuff and pile that on.'

The blood kept seeping out. Handing the gun to David, she took more fresh linen and replaced the sodden heap, then tearing lengths, wound them around. Whilst his brother held the gun, Alan suddenly jumped from the chair back and ran to the door.

'Sorry, I couldn't,' said David as his brother ran out. 'Jesus…' He pulled his jacket open. 'Must have gone through into my side.'

Valerie pulled his torn shirt away. 'It's okay, just a flesh wound.'

Taking the gun, she went to the door. Lawson was fiddling with the parking post when a bullet sank into the adjacent wall, sending brick dust into Valerie's eyes.

'They're after the Lambo,' said David, getting to his feet.

'Stay there!' Valerie ducked back, drawing a cuff across stinging eyes and shaking her head. 'You'll start bleeding again.' She took out her phone and dialled Claude. 'Here,' she said, passing it to David, 'when he answers, tell him what happened and get an ambulance. Postcode of this place is in the phone's diary somewhere.'

'What are you doing?' he asked as she kissed his cheek.

'What the bloody hell do you think?'

Trying to move, he winced again, as Claude answered the phone. 'Hold,' Preston told the inspector. 'Please hold.'

'See you later,' said Valerie. 'I'll be okay.' Preston spat out a combination of pain and anger then, reaching into his pocket, threw the Golf key across.

'Take the R, you'll never catch them in the Jag. And,' he added as she left, 'you'll have to catch them before they leave these side lanes. Let them get onto decent roads and you'll never see them again. One last thing,' he shouted as she sprinted across the grass, 'trust the car's computer.'

The Lamborghini was already setting off along the narrow lane when Valerie turned the Golf around in pursuit. One hand on the wheel, she put the little Volkswagen into "race". 'Which way? Which way?' she said, approaching the turnoff. 'Where the boat is.' She turned left and floored the throttle.

The narrow, twisting road gave her the only chance of catching them. After a few minutes, the lights of the Lamborghini illuminated the way ahead. Trusting the car's computer, she pushed hard to the end of the pedal's reach. 'More, more,' she said quietly.

At the sign of a double bend she had to brake, but it was not enough. With the ABS and computer losing control, the car started to slide on loose gravel, sending the offside wing mirror clattering into the wall, smashing a headlight and putting a gash down the side, but with the VW regaining its line, she again floored the throttle.

More bends and she was running down the lights ahead. Frantic turning, braking and accelerating were all sent down to the computer where, calmly shuffling power around in thousandths of a second, the electronics serenely sent commands to the wheels, keeping the car on the road. With the ever-narrowing lane down to single track, the driver of the Lamborghini was unable to unleash its full power.

'Hell's teeth,' shouted Valerie as the fuel warning light came on. 'Running on empty. You and me both, little Golf. Fifty miles left at most.'

Still the road remained her friend, twisting and climbing even as the trees gave way to open ground on one side and a stone wall on the other. Through the next bend and the Lambo was just one hundred yards in front, but as it reached a short, straight piece of tarmac, the powerful supercar leapt forward. Then, ahead, all went dark as the road disappeared and dropped around the bend.

No sign. Gone. Valerie was just about to gun the Golf again when a glint to the right caught her eye. Turning the Golf slightly, the remaining headlight picked up the big Lamborghini jammed in a ditch. Jumping out, Valerie tripped and slid the six or seven feet below road level towards the crippled car. In the passenger seat, Preston was dead.

The corner had been cut too close; a large protruding stone in the wall had come through the windscreen and crushed his skull. Lawson, dazed but relatively unhurt in the driver's seat, saw Valerie.

'Get me out of here!' she screamed in a mixture of panic and contorted pain. The ever-present smile was gone. Valerie moved back from the petrol pouring from the ruptured tank.

'In a bit of a mess, aren't we?'

'Anything Valerie, anything. You name it. Get me out of here! I'll give you anything.'

'Unto half my kingdom, is it?'

'You can have the whole fucking kingdom. Just get me out of here.' She leant forward and released the front boot. 'In there. Look. Go on. In the briefcases.'

Valerie pulled at the bent panel, took the large leather cases from the Lambo and flicked the locks, first on one then the other. The cases were full with bound bundles of fifty-pound notes.

'Half a million in there, Valerie, probably more. All yours. And much more, I'll get you more. Just get me out of this fucking car!' Valerie closed the cases, threw them up the bank and took a couple more steps away from the heavy fumes. 'I'm sorry about what happened, Alan forced me. Honest to God. He was behind the lights, you know, in the cellar? He had a bloody temper on him. Shit, did he have a temper. I'm sorry. Get me out.' She started banging at the door that was hard up against the small embankment. 'I'll do time, tell everything. The whole story. Bring down the lot.'

'And what about Ben?'

'I wouldn't have done it, you know that, all a big mistake. It was my fault you shot him, I know. I'm so sorry.'

'And Hardy?'

Lawson slumped back for a moment before starting to thump on the roof and door. Then, crawling over Preston, she started screaming, 'You fucking bitch! When I get out of here, you're dead. Do you hear?! There's nowhere you can hide. You're fucking dead!'

Valerie moved back a few more paces before taking a pack of cigarettes from her pocket. 'Sod it,' she said, throwing the empty wrapper into the pool of petrol.

Hate was overwhelming as she looked at the Zippo and growing pool of fuel. The temptation was pulling and grabbing, tempting and teasing as she rolled the lighter around with her fingers. An evil darkness hooked into her flesh, pulling her down into the sewer inhabited by the scum she had been chasing.

Now a decision as to which side to fall had to be made: climb out, or stay there forever with the rest of the filth. She pushed the lighter back into her pocket and reached for the mobile that wasn't there.

The ticking of cooling metal was silenced by a sudden ignition, then violent screams.

As Valerie scrambled away from the leaping flames, a lumbering milk tanker came around the bend. The driver, grabbing a small fire extinguisher, jumped from the cab.

'Bloody hell! What happened?!'

Holding a case in each hand, Valerie looked down at the small extinguisher. 'Not sure that will be of much use.' The screams diminished as the flames and thick smoke curled into the night. 'Besides, she needs to get acclimatised.'

TWENTY-FIVE

Looking at her watch, Valerie assumed the colonel would be an early bird and called into the department on her way back.

'Up with the lark?' she said, sitting down. 'Need something from the store, and as you're the only one here...' As the ashtray was empty and the colonel had a cup on the desk, she presumed the smell of cigar smoke lingering in the air was from the previous night.

'New coffee machine in the corner,' he said, leaving the room.

Going over to the dispenser, Valerie ran her finger through the capsules, stopping at an Americano. The aroma of a fresh brew momentarily overpowered the stale tobacco. Cup in hand, Valerie was falling in love with a painting of a ballet dancer when the colonel returned.

'Lovely, isn't it? Degas. It came in for cleaning, and I have the pleasure of its company for the next three days. Trouble is, if I want to keep on having the pleasure of these works of art,

I can't smoke in here anymore. Some little oik, that should still be in short trousers, laid down the law. The nicotine clings to the paint, apparently.'

'Bet that went down well,' said Valerie under her breath. 'So, what are you going to do?'

'I slept on it, and decided I can't live without the paintings, so—'

'The cigars go.'

'During the day, yes. Probably better for me, at least it's better on the wallet.' He put a small attaché case on his desk. 'Anything else?' he asked, pushing it towards Valerie.

She shook her head.

Thompson did ask, when she was halfway out of the door, but only received a smile.

'Think you'll have to trust me.'

***

After getting cleaned up and having three stitches put in her arm, Valerie was on the houseboat catching up on a little sleep. With the combination of two of the leftover painkillers and miscalculating how tired she had become, she awoke around six in the evening.

'Johnny,' she said to the sergeant, 'sorry to call you at home. I need to see Dennis.' Valerie wedged the phone with her shoulder and lit a cigarette. 'It's urgent. You know his address?'

'Got contact details for all of you, Valerie.' Seconds later he brought up the detail. 'Anything I can help you with?'

'No, no. Just need to see him before tomorrow. He might need to put a few things together quickly.'

***

It was no more than a feeling. Valerie had seen no one but could not rid herself of a sense that she was being followed. Leaving the lift that served the flats where Dennis lived, she spent five minutes looking from one of the windows along the corridor. Nothing caught her eye; the small, pebbled forecourt was deserted, and the only movement came from vehicle lights on the by-pass.

Valerie pulled the jacket away from the bulge by her arm, gave up scrutinising the deserted night and followed the numbered arrows to the apartment door. Not sure if the music signalled someone else was in the flat as the door opened, she shoved Dennis back into the room.

'All alone?'

'Valerie. How nice. What brings you here?'

Valerie pushed him again, this time into a chair. 'You can cut the niceties, Dennis. Are you alone?'

'Oh, Dennis.' A soft cooing came from the next room.

'Well, that's a no then.' Valerie released the door handle. A startled girl pulled a flowery sheet above her breasts.

Probably under twenty, she didn't believe that less is more when it came to makeup. Long chestnut hair hinted at the pretty young woman beneath.

'Better come in and join the party, after you've put something on.' Then, turning back to Dennis, 'Well, aren't you the one full of surprises? Didn't have you down as jumping into bed with a slapper.'

Dennis got to his feet and shuffled nervously. 'Now what's going on, Valerie?'

'Let's just wait for your friend, shall we?'

When the girl appeared, Valerie turned to Dennis. 'Well, be a gentleman. Give her the fare home.'

'This *is* her home.'

'Crikey, Dennis. You can do better than that.' She looked

first at Dennis and then the girl. 'Okay, give her a twenty for the pictures.'

Putting hands on hips, the girl scowled at Dennis. 'Aye, do you mind! I ain't off to no flicks while you give 'er one. If you're goin' to screw anyone, it's me.'

Valerie took a couple of twenties from her pocket. 'Always tell a Roedean girl.'

'Eh?'

'Okay, Tara Palmer-Tomkinson, make it the theatre.' Along with the notes, Valerie took a purple coat from the door and thrust it into the girl's hands. 'Take a hike, golden girl.'

'You goin' to let her chuck me out, Denny?'

'Denny ain't got a say in this.' Valerie held the door open and pushed her through. 'Now go find yourself another free ride. If you'll excuse the expression.'

Unsure of what was coming, Dennis slumped back into the chair and waited quietly until Valerie returned.

'Lost, aren't you?' she said. 'Hand the information on down the line, but when it comes to the lightning striking, you're out of fuel. Well, you bastard, it's struck me and you've been catapulted right into the middle. It's time to pay, and I'm the cashier. Now, on your feet.'

'Valerie…' Dennis made weakened legs work as he pushed himself from the chair. 'I…' He looked around for non-existent help. 'What are you talking about?' A strike across the face sent him back into the chair.

'Don't make it worse, Dennis. Don't take me for a prat. More than one person in this treacherous mess has made that mistake, and they're now on the wrong side of the great divide.'

Dennis held his arms out in defence. 'Honestly, Valerie, you're making a mistake.'

'What's the name of Preston's yacht, Dennis?'

'What?' He furrowed his brow at the seemingly unrelated question.

'It's a simple question, Dennis.'

'*The Sun Dancer*. Why?'

'*The Sun Dancer*. Exactly.'

Dennis pushed himself into the chair back. 'What the hell's this all about?'

'Up.' She caught hold of his collar, dragging him to his feet. 'Get your car keys.'

He fumbled through a few keys in a glass bowl before removing a BMW fob. 'Where're we going?'

'You'll see.'

Grabbing at the doorframe, he fell backwards as she propelled him into the corridor.

'How come all the bad guys drive Beemers?'

'You're making a mistake, Valerie. I'm not one of them. Honest.'

Valerie hit the lift button and pulled him towards her. '*The Sun Dancer*. It's *Sun Dancer* on the back of the boat and on all the papers. Only the Prestons and the ones involved in this call it *The Sun Dancer*. And that includes you.' She thrust him into the lift and put her elbow on the button sending them to the basement.

'And that's it?'

'Along with me falling into the wrong hands when no one else knew. It's enough.'

'When?'

'The bent inspector. He could have just brushed me off, no problem. Someone told him that I was more than from Special Branch or whatever. He was told I was close and to take care of me.'

'You're wrong. Honest to God, you're wrong.'

Valerie looked around the underground car park. 'Which one?'

He nodded to a blue 2-Series BMW. 'Over there.' Dennis dropped the key as he pressed the entry button. Valerie kicked it back towards him, then pushed him along.

Even though it had an auto box, Dennis's trembling foot had the car jerking towards the exit.

'Left.' Valerie pointed along the nearest turn as they exited the car park. With shaking hands, Dennis followed her instructions.

'Where're we going?'

'Drive.'

'What can I do to get you to—?'

'You can't.'

Valerie carried on with the directions until they pulled up next to the bollards where Jane had taken the beating.

'Out.' She followed him and, as he dropped to hands and knees, she gave him a kick.

'Valerie!' He fell back, supporting himself on outspread hands behind his back. 'It wasn't me!'

'In case they didn't tell you, this is where your friends battered Jane to within an inch of her life.' She flicked a cigarette out and calmly took the Zippo to it. 'Don't suppose you ever got your hands dirty, did you, Dennis? Just get on the phone then pick up your wages.' She blew smoke out towards the river, pocketing the Disque Bleu and lighter. 'Funny thing, life, isn't it? Most people don't get to choose which way to jump when the time comes. You did but decided to go the wrong way.'

'I didn't. Honestly, Valerie, I'm straight. You've got it all wrong.' Dennis pushed with his heels but just came up against one of the bollards.

'Not nice, is it?' She drew the Glock and, sitting on a bollard, rested it on her knee. 'Frightening when there's no way out, I know... I've been there.'

The night was cool but sweat was starting to gather on Dennis's brow and back. 'I don't know what to say, Valerie. How do I convince you that I haven't had anything to do with it?'

She drew the slide back and raised the gun to his head. 'There's three men dead, more if you count the sewer rats, all because of the filth you were mixed up with. A woman on the Exe has no son, to go with her dead husband. Give me one reason, doesn't even have to be a good one, but one reason I shouldn't pull this trigger.'

Valerie wasn't sure which she heard first, the footfall through the dying grass or the voice. 'I'd better take that.' An arm came from behind and gently removed the gun from her grasp.

'Think the sergeant told you before. Don't abuse it.' Simonds lowered the gun and sat on a nearby bollard.

'Not sure I'd have done it.' Valerie's laboured breathing eased as the gun was removed. 'Think I just wanted to see him sweat.'

'Not worked it out yet, have you?'

Valerie pushed her hair back and peered into the darkness. 'Worked what out?'

Turning to face him, her brain raced as she realised how far off-base she'd been.

Simonds stood up, raised the pistol and shot Dennis in the chest. 'It wasn't that useless public-school twat. Told you back in the office, I get to know what's going on long before it filters through to anyone else.'

'You bastard!' Valerie jumped up, but he moved quickly as she took a swing.

'I was told you were a bad loser, Valerie.' He gave Dennis a kick but, receiving no response, sat back down. 'Now what the hell am I going to do with you?'

With the barrel of the pistol, he motioned Valerie a few yards away as he lit a cigarette. 'Lost me a lot of money, you have.' He looked down at Dennis then back to Valerie. 'Well, we have this little turd shot with your gun, so where to now? Shoot yourself in a fit of remorse, maybe? Naw, shoot Dennis and then you disappear. Get into his car.' He raised the gun as he felt through Dennis's jacket for the key. 'Come on, move or you get it right here.' He threw the key across. 'You drive.'

Valerie banged the lock with her fist. 'The door's stuck.'

Coming around from the front, Simonds pulled at the handle. As the door flew open, Valerie hit him in the teeth and ran to the other side. The first bullet ricocheted from the car roof; a second went harmlessly into the night.

Valerie ran into the darkness between two lamps and crouched beside a pile of lumber. 'That's three. Don't forget it's a baby Glock. One in the barrel and six in the clip. Only four left.'

'I only need one for you, Valerie. You might be useful, but you can't shoot without a gun.'

She threw a chunk of wood across; it bounced from the wall behind the car.

'Have to do better than that, Valerie. You're up against a pro.' The voice was further along the path as she moved towards the edge of the embankment.

An involuntary curse left her lips as she tripped over an old warp, and two shots flew over her head.

'Just the two left now.'

'Then what? Going to take me on at unarmed combat?'

Searching between old crates and tyres for a few seconds, Simonds did not see as she ran back towards the car. Only when a bullet thumped into her shoulder did she change and swerve down an alleyway. Too late she saw it was a dead end, as he came towards her.

'Told you I only needed one bullet. Looks like I need two.' He raised the gun, only to be confronted with the slide in the rear position. The Glock was empty.

'Sorry, Inspector, I lied. It's one short in the clip.' Blood trickled down her shoulder; luckily it was numb as she drew a pistol from the back of her belt. 'All that crap you gave me back in the office, I believed it. You bastard.'

The inspector stopped and held up flat palms. 'Sorry, but bringing a second gun? Now that's cheating.' With little to lose, he slowly continued towards her. 'The thing is, are you going to use it?' The answer came swiftly as a bullet in the leg sent him to the ground.

She pulled the phone from her jacket pocket, but within the high walls the signal was absent. Quickly heading towards the alleyway entrance, Simonds made a grab at her ankle and sent her toppling into the dirt. He grabbed her thigh and the belt around her jeans, then pulled her towards him.

'Bastard!' The curse was spat out at the same time as she kicked him across the head. With both of them still on the ground, Simonds managed to twist round. Valerie screamed as he punched her wounded shoulder. The trickle of blood turned into a stream. At the same time, the gun fell from her grasp.

She kicked him again, turning back and forth looking for the pistol in the dim light. He managed to struggle to his feet, but his injured leg would not take his weight and he collapsed across Valerie's chest. Fighting to get free, an outstretched hand found the pistol. She turned, making a savage strike across the inspector's temple with the gun butt.

'Got other things in mind for you. Arsehole.'

She got to her feet and pressed speed dial. 'Need the cavalry, Claude.' She looked back down the alley at the semiconscious inspector. 'Suppose you'd better bring an ambulance as well. And I'm afraid we'll need a body bag.'

***

Valerie was sitting on one of the bollards when flashes of blue lit up the embankment.

'You all right?'

She had never seen Claude move so fast. 'Oh, you know,' she said, remembering something from a lifetime ago, 'clinging to the wreckage.'

'Trouble follows you around like teeny-boppers chasing Justin Bieber. What the bloody hell happened?'

Wincing as she raised her arm, Valerie pointed down the alley. 'Wounded one in there. Better get your guys to check him before letting the medics in. Dead one over here.' She nodded over her shoulder to where Dennis lay.

'And you?' Claude looked at Valerie's shoulder and called over one of the ambulance crew.

After removing her jacket, she handed over the holster and gun to Claude. 'You'd better look after this for the time being. There's another pistol down the alley with our friend. Don't lose it, that one's mine.'

'Been here before,' said Claude, turning his back as Valerie's T-shirt came off.

'Christ's sake, Claude, don't get so bloody prissy. I'm not going to take my bra off.'

The banter was interrupted by a shout from the medic at Dennis's side.

'This one's alive.'

TWENTY-SIX

Slumped in the chair across the desk from the colonel, Valerie was totally drained. The ever-present energy, mental and physical, was gone.

'You hung me out to dry,' she said, gently rubbing at the stitches under her jacket. 'Didn't care if I came out the other end or not. Just so long as you could keep on building your precious bloody Jerusalem.' Playing with a cigar cutter he said nothing, waiting patiently for her to continue. 'How's Dennis?'

'Okay. Hopefully. Bullet went straight through and didn't touch anything important. Poor little sod must have fainted with the shock. Lucky.'

'Very. He'd have had his brains all over the grass if Simonds had known he was still alive.'

The colonel put the cigar cutter down before spreading his fingers on the desk. 'I've made arrangements. That is, set up a pension for Ben's mother. Just said he had some sort of insurance. She'll be okay.'

'Okay?!' The blood in Valerie's neck flushed into her cheeks. 'Jesus bloody Christ! Her husband was dragged under a boat. I killed her son. How's she going to be anywhere near okay?!'

'Stay away.' He leant forward, fixing her with an uncompromising glare. 'Don't even think about going to see her. You'll make it worse.'

'That's a joke. Where in God's name am I ever going to get the guts to go and see her?'

'We've got all those that count.' He attempted a little graciousness with an understated smile, but failed, producing something nearer to a sneer. 'The ones left...' He uneasily cleared his throat, but Valerie felt no sympathy for the man obviously out of his comfort zone. She'd had to bear her part of the guilt and felt no remorse sharing it around. 'The few small ones haven't the brains to give trouble on this scale. They'll drift back into mainstream crime and be sent down sooner or later.'

'What about—?'

'The two from the east?' he interrupted. 'Gone. They're strictly mercenaries. With no pay they won't want to know. Probably sitting in the departure lounge at Heathrow reading *Vegan Food and Living* right now.'

Valerie pulled up the large briefcases that had been by her side since she had walked in. 'Present,' she said, dumping them on his desk.

'Cripes.' The colonel looked genuinely impressed at the tightly bound notes. 'Not sure I've ever seen that much in one place before.'

'The other's the same. Didn't know what to do with it all.' For the first time she managed a half-smile. 'Well, that's not strictly true. There were one or two things that crossed my mind.'

'How much?' he asked, thumbing the top pile.

'According to Lawson, somewhere around half a million. That is until I took a couple of bundles. Gave one to Jane. I've got something else in mind for the other... if that's okay?'

'Yes, of course.' Shutting the lid, the colonel dropped the cases to the floor. 'Sure... Can I ask you something?'

'If you want.'

He reached for the cigar cutter and started to use it like a bunch of worry beads. 'Why do you pretend to hate your country?'

'Pretend? Now there's a joke if ever I heard one.'

'You can't fool me, Valerie. If we were all out of ammunition and the enemy was charging up the beaches of our green and pleasant land, you'd be there... throwing rocks at them!'

***

'Conscience money, is it, gorgeous?' Dan looked at the pile of notes on the table. 'Pay-out for the boat is on its way, so I don't need it.' He pushed it back.

'It's to help you out. Get some modern equipment on board.'

'Ain't going fishing no more, getting too old.'

'Come on, Dan, don't be stupid.'

'Don't call me stupid,' he growled.

At a new low ebb, Valerie just sat there. All the friendliness, all the banter between her and the old man had evaporated.

'It wasn't...' She stopped as steely eyes burnt into hers. Only she, the colonel and Claude knew how Ben had died, and she had neither the energy nor the courage to explain. 'I'm sorry,' she said, rising from the table. 'If you don't want it, give it to the RNLI.'

She turned and made for the door of the small cottage.

'Goodbye, Dan.'

TWENTY-SEVEN

As the wind came around into the north, the chill of autumn was in the air when Preston walked along the towpath. The vibrant greens of the summer were gone, leaving the dead and dying leaves strewn around like decaying confetti. Blackberries and wild hips that had hung along the bushes had been plundered by blackbirds, the odd ones that had been missed now lying crushed in the mud.

The physical wounds had quickly ceased to bother him. The mental ones were deep and still seeped crimson pain. Now he only thought of the one person that had the power to heal, the only person that could haul him from the edge. But not too quickly. If she would be the one, then she must be given time to breathe, to come back down among the living. So, letting the dust settle, he had given it a few weeks before making the short journey.

With flowers and a box of Belgian chocolates gripped between arm and chest, he knocked on the houseboat door with a free hand.

'Oh, hello, come to see Valerie.' He looked quizzically at the tall, immaculately dressed West Indian, who made him feel like his own expensive suit had come from Oxfam.

'Janie,' Winston turned and shouted down the corridor, 'someone to see Miss Stone.' Giving a wide smile, he moved to one side. 'Come in man, come in.'

Jane, the bruises now diminished, was sitting in a worn, brown leather chair next to a wood-burner. 'It must be Mr Preston.' As if warming her hands, she cupped the mug of coffee.

Preston motioned her to stay seated as she started to rise. 'Come to see Valerie,' he said, slightly puzzled.

'Coffee?' Winston appeared with another mug. 'We're house-, er, boat-sitting.' He sat protectively on the arm next to Jane.

'Miss Stone's away for a while,' said Jane as Preston raised his eyebrows. 'Think we both probably know where.' Jane took a sip of her coffee and looked up. 'Why don't you sit down?' She waited until he took the chair opposite, then carried on. 'I think we both know she doesn't want to be disturbed.' Looking for reassurance, she took hold of Winston's hand. 'You've fallen for her, haven't you?'

'It shows, does it?'

'Oh yes.'

'Tell me about her, Jane,' he said, leaning back. Jane looked into the fire, saying nothing. 'Think I'm owed.'

Winston nodded.

Finishing her coffee, Jane put the mug on the table and once more looked at Winston for reassurance.

'It's okay, Janie, tell him. He could find out with a little digging. Might as well get the King James version.'

'It's not Miss Stone,' she began. 'It's Mrs Stone.'

Preston was about to speak but Jane quickly carried on. 'Where to start? Oh, Jesus.'

Winston made an attempt to lighten the situation. 'Start at the beginning, sweetie,' he said, squeezing her hand.

'Right,' said Jane, not sure of where the beginning was exactly. 'In-laws. You know the Queen owns half of Scotland?' Preston raised an eyebrow but smiled. 'Well, Valerie's in-laws own the other half. Or, to be exact, two hundred and thirty-four thousand, six hundred and three acres... give or take a yard. Plus West End property, and plus and plus and plus. I know you're not short of a penny, Mr Preston, but they carry your kind of money around like loose change. You get the picture?'

Preston's lips tightened into a wry smile.

'Valerie married the only son, Simon. Everyone was incredibly happy. The fairy queen had stepped down from the Christmas tree sprinkling gold dust everywhere. And after not too long she fell pregnant. Great jubilation, parties, celebrations, you name it. All was well with the world... offspring to keep the name and estates going, and of course, the child would be beautiful etcetera, etcetera.

'Anyway, when she was about six months, Simon and Valerie had been to his parents' place for lunch, some whopping estate in Surrey. Valerie was driving but has no recollection of what happened. She can remember waving goodbye as they drove off, but then nothing until she was in the ambulance. Some bloody lunatic came around a corner on the wrong side, according to Simon. Head on. Valerie lost the baby within a few hours.'

'They blamed her?' said Preston. 'For Christ's sake, why?'

'Apparently there were comments made over lunch that Valerie shouldn't be driving. You know, being pregnant. Simon jumped to her defence and nothing more was said.'

'That's ridiculous,' said Preston.

'Oh, there's worse. Simon spent most of the time with her after the accident, wouldn't leave her side. One morning he was rearranging her pillows and just collapsed. Aneurism from the accident. Brain damage. Severe brain damage. He was put on life support... still there now, after four years. Valerie won't give permission to turn him off. She visits him every week. Listens to the radio, reads him books, keeps him up to date with what she's been doing.'

Preston raised a hand to his forehead and pushed back his hair. 'Oh, Jesus Christ.' He paused for a moment, gazing unfocused out of the window. 'So why the life she leads? She can't be short of money.'

Jane shook her head. 'It's all family business, her in-laws' business, that is. When they were one big, happy family it didn't matter. But after the accident the family never forgave her and took the lot. House, everything. Now she rents this houseboat. She has the car, that was a twenty-first birthday present from Simon, and two wedding rings. They tried for the car but it's in her name.'

'And the watch?' said Preston. 'With the way she guards it, I imagine there's a story there too.'

'Yes,' said Jane, 'the other thing she treasures above everything else, the watch. One Christmas she asked him what he wanted. He joked that he wanted the same as James Bond wore. So, she went out and paid over ten grand for a nineteen sixties Submariner. She pays for his nursing; it takes most of her income every month.'

Preston rose to his feet. 'A small village just outside Worcester. Shouldn't be hard—'

'Won't be hard at all. Probably walking the family spaniel down a country lane right now. And if you come up behind her with your roses and Belgian Truffles, you might make her stop and think. But you have to make up your mind... how much of her would make you happy? Or more important, make her happy?'

'There were times.'

'I'm sure there were. I'm also sure they were total magic. But would you be happy with three quarters of her for the rest of the time? Could you bear to look at her and see she was somewhere else? I would have said you were the kind of man that wanted one hundred per cent of her, for one hundred per cent of the time. And another thing, of course... how long would it last?'

'Thanks.' Preston got to his feet and handed Jane the flowers and chocolates. 'Let me know if there's anything I can help you with.'

'Where are you going?'

Turning to the door, Preston shrugged his shoulders.